TO AVENGE A FAE:

A Reverse Harem Tale

ASSASSIN'S PULL, book 3

by

Rachelle Hobbs

TO AVENGE A FAE
A Reverse Harem Tale

ASSASSIN'S PULL, book 3

ISBN: 978-1-945893-35-3

Published by Untold Press LLC
114 NE Estia Lane
Port St Lucie, FL 34983

www.untoldpress.com

PRODUCED IN THE UNITED STATES OF AMERICA

10 9 8 7 6 5 4 3 2 1

Dedication

For my father. He'll never read about my sexy Assassins and Fae, but their books will still find a place of honor on his bookshelf.

Acknowledgements

First, as always, I want to thank the Untold crew for everything you do. You are the most generous people, and the support you give your writers is unmatched. I also want to give a massive shout-out to Dakota Brown and Aeryn Havens for being the best alpha readers on the planet. The feedback and encouragement you both give make the writing journey a little easier.

To the fabulous Becky Hodges, PA extraordinaire, and the Babes. You're the best bunch of women a gal could ask for. Writing is such a solitary job, but you all make sure we're not truly alone.

Finally, to me amazing family. I'm pretty sure I have the best children on the planet, and I'm so fortunate to have their unwavering support—even when Mommy is writing sexy-time books. □

Chapter 1

I don't want to be here. Not in this airy living room with its pastel furniture, white tile floors, and pictures of sailboats on the walls. The scent of jasmine incense filling the place makes my stomach churn. Even the crashing of ocean waves floating through the open window and the salty air breezing in make my skin prickle with the desire to jump on the first flight home. I want to be in West Virginia, cocooned in the woods, where snow has fallen. I want to keep hiding from the world and pretend it doesn't exist anymore.

But when you're waging a war with the Fae king, hiding in the woods is not an option. It doesn't leave many options for where you find your allies, either.

Luca, Ben, and I sit on a robin's-egg blue couch across from Madera, the Leader of the Pacific Northwest Order, her four Bonded sitting on either side of her in high-backed chairs with canary-yellow cushions like they're royalty. It's so haughty and egotistical and expected from this Order. They truly believe being Assassins is some sort of divine gift.

Irritating, but the unfortunate truth is we need them. They're the largest, strongest Order in the United States. On our side, they're a powerful ally. On Oberon's, they'll be the first Order called to take us out as soon as the king feels comfortable enough to attack us again.

Finn stands at the window in the decadent beachfront home, fingers laced behind his back and face pensive while studying the waves hitting the sandy shore. Jessie, another woman in my Order, cut his silver hair a couple weeks ago, and the short style gives him the look of a sophisticated Wall Street trader–if humans had slightly pointed ears. He's beautiful. Perfect. And his presence is driving Madera crazy. It's obvious by the way she darts furtive glances his way when she doesn't think I'm paying attention. We told her we'd have an Unseelie with us during our visit; he's no surprise guest.

She hasn't asked about him, though. The Leader of a powerful Order would never give his presence the dignity of her actual attention.

That's fine. Madera will grovel at his feet soon enough. In her arrogant, aristocratic way, of course. But after he reveals who he is, hopefully they'll see the atrocities King Oberon has committed as the horrors my Order believes them to be. Killing innocents, including children. Capturing Mages like Finn. Wanting to kill Alexie, our little Fae queen we've miraculously been able to keep hidden from him.

Killing my father.

We don't jump into the horrid truth or the Finn Show right away. Instead, we've spent the better part of an hour skirting the reason we're here with pleasantries and the obligatory condolences they give for Topher's death.

When they say Topher's name, speak of him, I smile, accept their kind words, and dig my nails into my thighs. Empty platitudes are useless. My father's dead, and Oberon took Pia, my best friend in the world. She's probably dead, for all I know.

It's been sixty-one days, five hours, and forty-six minutes since I last saw my friend. Since I last saw my father alive.

I squeeze my eyes shut for the barest of seconds. *No. Don't go there. Don't.*

Madera's not the only one doing a poor job of ignoring Finn. None of her Bonded acknowledge him, but they're aware of him.

All four have their daggers out. Sunbeams shoot through the window and glint off the iron blades. Her men are all big and strong and trained. And they're not huge fans of our Order. Call it a rivalry, I suppose. But we will let bygones be bygones to get what we want. Who knows what side Madera will land on once we're done explaining everything, but I fucking hope it's with us–after she sees what Finn can do and hears his story.

I'm also looking forward to Finn revealing those iron weapons have no prayer of hurting him, not with his power and the red pill he's taken. One of the few things I've done right is steal those anti-iron pills from Julius, a target in New York we took out after discovering his Fae den. We haven't gotten more yet, and the effects only last about four hours, but the pills give us a huge advantage.

"How does it feel, Nora?" Madera asks, after offering beverages we decline. Her voice is a purr. "To finally be Leader?"

I wince inwardly. Leader. The title is tough to hear, especially because I don't deserve it. But I'm the strongest, now that I've Bonded with Luca and Ben, and my family's women have run the East Order since its inception, apart from Topher.

I dig my nails deeper into my jean-clad thigh as my father's face flashes through my mind. *Don't. Lose. It.*

Luca's warm hand presses against my back, while Ben gives me a soft smile. Their encouragement streams through our Bond, and it helps. A little.

I clear my throat, release the dagger-grip on my thigh, and cross my legs. This arrogant woman won't see me rattled. "It's been an adjustment, but I feel right at home."

She nods. "I'm glad to see you're taking the mantle… albeit under grievous circumstances." Her lips twitch as if giving faux sympathy amuses her.

Oh, I can't wait until they find out they're not the most powerful bastards in the room. "Yes, well, that's why we're here," I tell her, my voice surprisingly flat.

"Is it?" Madera gives Finn a cursory glance. She can't hide how her pupils dilate at the sight of him, taking in his solid frame, his perfect posture.

I tamp down the jealousy her covert admiration generates inside me. It's irrational and a byproduct of the Pull I have with him. He's mine, even if he isn't truly mine. Not yet.

Good thing his back is to us. She'll be trying to find her tongue once he pierces her with his undiluted attention. The man is a physical masterpiece, like most Fae, but he's got a dangerous edge to him, one that's both intimidating and sensual.

I touch my stomach when the Pull for him dances there, and then try hard not to snap my fingers to get Madera's attention off Finn and back on me. "It is," I say with a harshness to my voice. It's enough to get her focus again. "The way my father died, it should scare the shit out of all Assassins and Fae."

"I heard it was an accident," she says, brow furrowed. "A car wreck on those atrocious mountain roads."

I tilt my head, biting the inside of my cheek to keep a sharp laugh from escaping. Not one thing about my father's death is funny, but shock makes you react in crazy ways. "Who told you that?"

"Our Messenger. She said it was tragic, a true devastation to our people."

Looks like Oberon is on clean-up detail, ordering his Messengers, Seelie who bring our target scrolls through the Window from Etherias, to spread his false narrative. How desperate. How arrogant of him to think we'd accept what he's done and hide.

I stare at her for a second, feel the anger seeping from Ben and Luca and infecting me. "She lied to you."

Maybe it's the rage in my voice, or how my lips tremble, that gets her attention. She straightens, joins hands with the Bonded closest to her. "I'm listening."

I take a deep breath, focusing on the warmth from Luca's hand on my back. Ben's hand, too, which is now on my thigh. Then I give her everything. I start with how Oberon uses us to take out innocent Fae who've done nothing but escape Etherias to come here, hoping to live without hunger and fear.

She flutters a hand to her collarbone, her only tell the news disturbs her. She says nothing for a moment as her Bonded drill me with all their disbelief. Then, "We are the guardians of our secrets, Nora. If what you say is true, for every innocent we kill, a hundred are not."

I force myself not to reach across the coffee table to strangle her. "Even one is too many."

"I don't see it your way, Leader," she says, her tone formal.

Okay, fair enough. Let's give her something meatier. "Oberon killed my father, right in my backyard." I purge the entire battle, give her all the dead bodies on my conscience.

This gets her attention. She leans up, her eyes wide with surprise she doesn't suppress. "Oberon brought his army to your home? His army from Etherias?" She shares an incredulous frown with her Bonded, who all mimic it like parrots.

"He did. Hundreds of soldiers came through the Window, intent on slaughter." I swallow, trying to keep emotions from skipping my voice. Still, when I close my eyes now, I see that morning as if it happened hours ago. All the death, all the destruction.

My father's lifeless eyes staring up at me as he lay in the blood and mud of battle.

"What would make Oberon do such a thing?" She's no longer the affable Leader with faux grief for a man she barely knew. Her eyes narrow at me as if I were already her enemy. "What has your Order done to bring the king himself to this side of the Window?"

That's Finn's cue.

His shoulders lift with a heavy sigh before turning from the window to face the shell-shocked Pacific Northwest Order. "Their crime was hiding me."

Madera gawks at him, her jaw slack. "What? Why? What rule have you broken?"

13

She's talking about the rules we live by. Number one: never reveal our world to humans. Number two: never kill one of our own without permission. That's it. End of list.

Oberon has folded lies into those rules. He's had his Assassins kill innocents for infractions that have nothing to do with surviving in this world.

Finn smiles at her, a gorgeous smile that promises things. "Living is my crime, Leader. Plain and simple."

Ben, Luca, and I stand, which confuses the fuck out of Madera's Bonded. Yes, it would appear ominous, an Unseelie staring right into Madera's soul while the three of us stand and laser in on the four strapping men with iron daggers. But we're not here to hurt anybody. We're only making sure no one tries to come at Finn. Better we sit them back on their asses than Finn using his magic to really make them suffer.

"What the hell is he talking about?" Madera says to anyone who will answer while never taking her eyes from Finn.

"I reckon he's about to show you," I say, keeping my attention on the largest of her Bonded. "Relax, everyone."

The large Bonded stands and takes a step toward Finn. "Fuck this, Madera. They can't come in here and feed us bullshit with an Unseelie criminal."

"You'll want to stand down, mate," Luca says, his brogue thick, voice gravelly.

When the guy ignores him, Ben adds a singsong, "You'll regret it." He might sound flip, but Ben is ready to rip off faces if these fellas get ballsy.

When the guy hesitates, a white-knuckled grip on his dagger, Finn tilts his head at him, meeting his stare with a dangerous grin.

"Sit, Ryan," Madera says. "This isn't getting us anywhere."

Like a scolded dog, Ryan takes his seat again, chest puffed and neck red with what I'm assuming is embarrassment for the public chastising.

Madera frowns at me. "What does he plan to show us?"

Finn saunters in front of Madera, his right hand out. A ball of light floats above his palm. "*He* plans to show you some truth, Leader." The arms of their ridiculous chairs ice over after he murmurs a chant. Then, "Let me tell you a story."

Chapter 2

Days later, and two more Orders visited, we're finally leaving the West Coast.

The Leaders of the two other West Coast Orders we visited after Madera's had reacted relatively the same when Finn showed them what he's capable of. It's not every day you find out Unseelie Mages exist, and especially ones as powerful as Finn. Thankfully, the West Order and the Southwest Order have aligned with us and agreed to allow Finn to close their Windows, like the Pacific Northwest Order has. They agreed to halt any Fae killings, too, even if only temporarily.

Last week, we left home for this most recent campaign to gain allies, starting on the East Coast and ending here. Many of this country's brethren are with us, especially after finding out the lie Oberon is spreading about my father's death. That information was even stronger than Finn's revelations in some ways. Quite a few Orders live in secluded areas like we do, where no human eyes are present. Who's to say Oberon won't try to punish them in the same way in the future?

All in all, a productive mission. One I'm desperate to end. I want to be home. I want to be surrounded by Topher's things and fading scent.

"I'd call this a success," Ben says as the four of us stand in line for security at LAX airport. "Three more Windows shut, plus the three from the beginning of the week, and a few more Assassins aware of reality."

Luca nods, adjusting the strap of his bag resting on his shoulder. "Aye, a success, especially if ye count four strapping Assassins squealing like wee bairns at the sight of frozen furniture." Madera's Bonded were the only ones who showed blatant fear. Funny, since their Order is most respected for their strength.

Ben shrugs, nudging Finn's shoulder. "You should have frozen their balls, brother. That would've shut them up."

Finn smirks while staring straight ahead at the metal detectors. "What, and condemn poor Madera to a life with eunuchs? The woman is far too sensual for that. Not her fault she's Bonded with screeching fools."

The three of them continue bantering, quietly so as not to alarm any humans close by. They laugh and act like they came from the same womb. My Bond with Luca and Ben, as well as the Pull with Finn, has done this. Created a weird family of unmatching puzzle pieces.

This connection I share with these men is the only thing keeping me going. The. Only. Thing.

I don't join their conversation as we shuffle closer to the front of the line. Yes, this past week has been a success of sorts. Yes, it was worth leaving the comfort of Topher's room, which still smells faintly of him. But my ability to find joy has decayed away. My father's still dead, and Pia's still in Oberon's clutches. The reasons he wanted her and how she knew he wanted her are still a mystery. No amount of success in this world will erase the devastation and painful questions that coat my heart like thick tar.

Once we're on the plane, I breathe a little easier. Only six hours away from West Virginia, plus another two-hour drive from the airport, and then we'll be home. Eight hours until I can hide under quilts and sleep another day off my calendar. I can't stay in bed forever, as much as I want to. I'm Leader now, and there's a fuck-load of people back home waiting for me to fix every broken thing.

I sit next to Finn. Ben and Luca are paired off across the aisle from us. My gaze drifts to Finn's profile as he listens to the flight attendant go over the safety rules. Such an arrogant man. Such a compassionate one. He's frustrating. Secretive. So compelling. I can't deny the Pull anymore. I want to know everything about him. I want him to give me details of every year of the thousand years he's lived. I want him to know he can trust me.

It's only been a few weeks since I've found the courage to be alone with him. Yet, he's not the same man who would trap me with looks or a searing touch to get me to admit our connection. He treats me with kid gloves, keeps an emotional distance.

"You're tired," I whisper to him, resting my head on the back of my seat.

His gorgeous face is drawn, with faintly mottled circles under his eyes. I'm not so self-absorbed as not to notice the toll this trip has taken on him. He's still recovering from taking down Julius's Fae den—and saving us from Oberon's army. I'm asking too much of him. Treating him like a show pony to convince the masses. I hate that it's necessary.

He brushes a gentle thumb under my left eye. "As are you, love." He then cups my cheek and kisses my forehead in an innocent way that doesn't feel innocent at all. "Sleep. You'll be home soon."

I nod. As the plane taxis on the runway, I close my eyes.

Mistake.

The image of Topher's lifeless body lives on my eyelids. The only thing that blurs it is the sting of tequila at the back of my throat—a lot of tequila. That's also waiting for me at home. Tears prick my eyes, which makes me squeeze my lids tighter to hide them, torturing myself.

Finn isn't fooled. But he says nothing. He simply takes the hand I rest on my lap and laces his fingers with mine.

As the plane leaves solid ground, I concentrate on the feel of his skin. On how his warmth invades my body, soothing the perpetual chill that hasn't left since that horrible morning. After deep breaths, and Finn's thumb tracing gentle circles on the top of my hand, the tears stop threatening to spill. And when I squeeze his hand, he inches closer until our shoulders touch.

For a few moments, the demons ravishing my mind crawl back into their cages.

Chapter 3

We've been home for three days, and sleep has evaded me. That's right. Sleep and I aren't friends anymore. It runs away every time I chase it. And as much as I'd like to, I can't catch it at the bottom of a bottle. Not anymore. My Order indulged my drunken state for almost a month after... that day. I can't expect them to keep granting me an escape from my pain. What kind of Leader would I be if I were perpetually drunk while Oberon lurks only a Window away?

No matter. I'd rather be exactly where I am now, in the kitchen at 2:00 a.m. This outdated room is the place where I feel Topher most.

I bend in front of the old cast iron cookstove, open the firebox, and strike a match against the scarred floor. Sulphur wafts in the air as I work to build up the flames with a fresh piece of dry wood. When an orange blaze crackles and sparks, I close the firebox. And stay on my knees as I listen to the fire eat the wood. I don't want to cry; I've done too much of that lately. Tears burn my eyelids, anyway.

Damn it.

Sighing, I force myself up on my feet and rummage through the distressed green cupboards for my favorite ceramic mixing bowl, the sifter, and everything else I need. I'm on autopilot, muscle memory guiding me around the kitchen I've known since the day I was born.

Nothing has changed in here, not where my father stored the pots and pans or the chipped dishes that have been in my family for generations. Even the heavy fridge is the same. The last time a new one graced this kitchen had to have been in the eighties. Everything is old, outdated, broken–and I love it. All of it, including the slight musty smell usually masked with burning wood and the threadbare drapes over the iron-shuttered window.

Everything.

I wipe my wet cheeks with the back of my hand and pour flour into the bowl. Next, the baking powder, and so on and so on. The dough is cool against my hands as I knead it into submission. This I do from memory, too, make my father's cinnamon rolls. I've made so many of them lately. Ben has begged me to stop.

I wish I could stop.

"I hope I'm not intruding."

I don't turn from my work to face Callum, the Seelie we've adopted into our Order–after I cut off his hand. Another something to add to the guilt pool I drown in. "You're not."

"More cinnamon rolls? We do quite enjoy them. Helene and Alexie missed waking to the smell while you were gone." Helene and Alexie are two more Fae we've welcomed into our fold, along with Seamus. The warrior Pixie, the child Unseelie Mage who is the rightful heir to Etherias's throne, and the foul-mouthed teen Haunt I've come to care about as if he were my own kin. It feels like years ago when we first encountered them, intent on killing them. But it's barely been four months since that fateful day in the Pocono woods when we all fought and then came together within minutes.

I work the dough into a fluffy pillow. "Glad someone's eating them." I had to tweak the recipe a bit, seeing as Alexie and Finn have a severe allergy to any pastry made with yeast. It's like eating rotten chicken to them, the yeast giving them the same symptoms as a bad case of food poisoning.

No matter. They still taste like my father's recipe.

"It's been a treat, I assure you." Callum's sigh fills the kitchen as he pulls out a chair at the table, the wobbly legs creaking in protest.

I let the room fill with silence as I continue to work the dough. I won't kick him out of the kitchen; this is his home now, after all. But I won't force myself to engage in conversation to meet some expectation of politeness.

"I wanted to tell you," Callum starts, marring the quiet. "I've never found the right opportunity to express my sadness for Topher's passing." He pauses. "He was proud of you, Nora. Even for the short time I knew him, it was clear."

I press down on the dough, let it ooze between my fingers. "Stop talking about him, Callum," I whisper. "Please."

"I did not mean to–"

"It's fine. Really." I wipe a shaky hand across my forehead and leave a trail of sticky dough behind. Being mean to Callum is like kicking a newborn puppy. He's nothing but kind and sincere, and he adores Alexie, Seamus, and Helene. He's like their surrogate parent, though he can't be much older than they are.

"I do not mean to cause you more pain."

"You're not." My voice comes out broken. "I can't deal with more sympathy. Not in my own house."

"I understand."

Quiet separates us again as I roll out the dough and spread on melted butter, cinnamon, sugar, and nutmeg. The nutmeg is Topher's secret, the reason these things taste so good.

Shit.

I stop, press my hands against the counter, and close my eyes. Nutmeg *was* his secret.

Was.

Callum gives a polite cough behind his fist, reminding me that he's still sitting at the kitchen table.

I finally give him the respect of my attention. He deserves it, even if I'm in no mood to give it. I pull a kitchen towel from the oven handle and turn to lean a hip against the counter, wiping dough from my hands. Callum is gorgeous, obviously. The

23

adjective is a given at the beginning of the physical description of every Fae. His fiery hair that's long and always braided, chocolate-brown eyes so much like Pia's, slight build, and delicate features aren't striking like Finn's or Helene's. Looking at him, being near him, he's pleasant to be around in the way a favorite blanket comforts, if that makes sense. His kindness is his most remarkable attribute. His ability to forgive and carry on is something I've had firsthand experience with. He's never resented me for taking his hand. Every time I've apologized–and it's been many, *many* times–he tells me I was justified. The situation demanded it.

Yeah, I call bullshit on his reasoning, but I'm grateful for his compassion.

Anyway, I owe him my attention when he subtly asks for it, like right now. I'll owe him for the rest of my life.

"Did you want to talk to me about something, Callum?"

He shifts his gaze to his drumming fingers on the table with a contrite smile. "Am I that obvious?"

His smile is contagious, and it feels good on my lips. "It ain't every day you seek me out."

"I don't want to take up much of your time."

"It's fine. Really. Always feel free to speak with me."

"Thank you, Leader." He continues to tap his fingers, studying their movement. "What I'm to tell you... I'm fully aware of overstepping my boundaries, and this will no doubt anger him, but I wanted to express concern for my lord Finn," he says to his tapping fingers.

I tilt my head, tossing the towel onto the counter. "Finn? Why? Is he okay?"

"For now, I believe he is," Callum says. He lifts his attention to me. "I've studied Mage history, especially once I met our sweet Alexie and found out who she is. It's fascinating material. Finn is part of Mage lore, you see. He's spent the better part of two centuries spiriting Fae through the Windows in search of a better life."

Now, this is interesting, and a part of the Finn puzzle I want to know. "So, he's... what, to Fae, exactly?"

Callum smiles softly. "A hero in fairytales. When Alexie's mother revealed to me that he's indeed real–alive–and that they shared a lineage... Well, as a scholar, it was as if she gave me fuel to find everything, search out any and all knowledge of him. He is a hero. A quiet hero who has worked tirelessly to help our kind. But..."

When he stops talking, I realize I've barely taken a breath since he mentioned Finn's name. My body is tense and feeling not my own. I sit next to Callum, cover his white-knuckled hand. "Tell me."

"It's his power, Nora. He's taking longer to recuperate. When you came home, he seemed horribly drained. And he's slept for longer than what's normal."

It doesn't surprise me that Callum watches Finn. The man is in awe of him, and now I understand better why.

"It was a whirlwind of flying and persuading and downright begging at times," I say, trying to convince myself as well as Callum. "He shut a lot of Windows, too. We're all tired."

Callum actually shows some irritation with me, snatching his hand from under mine. "You don't understand, Nora, and I'm sure he hasn't told you. It is not *normal* exhaustion."

"What kind of exhaustion is it, Callum?" Ice snakes its way inside my gut.

He bites on his lower lip. Then, "I believe he is iron-touched."

I tilt my head, scrunching my brow. "Iron-touched?"

"As Lord Finn told everyone months ago, iron has a more debilitating effect on Mages. It not only makes their magic unusable, being in iron shackles too long drains their very life. Lord Finn's incarceration, the five years he spent in Oberon's dungeon bound in iron, has had a much more dire effect on him than he's let on. I see that now."

Panic builds inside my chest. "How do we help him?" *Fix him? Make him whole? Save his life?*

"I... If what I surmise is true, he needs a Healer."

"I don't–What the hell are you talking about?"

"He requires a Healer. One like King Oberon's. They are rare, and I do know of another besides the king's, but..." He worries his bottom lip again.

"What happens if he doesn't find one of these Healers?"

Callum finally gives me his complete attention. "If he stays here and continues to use his magic with abandon, he'll die."

Chapter 4

I leave Callum in the kitchen and take off upstairs. My ears ring with his last two words. They make my clothes too tight and my lungs too small.

He'll die, he'll die, he'll die…

Callum didn't need to give more details. He didn't need to explain *anything* after those two words. He'd already given a solution: Find a Healer, save Finn's life. Period. Full stop.

When I reach Finn's bedroom door, my heart thuds painfully. It stings from the gash left by Callum's warning.

Finn won't die.

I won't let him.

I wrap my hand around the doorknob and close my eyes.

Deep breath in, slow breath out…

I'm quiet, respectful of the others sharing the room with Finn, but I sure as hell don't knock before I open the door. It takes a second for my eyes to adjust to the pitch black, the only light filtering in from the hallway. The room is huge, with two double beds and two sets of bunk beds. I don't need to search each bed to find Finn. He's claimed the double bed by the window since he's gotten here. After Topher let him out of the basement cell, of course.

Callum has claimed the other double bed, an upgrade since Luca left this room to sleep in Topher's old room, usually with me. Ben is still in my old room. And I… Well, I've been sleeping with Luca. His past grief and mine make good company.

Anyway, Seamus sleeps on the top bunk of one set of bunk beds, his phone tucked in his hands as he snores, and Malcolm, a half-human Assassin, sleeps on the bottom bunk of the other set. Both sets butt against the far wall, and all the beds sport quilts that have been in my family for ages. It's not five-star accommodations, but it's comfortable.

I try not to make a lot of noise as I go over to Finn's bed. Try. My fear makes it challenging. The old floor protests under my heavy footfalls.

"What the fuck, Nora?" Seamus hisses from his bunk. His thumbs are already going over his screen even though he's looking at me. Teens and their cell phones, man.

"Go back to sleep," I hiss-whisper back.

"Whatever. Damn." He turns to face the wall, his phone screen flashing in the dark.

I ignore him and stand over Finn. Some of the fear-induced anger diminishes as I watch him sleep. He's so beautiful, even while sleeping. Even with the dark circles under his eyes that the hallway light and Seamus's phone screen catch. Not even sleep rids his skin of them. I should have paid more attention, saw his exhaustion for what it is.

Instead of shaking him like I'd planned, I bend to whisper in his ear. "Finn."

His eyes flash open in an instant. They're glittering silver shards of glass cutting through the dark. They're also filled with confusion and panic. Before I have time to react, he grabs my wrist with surprising strength. His grip is so tight, I feel my bones crack under it.

What the hell?

"Hey!" I say a little too loudly, which wakes up Malcolm.

"You okay over there, Nora?" Subtle warning fills Malcolm's question. I appreciate the sentiment, though he has no chance to save me if I actually needed saving. He's a sweet guy, and his parents are great–parents who are in the room across the hall, I might add–but he's weak. Ben and Luca have been working with him. So has Jessie. Yet, no amount of skill can erase his humanness. That part makes him fragile. Physically, anyway.

"I'm fine," I say through gritted teeth. "Go back to sleep."

Damn, I fucked this up. So much for a stealthy Finn extraction.

The grip Finn has on my wrist loosens and his eyes are instantly softer, full of alarm. "Did I hurt you?" The anxiety in his voice isn't normal. Not for Finn. It makes him vulnerable, like the dark circles under his eyes.

I pull my wrist from his lax grip, rubbing where I can already feel my body healing. "No." As he opens his mouth to speak, I lift a hand. "I need to talk to you."

"In the dead of night?" He throws the quilt off his legs despite his question and stands. He only wears flannel pajama bottoms. His chest is all sinewy muscle, muscle that also ripples across his abs. His skin is tan, which makes his gray eyes more noticeable, more vibrant; it makes his delectable body more mouthwatering, too.

I lick my lips, trying to muster up some of the angry fear that brought me up here. "Yeah, right now." I head for the door, fully expecting him to follow me. "Downstairs."

"Easy, love. Let me don a shirt first. I wouldn't want you to be distracted during our secret conversation."

I roll my eyes–and feel my face heat. Looks like he's back to himself. And yup, he caught me eye-fucking him.

I don't miss Seamus's snicker, either. "I'm shutting off your phone," I mutter to him as I escape into the hallway.

Once downstairs, I grab coats for me and Finn off the hooks by the living room door and remove the barricade to the porch. The cold instantly seeps into my bones, and I still get triggered by its bite. Since Alexie used her magic on me, I can't be cold and not have flashbacks. Mild flashbacks, but there all the same.

I slip on my coat as Finn comes out, and then toss Topher's heavy Carhart to him. Without a word, he tugs it on as he takes in the darkened yard. White mounds of snow glint like diamonds in the moonlight, and stars twinkle brightly in the sky. Only two months ago, blood and the dead covered this yard. Mostly hapless Fae and Oberon's soldiers.

And my father.

Damn it!

No.

I can't let my mind go down that path. Not now. Not during an imminent crisis, like Finn's finite time on this side of the Window.

"I'm sorry, Nora, for grabbing you." Finn's words are soft and full of regret, and he still doesn't look at me. "It seems five years of incarceration made me more than a little untrusting."

I rub my wrist, already healed and perfectly fine. It's difficult to remember this man has demons haunting him. He's always so confident. "Yeah, no, don't apologize. I shouldn't have woken you that way." In hindsight, a rash move on my part.

"Why *have* you awakened me, love?" He zips the Carhart to his chin and finally looks at me with a subtle grin. "Not that I don't admire the dramatics, but you must work on your delivery."

Nope. I will not fall for his charm, despite his perfect smile, showing his perfect teeth, and revealing the perfect dimple on his perfect right cheek. "Callum told me about you. About using your magic. How it..." I force myself to say the next words without my voice hitching. "How it's killing you. He told me you were iron-touched."

His smile doesn't waver, but humor leaves his eyes as they turn hard and as glittering as the snow on the moonlit ground. His reaction confirms everything Callum said. "Callum is a busybody, it appears. Perhaps I should have a talk with him."

I try not to stomp my foot. Failing. "You'll leave him alone, and you're focusing on the wrong part of what I said. Why wouldn't you tell me?"

He raises a perfectly arched brow. "Would you worry about me? Ensure that I'm tucked away safely in a bubble of Assassin protection?"

"Yes!" I close my eyes against his patronizing tone. "Yes, damn it. That's exactly what I would do."

30

"Well, then. You've answered your own question."

He's so insufferable! I find myself always on the verge of smacking that supercilious smile from his lips or kissing it away. I believe the latter would shock him more.

My brain floods with a huge pool of…something for Finn. Something I'm not ready to decipher. No, I won't hit him–or kiss him. I'll give him my fear. "I can't lose you, too, Finn. I won't."

There. I said it. This infuriating man has burrowed under my skin so deeply, I'd hemorrhage if he were ripped out of me. I want our Bond complete. I need it.

How did that happen?

I open my eyes to find the pretentiousness he wears like a mask has melted away. He's staring at me, his face soft and so striking without a glamour, even with the dark circles marring his skin.

"Nora…" My name is a whisper on his lips as he takes the wrist he'd hurt in his warm hand. His fingers are long, elegant like a pianist's fingers. Graceful. And his touch activates the Pull melting my stomach. He slides his thumb over my skin, and I feel it all the way to my bones. "I will never hurt you." He pauses as he examines my healed wrist. "Not intentionally."

"Your death would hurt me, Finn."

He *tsks*, his silver gaze never leaving my wrist. "You mustn't get attached to me, love. *That* will hurt you."

"Whether or not I like it, biology has dictated I'm attached." I take my wrist from his relaxed grip. "And, yes, I admit it. There's a Pull. Happy?"

"Absolutely not." He sighs and moves to the steps, sitting on the first one. "Sit with me. Please," he adds when I don't move.

Sighing, I tuck my hands in my pockets and lower beside him. The cold from the freezing boards bleeds through my yoga pants, making my ass cheeks numb in seconds. His answer confuses me. *Absolutely not*? I always got the feeling he wanted to connect with me. He's made moves, shown compassion, knowingly turned me inside out with a touch.

"Finn?" I keep my voice soft. "Do you… want to Bond with me?"

31

He studies the yard as sadness dims his contemplative expression. My heart breaks a little without him having to say a word. I already know the answer. Finally, he says, "It's not a matter of want, Nora."

I swallow, my gaze cemented to his profile. I couldn't look away if I wanted to. "Then what is it?"

He finally gives me his attention, and his face is tight with regret. "We could never–A Bond with me will only cause you pain. I... I can't give all of myself."

"Because you're sick?"

He gives his attention back to the yard and says nothing for so long, I wonder if he heard me. Then, "Yes, among other things."

"What other things?"

He tugs on his coat sleeves, concentrating on the task. "I'm needed elsewhere, love. I'll always be needed elsewhere."

The pain in my chest is quick and sharp. I press a hand to my heart, already feeling the loss of what I never had. I try to say something, *anything,* that would let him know I understand, but I fail. My brain understands, but my heart is confused as fuck.

After a few moments of silence, I clear my throat. "How long before you...?" I can't even say it.

The sadness on his face washes away with relief when I change the subject, and fuck, that hurts even more. "Perish? Die a fiery death? How long before this world drains every ounce of life from my poor, withered body?"

"All right, stop."

He chuckles, still admiring the snowy yard. "I've lived over a thousand years. It'll take a lot more to do me in."

"How long?"

His quiet contemplation of the yard answers me loud and clear.

"You need to go back."

"How do you propose I do that? Our Window is closest to Oberon's palace. I can't just traipse through now, can I?"

Yeah, I know that. Of course I do. It's no secret where our Window leads. It's the very Window from where Finn escaped

Etherias–which brings a long-awaited question to my mind: "How did they capture you?"

It's something I've always wondered, though never came close to asking. When I first met him, starving and close to death with iron cuffs on his wrists and a busted leg, I didn't like him enough to care.

Now?

Even if he can't Bond with me, I still want to know all there is to know about him.

"Unseelie magic created the Windows," Finn says after a moment. Finally, he gives the yard a break to look at me, his face gorgeously sincere. "When a Mage crosses, the Windows tend to… feed from us. Drain our powers. Only for seconds, but those seconds were all it took. Trackers must've caught wind of my impending return to Etherias after meeting with your mother and knew where I was entering." He pauses to tuck hair behind my ear with a sad smile. "Oberon's Guard was waiting for me with an iron blanket, and that's all she wrote, so to speak."

I take his hand and hold it on my lap. I need to touch him now. Need to feel the heat of his skin. "And the way you escaped… after all those years?"

"I was honest when I told everyone my cell door was left opened one day." He wipes the corners of his mouth with his free hand. "I couldn't believe my fortune. And when I found the Window leading to your land left unguarded…" He lets out a dumbfounded scoff. "Someone helped me escape, Nora. Someone risked their life to make sure I came here. I'm sure of it now." Finn's eyes are wide with gratefulness. It makes him vulnerable, and fierce protectiveness washes over me.

And it solidifies my decision. "We'll find another Window. We need to go. *You* need to go."

"I've closed every Window remotely near us."

"Yeah, and it's taking a toll on you to keep them closed."

"Yes, it does, and the only other person capable of maintaining the magic locks on them is Alexie. A child, untrained and incapable of keeping multiple Windows closed." He says the last part as if I've forgotten the girl is only eight.

"And it will be even more complicated to keep them closed in Etherias."

"We can–"

"I can't keep them closed forever, and Alexie is not ready to take over the task. She's capable of maybe keeping our Window closed, and that's it. When my magic fails, they'll be coming for you. I won't be safely tucked away while you're in danger."

See? This is so damn confusing. He can't give himself to me, but he'll risk his life to protect me?

"You're not making sense, Finn. How can you help your people, *give* yourself to them, if you're dead?"

He stands and bends to kiss the top of my head in a placating way that infuriates me. "I'm not leaving, Nora. End of story." He stops before opening the door. With his back to me, he says, "I've been there for you when you needed me. Given to you without question or complaint."

I stare at his rigid back. "I know, and I'm thankful. Grateful for all you've done."

"Then as a favor to me, do not speak of my illness with anyone else, not even Ben or Luca. Can you do that?"

"What you're asking is almost impossible. They'll–"

"Yes or no, Assassin."

I take a deep breath and close my eyes, regretting what I'm about to agree to. "Yes, Finn. I'll keep your secrets."

"Thank you." Finn slips back inside without another word.

Chapter 5

Four days go by, and it's mostly a blur. Like most days. We train, eat, strategize. Mill around aimlessly in times of quiet. A lot of boredom takes place during a war.

For the most part, Callum avoids Finn like the tattletale he is, and Finn avoids me like the infuriating Unseelie he is. He spends most of his time with Alexie, teaching her, showing her how to control her power.

Only one blip ruffles our routine. Malcolm's parents left two days ago. I decided they'd be safer somewhere else. More specifically, I felt they'd be safer in South America. They agreed with only a little pushback. Our Order paid for the trip, and it was worth the cost. We can't be worrying about people who can't take care of themselves, not when we've got a child queen to look after.

I bake at night. It's a hard habit to break, and the one thing that brings me closer to Topher. Closer to Pia, as well. I haven't given up on her. I don't know what the hell happened, and what connection she has with Oberon, but I refuse to believe she's dead. I refuse to believe she's anything more than a friend who tried to help.

Tonight, I lie in bed next to Luca in Topher's room and wish for sleep. Honestly, making more pastries at this point is wasteful. Too many baked goods flood the kitchen. They'd feed the house for a month. Even Seamus and Luca, who can plow through some shit, wouldn't put much of a dent in the supply. The freezer is full of muffins, cookies–and yes, cinnamon rolls.

I blink into the darkness, stare at the shadowed cracks in the ceiling plaster. While we were out west, all I wanted was this bed and the bottle I have stashed under it. Haven't touched the bottle, and sleep is still being a fucker. Every time I close my eyes, I see my father, Pia–and Finn. They all stand in a line, pale faces and accusing sneers aimed at me.

I rip the covers off.

Can't do it. The freezer's going to get fuller.

I move to get up–and a well-muscled arm wraps around my waist, trapping me to the mattress. "Stay, Nora. Sleep." Luca's husky voice fills my heart, and his touch feels so goddamn good.

I hate how I can still feel so good when my father's dead and Pia's gone. "I can't sleep."

"Try."

"What do you think I've been doing?"

My attitude doesn't faze him. No, he nuzzles my neck, kissing the sensitive spot behind my ear. "You've been staring at the ceiling, letting your brain take you down a rabbit hole."

Okay, so, yeah, his analysis is spot on.

I huff out a sigh and relent to Luca's touch, nestling to his side and stealing his strength, wishing I still had my own. I can't help the guilt invading me. Can't stop feeling as if I need to continue the self-imposed punishment of not being with Luca or Ben–and I haven't been with them. Meaning, no sex. None. Even though my treacherous body screams for it.

"I'm sorry, Luca." My voice is barely a whisper, barely a sound at all.

"You've nothing to be sorry for." He adjusts us until I'm fitted perfectly in the crook of his arm as he lies on his back. I regret having the iron shields up to keep the monsters away. They block the moonlight from sneaking through the windowpanes. I want to see Luca's bare chest. Read the tattooed names of his family. Show my love for people I'll never meet.

"I do, though. I've neglected you… and Ben."

"You've done no such thing, lass. 'Tis not your job to service us."

I grin against his chest, absorbing the warmth of his skin against my cheek. He's irritated with my words. His gruff, old-man voice is a dead giveaway. "I love you, Luca." So much. What I feel for him and Ben, what the Bond gives me, it swells my damaged heart, makes the ache less painful.

"And I you." He runs his fingertips over my arm in gentle laps, creating a trail of goosebumps.

"I know."

I move closer to him, his heat extracting some of the toxic thoughts from my body. The kind of toxins that jam ugly, gruesome pictures through my mind. The guilt is there still. It's a nagging voice telling me I don't deserve a respite from the chaos in my brain. But it doesn't roar loudly in this quiet moment, not while I breathe in Luca's spicy clove scent and concentrate on the steady *thu-thump* of his heart. The guilt reduces to a whisper, a shadow of its former self. I miss physical contact; miss the relief it gives. I miss how it softens edges and soothes grief, no matter how temporary.

I press my lips against Luca's rib cage, savoring how this one touch makes his breath hitch. His fingers go from lightly scaling my arm to sliding down to my waist. He doesn't tuck his hand under my T-shirt, doesn't take his touch further, but the pressure of his hand, the way he kneads my muscles, ignites a flicker of heat I can't bring myself to extinguish. Not tonight. I want the flicker to flame and explode. I want it to burn away the guilt and sorrow and abject fear of not knowing what the hell I'm doing.

My tongue darts out, tasting the heat and saltiness of his skin. His grip on my waist tightens, and his heart beats faster. Luca's instant reaction feeds the flicker like oxygen.

I use my hand to see what the iron barriers steal from my eyes. My palm travels over Luca's muscled chest, all the dips and sleek angles. I know the names he's tattooed on his body like my own family. I've memorized them, revered them. During quiet, sleepless nights, with only dim light from an oil lamp, I'd watch

Luca sleep, studying the inked map of his kin and Order on his fair skin.

Before we went west, he had Topher's name inscribed below his family's names. He didn't tell me he was going to do it. I found his new tattoo one morning while in New Mexico with the Southwest Order. It broke my heart and filled it at the same time. I didn't believe it was possible, but I fell more in love with him after that. My patient, thoughtful giant.

I press a hand to Topher's name now, not requiring light to know where it is. My lips don't leave Luca's skin as I explore with my hand. He's so warm and hard, and the only thing in the world I want right now is his weight on top of me.

My shirt gets in the way, my skin pleading for a connection with his. I sit up long enough to lift the fabric over my head, and almost cry out when I come back down on his chest, my nipples taut and sliding over him. My core throbs with need.

He growls, no longer allowing me to explore. He's a man starved. With a tug at my waist, he switches our positions. His hand slides down the length of my side, and his luscious weight presses me into the mattress.

Tears spring to my eyes then. I wrap my arms around his neck and run my fingers through his short hair. I bring him so close we're no longer two people.

Luca cups my face between his large hands, and even with almost zero visibility, I can see his whiskey eyes taking in mine. He leans in to kiss the wetness that slips to my cheeks and whispers sweet words in his lyrical accent. My giant doesn't give me empathy words I've heard a thousand times already. He gives me himself, and it's exactly what I need.

His erection rests against my stomach while he shows me compassion, his love. It's so intimate, so raw, this dichotomy. It's absolutely, unequivocally, who Luca is.

I arch my back to get closer, reveling in how he feels, the silkiness of his skin. He groans when I rotate my hips so that he's nestled between my thighs. His gentle kisses on my cheeks become more demanding when he reaches my mouth. His hips, now in sync with mine, fan the fire hotter inside me. I need him closer, need him to give me release with quick, deliberate strokes.

Yet, he takes his time. Shows restraint I never have. And I love the sweet torture of it.

He smiles against my neck when I huff out impatience. "I'll take care of you, lass. I promise." His voice is a low rumble, filled with the brogue that drives me to the brink. His voice is music and poetry. Kindness and honesty.

My fingertips glide over his shoulders and travel the rippling muscles of his back. He feels *so* damn good, his weight, his mouth now skimming my collarbone, his big hand lifting my thigh to bring his cock closer to my wet folds.

I squirm to get him inside me, but he holds himself back. He's in control, and it's hot and frustrating. Luca's the calm to my storm. Has been since I met him.

His mouth finally connects with a nipple, and I moan out my pleasure when he nips and licks. I push on the back of his head, coaxing him closer. When he does, my eyelids shudder in bliss, and I close my eyes to absorb all of it. Gods, I miss this. I *have* neglected my men–and my own body. Luca is mending the jagged edges with every touch. I only hope I'm doing the same for him.

He moves lower down my body, his hands now on each side of my rib cage. I concentrate on the feel of his fingertips against my skin, the way his large hands can almost meet on my breastbone. His thumbs brush my nipples as he trails slow, savoring kisses over my abdomen. I can't stop moving underneath him. My skin is sensitive against his silky hardness, and it ignites every nerve ending.

"You're ready for me, are you?" He chuckles at my insistence, and it's not only humor filling the sound. His relief gushes through our Bond. I know he can feel my desire to heal, to become active instead of a passive participant in life, as I have been for over two months.

A smile–a genuine smile–curves my lips as I lace my fingers in his hair. "Slip into me and find out if I'm ready."

"Oh, I'll be doing that." He plants a kiss on my inner thigh. "As soon as you're screaming for me."

And then his tongue flicks my throbbing clit.

Ahhh!

My mind is gone, replaced with feral need as Luca's tongue moves fast and slow, fast and slow. I rear off the bed when his lips join his tongue as he sucks, sucks, sucks until I'm screaming. Writhing. And exploding against his mouth as I come and come. Release brings clarity. Beautiful blue clarity, like the clearing sky after a thunderstorm. I feel... alive again. Myself.

And I pray to any gods listening for the feeling to stay with me, even a small piece of it.

Luca again brings his body flush with mine. I can't quite see his smile, but I can feel it through the Bond. He smooths hair from my face, kisses my forehead, my cheeks, the tip of my nose. And as he presses his lips to mine, he finally, *finally*, drives into me.

I gasp in surprised pleasure as he stretches me. He's big everywhere, and he fills me up. My body arcs to meet his slow thrusts, and as he moves, another climax builds inside me. His ragged breath wafts against my neck, his face buried there as he rolls and circles his hips, finding my G spot in that expert way he always does. Sweat slicks his back, his chest. His skin is wet heat against mine, and I bring him as close as I can, my hips moving to match his pace.

My body is pleading for release as my climax builds and builds. "Luca," I breathe. "Please."

This time, he listens. His control snaps, and he drives into me faster. He palms my ass, bringing me closer, his rhythm jerky, impatient.

I love his control.

And I die for the moment when he can no longer keep it.

He groans out his pleasure, his voice deep, guttural. My sounds mimic his as he takes me higher and higher. "Luca... I'm coming. Luca!" I yell into the darkness as my body explodes for the second time. It sends rivulets of pleasure to every nerve, every single pore.

His moan of release follows shortly after, and I bask in the way he throbs inside me as he pumps out his orgasm. When he stills, he rains kisses on my face, my neck. It's as if he's memorizing me all over again. His breath is a rough symphony against my skin, his glistening body a clove-scented weight keeping me anchored in the here and now. At this moment, when I close my eyes, I see him. I see Ben. Finn.

I see what I need to see.

"I've missed you," he whispers into the darkness.

I tighten my arms around him, burying my face in his neck. "I'm back, Luca. I'm back."

Chapter 6

Daylight brings a heaping amount of determination with it.

I wake to the iron shields up and Luca gone. We always open the shields during the day while we train, and it's been me opening them lately, seeing as I'm usually still awake. Not today, though. Someone else took the liberty and let me sleep. Luca or Ben, probably.

I stretch out the kinks, my arms high over my head, and feel deliciously achy from last night. For once, I'm rested. Alert. Exhaustion doesn't chase me this morning. Neither does misery.

Sadness is still there. It lingers in the recesses of my mind, waiting for a chance to pounce on all the progress I've made in the last ten hours.

I won't let it.

At least, I won't kneel to it and give in so easily.

It'll have to fight me to get another good grip.

I pull the quilts to my chin, smell Luca on the worn, soft fabric as I peer out the window. The sounds of training travel through the thin windowpane: knives clashing, Ben ribbing Seamus, and Seamus comfortable enough to tell him to fuck off with a laugh. Alexie's little voice tinkles like music, filled with glee, as she cheers on Ben, who no doubt is kicking the shit out of Seamus. Luca's thick accent rumbles in the mix, his cranky directions to Seamus to dodge and move making me grin. Helene also gives gentle guidance to Seamus—and he doesn't swear at her when she does. Maybe he's more afraid of our warrior Pixie than two Unseelie Mages and a few Assassins.

A contented sigh drifts from my mouth as I tune in to my Order. My family. They're worth fighting for. Worth getting out of my head and figuring out a way to keep them alive and safe.

My father would want me to do exactly that.

It's not Topher's death I think about now. I think about how he lived. How he persevered when so many of us didn't after Mama and Casey died.

If a place exists for pure souls beyond this plane, Topher's there and probably itching to leave its comforts to come kick my ass. He wouldn't have taken two months to wallow in despair. He'd already have a plan to get Pia back and stick it to Oberon.

Deep breath in, I throw the covers off me and head up to the bathroom to pee, shower, and brush my teeth. Today is going to be the first day on the road back to normalcy. Some won't like how we get there, but damn it, I'm Leader now. It's time I act like it.

When I get into the kitchen, Jessie is there with Callum. Both sip coffee at the table and talk in quiet tones. They've gotten close in the time we've all spent together. Not on-the-verge-of-fucking close, mind you. More like friends. Confidants.

Can't say it surprises me. Callum has an easy way about him, a calmness and intelligence that radiates in a quiet, powerful glow. And Jessie? She might be all sarcastic and sexy on the outside, but we depend on her brain. She runs a huge securities company in Pittsburg, and she knows everything there is to know about weapons and explosives. Her area of expertise and Callum's go together like peas and carrots.

I swallow, not really knowing how to act, when I go for the percolator on the stove. Their conversation has gone silent, and their pity for me slams into my back. Everyone's on eggshells. Everyone's treating me with kid gloves.

I pour a cup of coffee and dump in creamer from the ceramic, cow-shaped creamer pot on the counter. With feigned nonchalance, I sip and stare out the window, taking in the smell of burning wood from the stove and trying to ignore the loud silence behind me. After another slow sip, I turn to the kitchen table, lean a hip on the counter, and find empathy smiles.

Jessie doesn't wear that stiff smile well. It doesn't suit her. I want the Jessie everyone else gets. The bitchy, fierce fighter who doesn't put up with any shit.

"Morning," I tell their ridiculous expressions. I'm surprised by my voice. I sound like me. For the first time in a while, there's energy behind what I say.

And they notice, their stiff smiles slipping into more relaxed ones. Relief smiles.

Jessie wraps her hands around her mug and leans forward. "How you doing, chick?"

I take another sip. "Better," I say and mean it. "Much better."

Jessie gets up and drapes her arms around my shoulders. She smells of expensive perfume and leather, and her silky black hair tickles my nose.

I wrap my free hand around her, squeezing as tightly as I can. "Sorry it took so long."

"It took exactly as long as it needed." She gives me one last squeeze before pulling away. Tears glisten in her dark eyes. No need to bring it to her attention. She'd never admit it. "Right. Okay, yeah. Ah… I need to get out there, help Helene show those boys how it's really done." Jessie waves to Callum. "Coming?"

He gives her a subtle nod and tucks his hands–shit–*hand* on his lap. "In a moment." If I didn't know any better, I'd say he was trying to hide his nerves. We haven't spoken since he let the cat out of the bag.

Jessie opens the kitchen screen door. "Don't be long."

When Jessie leaves, I regard Callum with my head tilted, tapping on my mug. His skin pales a bit, but he meets my gaze. He's not a warrior or a fighter, but he's no coward.

"I'm not mad, Callum. I'm glad you told me, despite how irritated Finn is about it."

45

"I have no regrets, Leader," Callum says in his quiet voice. He lifts his chin. "If I am able to save Lord Finn's life by revealing his secrets, so be it."

It took guts for Callum to tell me what he had. Finn would never hurt him or anything like that. It's more complicated than fear of physical pain. Look, it might seem odd, but Callum idolizes Finn like he's a king. To betray one's king is a pretty big fucking deal. We all found that out the hard way.

"Finn will get over it," I finally say. "Don't sweat it, okay?"

"What, exactly, am I to get over, love?"

I peer up from Callum's now whitened face to find Finn leaning against the archway between the kitchen and living room. Shit, man. He can move like a ghost when he wants to.

And Finn's smile could freeze the Atlantic.

I inhale at the shiver tapping up my spine. I wouldn't want to be the person this man is pissed at.

Damn, I feel sorry for Callum.

But our resident Seelie doesn't cower, doesn't shrink into himself. Instead, he stands, pulls his handless right arm behind his back, and gives Finn a slight bow. "I've been meaning to speak with you, my lord."

Finn shakes his head with a dramatic eye roll. "*Finn*, Callum. That is my name. Not 'Lord,' or any variation of it."

Callum says nothing when corrected. No matter how many times Finn has tried, Callum hasn't listened. He respects Finn too much to respect his desire not to be called a lord. Weird, I know.

"May I have a word with you?" Callum says. At least he skipped the formal address this time.

"What would you like to talk about, *hmmm*? How you decided to speak with Nora before consulting me?" Finn keeps his hands folded in front of him. "Did it even occur to you that I might listen to what you have to say?"

Confusion ripples through Callum's eyes. Nope. That obviously never crossed his mind. "I... Well..."

Time to save the day. I know a cornered animal when I see one. "Callum, go on outside. Help occupy Alexie for a while."

Relief floods his face. "Yes, of course, Leader." He gives Finn another bow and stiffly walks outside.

When it's only Finn and me, the kitchen becomes smaller. Quieter. The smell of coffee wafts between us, and the one sound puncturing the silence is the old clock on the mantle in the living room tick, tick, ticking away in soft defiance.

Finn's icy smile morphs into something different, more predatory. His eyes glint like sunbeams on silver, his lips curved slightly. Challenge brightens his face. And maybe something more… wild. "Are we to stare at each other all day?" He pushes off the wall and takes a few steps closer to me. A silver lock slips to his forehead, and he runs his fingers through his hair to put it back in place. Jesus, his new style suits him. All sex and sophistication. "Not that I mind this game. I quite like staring at you."

When he's close enough, he runs a finger from my cheek to my collarbone. His scent, like a frosty, clean winter morning, assails me, seeping into every pore. Tired circles still paint the tan skin beneath his eyes, but he somehow makes it impossible to focus on his exhaustion.

I close my panting mouth, step back until my hip bumps the warm stove. This Finn, I'm uneasy around. He's sex and lust and makes my breath catch in the back of my throat. He's intimidating, I hate to admit.

And also, fuck him for doing it. He plays these games I now know are only games. He has no plans to Bond with me.

"You say you don't want to Bond, but you still do this shit. Stop," I tell him, my voice a shadow of its usual timbre.

He tilts his head, takes another step closer until I'm pressed against the warm face of the woodstove. Still keeping me hostage with his silver gaze, he places a hand on my waist and gently guides me away from the hot surface to lean against the counter. "I believe I said 'can't,' Assassin."

"Same thing."

His face finally takes on a serious frown. "It isn't. I assure you."

I close my eyes against his sincerity. It's so much stronger than his empty seduction. "That doesn't matter now. You made yourself clear." No, he really hasn't, but I know better than to expect him to be clear about anything. "We have things to discuss."

My words act like cold water dumped on his head. He steps back. Oh, yes, those dark circles are more noticeable now. Arrogant Fae. Just because he can make my panties wet *and* my heart ache for what could've been, it doesn't mean he can steamroll me into forgetting his time on this earth is frustratingly finite.

He huffs out a sigh and reaches behind me for an empty mug. His shoulders are centimeters from my face, and I take a selfish moment to breathe him in. As he grabs the percolator to pour himself coffee, he says, "You look… better."

"I feel better, thank you." My tone is now all polite formality while I sip on my coffee. I can ignore the electricity his nearness sets off in my nerve endings. "And we still need to talk about your situation."

"We don't, Nora. Leave it alone." Warning coats his voice. "As delightful as your new position is, you are not my Leader."

I meet his intense gaze even though it makes sweat pool at the roots of my hair. I try to funnel some of my father's authority into the way I stand, the way I answer him. "When you're in this house, and the safety of my Order is at stake, I'm a fucking god. We don't do democracies here."

His face becomes stone, and I hate to admit it scares me some. He's dangerous when he needs to be, and despite how my body reacts to him, despite the Pull, I can't forget that.

"We'll see about that, little Leader." He takes one slow sip of coffee, sets his half-full mug in the sink, and slips out the kitchen screen door.

Holy fuck.

My mug clatters to the counter, thanks to trembling hands. I grip the edge of the sink for support, digging in my nails until they bend against the unforgiving porcelain. As I peer out the window, watching everyone train, my gaze drifts to Ben and

Luca, who are now joined by Finn. They move off to the side yard, away from the mock fighting, talking with their heads tilted toward one another. Who knows what they're talking about?

I bet they're not talking about how Finn turned me inside out.

My attention is ripped away from them as Helene lets out a high-pitched scream. "No!" she yells. "Alexie, stop. Don't touch it!"

Fear burns through my veins as I race outside, following the screams to the shed containing all our weapons. Ben beats me to it, Alexie in his arms in seconds. He holds her close, panic in his green eyes as he inspects a small bleeding cut on her index finger.

My own panic churns in my gut as I focus on the three swords hanging in the shed next to two sets of almost impenetrable lirium armor. The three swords we'd salvaged from Oberon's attack.

The three magic-bound swords.

One touch, one tiny nick, and these things will kill you. Kellen wielded one exactly like it, one that killed my father. My gaze darts to the lock on the shed, a lock Alexie's magic broke.

Fuck!

"What were you thinking?" Ben demands of her, his fingers shaking around hers. Helene cries silent tears beside them, her hands roaming over Alexie's slight body, pressing against her tiny chest as if feeling for a heartbeat. Luca scowls at the swords, while Finn, Seamus, Jessie, and Callum surround Ben, all concentrating on our child queen.

Alexie smiles at Ben and lifts a finger for all of us to see. "They were dangerous, and so I fixed them."

"Fixed them?" Finn's voice comes out strangled, fierce. "You do not know how to–"

"I do, my lord cousin. I've been working to break the spell, and it finally came to me." She then whispers an incantation to him, and as she spills out foreign words, Finn's frown transforms into a radiant smile. It almost masks the exhaustion plaguing him. "You see?" she finishes puffing out her chest in Ben's arms. "It works. I'm still alive."

49

"That you are." Finn brushes silver hair from her forehead as everyone lets out relieved chuckles and sighs and, in Luca's case, grumpy words about naughty girls. "You're brilliant, little queen. Positively stunning."

Chapter 7

Hours later, after Alexie regales everyone with her breakthrough spell while eating supper, I stand in the middle of the living room on the old rug with everyone waiting for me to speak. It's completely surreal in the worst way possible. Déjà vu strikes me as I take it all in.

Luca sits in the rocking chair by the window, and Jessie slouches on the oversized window ledge beside him. Helene, Callum, Seamus, and Alexie are at attention on the couch, patiently waiting for me to speak. Well, all except Seamus are patient. His face is buried in his phone as he sprawls at the end of the couch, acting as bored as he probably is. Good thing I love the kid. Malcolm hangs by Ben near the archway between the kitchen and the living room, the spot I used to occupy before–

Yeah. Before.

I smile at Ben, who winks at me. I miss him. Miss being with him. And I plan to remedy that tonight. That is, if he's not too pissed at me after this meeting.

Anyway, apart from Finn, everyone waits for me to speak, as we all would wait for Topher to speak during these house meetings. The craving for my father's presence in this moment overwhelms me. He was always so calm, so sure of himself when he'd address us. Nothing like Mama, who used her passion and let her emotions carry her away at times when she was Leader. However, like when she was in charge, what Topher said went, and he was confident enough to look us all in the eye when he gave us our orders.

What I'm about to tell everyone saps the confidence from me. I don't show my trepidation. A weak Leader is like blood in the water, even with an Order as close as mine. No one will listen to a wilting flower tell them what needs to be done. I wouldn't in their shoes.

I can't be passionate like Mama was, though. She might have gotten carried away, but she never lost control of the room. I don't have that kind of restraint. So, faux calm matching my father's real calm it is.

All I'm waiting on to get started mapping out our next course of action–which at least three people are going to have a serious issue with–is for Finn to get his ass in here. He's one of the three. I'll give you two guesses who the other two are.

When Finn graces us with his presence, he waltzes in as if we're doing nothing in here except playing Scrabble or something. "Sorry, I'm late. Horrendous traffic."

Ben snorts, and I shoot him a scowl. He gives me an innocent, wide-eyed look. Then Seamus snickers, and I feel my control slipping.

Luca, my grumpy savior, speaks up. "You're about as funny as the lad, mate." He points to Seamus, who doesn't look up from his phone. "Sit so we can sort out this mess once and for all."

Finn raises his hands in mock surrender. "Touchy, aren't we?" He then takes his place on the arm of the couch, hands resting on his hips and ankles crossed. He stares at me with a face full of subtle warning.

I swallow. Right, then. Time to agitate the hive.

I cross my arms over my chest, relax my stance, copy every bit of body language I can remember from my father while he stood here. I won't apologize for being an absent Leader since inheriting the title. It's a small miracle I recovered as much as I have.

Instead, first things first: "Seamus." I wait until he looks up from his phone. "Give us an update on the New York situation."

Seamus huffs out a sigh as he pulls up a video to show me. "This is trending on TikTok. Pretty fucked up."

I take a few steps forward to get a better look. Ben, Luca, and Finn move in closer with me. I ordered a bunch of hotspots for the house, which helps with the shitty internet issue. It also helps Seamus keep track of the mess we left in New York.

A short video of a dude who's clearly a Pixie sits in Julius's living room with some song about "money and bitches" playing as background music. No surprise, the video is trending. A beautiful, slender man with slightly pointed ears gives pouty lips while showing off all those Rococo paintings and iron statues. At least his wings aren't out. A slight relief.

"Fuck me," Luca mutters, snatching Seamus's phone for a better look.

"Dude," Seamus says, his hands out and voice whiny. "Not cool."

Luca ignores him and pins me with a concerned frown. "We cannot let this go on, Nora."

Helene stands to get a look at the video. Her full lips twist with disgust. "Where is his honor?"

Honor. What everything in life boils down to for her. She is a warrior, after all. She'd fit in with Arthur at his Round Table.

"He's obviously lacking in that department," Luca tells her, squeezing the phone in his large palm.

"Uh… yo, can I have that back before you break it?" Seamus asks. His irritation makes Luca's knuckles whiter as he adds pressure. "Hey, sorry. Sorry! Just…" He's pleading like his cell phone is an abandoned infant as he reaches for it again.

Luca glares at him a second before tossing the thing back on the kid's lap. "Next time, tell us sooner when the todgers are wreaking so much havoc, ye eejit."

"Okay, enough," I say when Seamus opens his mouth to retort. It doesn't take much for Luca and Seamus to go at it. I clear my throat. "Luca's right. I've ignored the mess in New York for too long, especially now that Fae are camping out at Julius's."

Where the only known supply of red pills is located, by the way. I hope like hell they're not gone. Our stash is low.

I give Luca my full attention. "I need you to go back there with Malcolm and Seamus. Secure the pills and take care of the threat as best you can."

The room is quiet, a tomb.

Wait until they hear the rest of the plan.

Finally, Luca kisses my cheek, and whispers in my ear, "Smart, lass."

It's a simple compliment, but I flush with appreciation for it, anyway. It's good to feel in control again, even if I fight grief to maintain it. I tip my chin at him with a small smile, and then find Malcolm and Seamus. "You two up for it?" Not that they have a choice.

"Definitely," Seamus says, his glowing violet eyes blazing with purpose. "I need to get the hell out of these woods and rejoin civilization."

I smirk at him. The kid hates the city when he's in it and hates the woods when he's stuck in them. I need a teen decoder ring. "What about you, Malcolm?"

Malcolm crosses his arms over his chest, a grin on his face. "I'm with the kid on this one. Would love to dole out a little payback to some of them assholes."

I don't blame him. When Malcolm was blackmailed to work for Julius, the Fae's followers weren't exactly respectful to him. Being half human in our world isn't easy. Hopefully, this mission helps him leave a mark.

"Good. Y'all can leave tomorrow. Stay at Gerald's if it's still vacant. If not, use this for a hotel." I pull the Order's credit card from my back pocket. It's weird to oversee our finances now, and I'm more than relieved at how well Topher managed our payments from Oberon when I scanned the books. My father invested a good portion after paying us for our kills. We won't have to worry about money for a while if we're careful. "Seamus, take enough pills to last you about a week or two. Use them sparingly in case we have trouble procuring more."

With that settled, the room gives me their undivided attention again.

Okay, easy part buttoned up. *Deep breath...*

I steal a glance at Finn, who gives me silver daggers. No, I won't divulge his secrets, but I won't ignore what needs to be done, either.

I focus on Helene then, for no other reason than it's better to not look at Finn–or either of my men when I say, "I'm done sitting here, waiting for Oberon to come at us again. We've managed to temporarily close him off to this world in some areas, but he's got Windows all over. And we only have ten Orders in the States with us. That leaves two here who've more than likely put targets on our backs. I'm assuming the payout for getting rid of us is enviable."

"What do you suggest we do, Nora Jean?" Ben's voice is quiet, matching the vibe in the room. Oil lamps on end tables flicker soft light, also complementing the mood.

I brace myself for what I'm about to say. "I'm going to Etherias." Another deep breath. "I'm getting my friend back." I pause. "And I'm going to do what Topher had planned and recon the world. Maybe we can find others willing to fight with us there. Maybe we should bring the war to Oberon. This needs to end, and it needs to end on our terms."

If shock were a sound, it'd be the tense silence saturating this room. The mantle clock continues its defiant ticking, and a few audible gasps cut through the quiet. I keep laser-focused on Helene, who holds her head high. Approval glows on her face, the desire for action. Maybe she'll come with me–because asking her to come was at the forefront of my mind while cooking up this plan.

"Have you lost all your sensibilities, love?" Finn's attempt at cold ambiguity falls flat. His voice is full of threat and promise, and I ignore the warning shiver tingling my spine.

"It's the only way to end this." I brave a look at him and wish I hadn't. His tired eyes narrow, and his hands no longer rest on his hips. They're balled into fists at his sides–with glowing blue light illuminating his fingers. Shit. Would he really use his magic on me? "And… you can't keep these Windows closed forever. Once your magic lets up, Oberon will come back and finish what he started."

"There are other ways," Luca adds, his voice a low growl. "You cannot be putting yourself in that kind of danger. 'Tis reckless."

I swallow and swallow. I'm losing the room. Losing my Leader cred. Losing my goddamn nerve.

"It's fucking bullshit is what it is, Nora Jean." Ben is no longer the affable man I depend on. No longer the perfect soldier. He's the dangerous Assassin, ready to pounce on my bad decisions.

And as much as I love Ben and Luca, they will not undermine me in front of our Order. And they won't change my mind.

I lift my chin, pinning them both with a resolute frown. "Whatever y'all think it is, it don't matter. I'm going. End of story."

"I'm going with you, then," Ben says. Gods, he's angry. His fury burns me, even though I'm feet away.

So, let's add a bit more fuel to this fire, shall we? No need to stop while I've only started adding the kindling.

"No. I need you here," I tell him, my voice unwavering. I then nod to Jessie, dismissing him. "You stay here with him. We can't leave Alexie unprotected."

Before Jessie can acknowledge me, Finn stands, shaking his head as he steps toward me. "You can't–"

I lift my hand, effectively stopping him and his words. "I can, and I'm asking you to come with me, Finn. Callum and Helene, too. Y'all know the world better than any of us, and I need all the help I can get."

"Nora Jean."

I turn to Ben when he says my name. "Yes?"

He stands straighter. His eyes burn with green fury, but he doesn't say another word as Alexie slips off the couch and runs to him, wrapping her thin arms around his waist. He hesitates for a moment before patting her back, his anger still pointed at me.

56

His message through the Bond screams that this isn't the end. At least he's waiting until we're alone to rip into me. I respect that.

Luca, on the other hand, moves beside me. He runs fingers through his short auburn hair, making it stand on spikey ends. "You're asking for death, lass. Running straight into its mouth."

I return my gaze to Finn in case he tries to pounce. Because, believe me, he looks ready to beat the living shit out of me. "I won't be, though. I'll have Helene and Callum. Ain't that right?" I ask them, eyes still locked with Finn's.

"Of course, Leader," Callum says, his voice full of relief. He understands what I'm doing, after all.

I'll save Finn, no matter the cost. No matter if the insufferable man decides to hate me until the day I die. At least he'll be alive to do it.

"It would honor me to help you fight, Nora," Helene says, her voice pure confidence. "I'm tired of living my life on the fanatical whims of a tyrant king."

I force a smile as Finn sneers at me. "Good. Thank you."

I channel my father one last time, even though it's almost painful to do. I turn my back on Finn and ignore Luca's and Ben's emotional blasts pummeling me through the Bond. My gaze finds Jessie. "You good with this, then?"

She doesn't stare at me with incredulity. Pride shines on her face, and by damn, I need the jolt. "I'm with you… Leader."

"Perfect." I clap my hands together, hope their trembling isn't visible, and head to the kitchen door. As I release the shield latch, I turn around to face my stunned crowd. "Meeting adjourned."

Chapter 8

I keep my gait steady, not rushing across the backyard.

Don't want it to look like I'm making a great escape.

I am, but they don't need to see it.

Their stares pierce my back, angry heat rolling out the kitchen door like a grease-laden stovetop fire. As my father used to do, I ignore the frustration my orders create and let them work it out for themselves.

On the outside, anyway.

Inside, my lungs are the size of raisins, and all I want to do is give in to the panic roiling in my gut. Ben and Luca feel it. I can't keep it from them, unfortunately. And I'm sure they have plenty to say, but again, I'm thankful they kept a lid on it in there. The last thing I needed was the meeting to devolve into a lovers' spat, especially while sharing the first major decisions I've made as Leader.

And *fucking* fuck, I didn't think to grab a coat—or slip on some shoes. There's only about a hundred pairs beside the door. *Stupid!* The cold is one thing. The snow-covered ground under sock-covered feet is something else entirely. But I sure as hell can't go back in there and meekly put on shoes like the shivering coward I am.

Blood in the water, people. It's no joke.

I make a beeline for Topher's woodshop and yank open the door, flinging myself inside. After tugging off my wet socks, I flick on the light. Nothing in here has changed since Topher last graced this shop. His tools are still where he left them. His mug, half-filled with frozen coffee, sits near a piece of sandpaper and a toy sword on his bench. A toy sword he'd meant to give Alexie.

Everything screams Topher, as if he's still alive and fixing to walk through the door any second.

I close my eyes and concentrate on the wet snow pelting the window with a *tink, tink, tinkle*. It's a soothing sound, soothing like the smell of cedar and sawdust assailing my nose. I love this space. Love how it felt to be in here with Topher as he worked at his bench while I sat on a stool behind him. It was peaceful.

Now, it's freezing.

I force my eyes open to search for instant warmth. Thankfully, a thick blanket is draped over one of my father's unfinished projects, and a moan of joy crackles out of my mouth. Sawdust sticks to my wet feet as I shuffle to the far end of the shed and slide the blanket off whatever's underneath.

Tears threaten for the millionth time as I wrap the blanket around myself and inspect what it hid. A toy cradle. He hadn't only intended to give our queen a sword. It's like he was busy fulfilling a holiday wish list for her. He was Alexie's very own Santa's elf.

Topher was our Leader in the middle of a rebellion, and yet he still found the time to carve toys for our resident child queen. Both are already sanded and smooth. All they need is a few coats of stain.

He did the same thing for me when I was a child. Every holiday, Topher made me something that came directly from his heart. None of my other fathers took that time. Not even my own mama. Much easier to buy presents off Amazon and have them shipped.

I give the cradle a gentle push. It swings silently to the rhythm of the tinkling snow against the window. Maybe I'll finish it for Alexie once I get back from Etherias.

If I get back.

The door swings open, and I turn to Ben shutting the door behind him. He carries my winter coat and a pair of boots.

"You forgot these," he says, handing them to me. Malice doesn't trace his words. Neither does rage. Confusion, maybe. Love, definitely.

I wipe errant tears from my cheeks and accept his offering. "Thanks." I push on the boots and let the blanket fall long enough to slip on my coat. The fur lining in my boots is heaven on my icy feet, and I stifle a groan of relief as they warm up. "I didn't think that exit through too great."

He watches me, his dark hair, shaggy and wet from the snow, falling over his forehead in a way I shouldn't find imperfectly beautiful right now. No, I should be bracing myself for the inevitable argument we're about to have, not contemplating how ridiculously gorgeous he is. What I wouldn't give to be in our old room, listening to him play his guitar, and feeling his hands on my body. His mouth pressed against my skin.

"Why're you doing this, Nora Jean?" he asks softly.

I stand straighter and hold the blanket so tightly over my shoulders my fingertips go numb. "I have to."

"You don't."

I hate the space between us. The ten feet of literal space and the thousand-mile figurative gap. I've let us drift apart, and I need to do better. *He* deserves better.

Now, though, I need to make him understand.

I open my mouth to explain, to give him the best reason I can, without betraying Finn, but he lifts his hand–like I did during the meeting to stop him from talking. "You're doing exactly what your mother did. Do you realize that? You're cutting us all out, not trusting us with your reasons, and putting yourself in needless danger."

If he were to have punched me in the gut, it would've hurt less. "I'm *not* my mother, Ben, and fuck you for saying it."

I regret the words as soon as they fly from my mouth.

Ben's face registers shock, hurt, and then pure pissed-off anger. He smiles a cold smile that numbs my body faster than

61

snow ever could. "Is that how it is, Nora Jean? Is this where we're at now?"

Unfortunately, yes, I guess we are. And once I get started, I can't seem to shut it off. "I don't know. Is it? Is this where you tell me I'm a selfish asshole and only think of myself?"

He tilts his head, shoving his hands in his coat pockets. If he'd just stop looking at me like he doesn't know me! "You're a selfish asshole who only thinks of herself."

Damnit. Damnit! Damnit!

I close my eyes and focus on our Bond, feeling his love still flame under his rage. It calms me enough to at least try to deescalate the situation. "You have to trust me," I finally whisper. I keep my lids shut tight. I don't want to see the doubt that still reverberates off him.

"Maybe I could if *you'd* trust *me*. Help me understand. Just… Why the hell would you risk going there? What do you think you'll accomplish alone?"

"I won't be alone."

He scoffs, and I wince at the sound. "So… you think the four of you can take out the fucking Fae king, huh? Maybe start some Fae revolution? Your heaviest hitter hasn't even agreed to it yet. That leaves you with a Pixie, and a Seelie who's more comfortable with a book than a sword."

Slowly, I open my eyes, and breathe out relief to find his frosty smile gone. The concern now softening his features isn't much better. "Finn will come with me."

"You know as well as I do that Finn will do whatever the fuck he wants to, and he didn't exactly appear onboard with your idea in the house."

I let silence answer him.

Ben lets out a frustrated sigh and swipes wet hair from his brow. "Look, you can kick some ass. I don't doubt your abilities for a second. But are you forgetting what happened, right here in our backyard?"

Heat flashes through me, a mixture of shame and anger. "Don't patronize me," I say in a low voice full of warning. "That's *all* I can think about."

"Really? Because what we went through is only a fraction of what's waiting for you in Etherias. Even if Finn decides to go, he can't take on the army by himself. And not one Etherian Fae is going to side with an Assassin against the king to start some mythical rebellion. We're just as repulsive to them, maybe more so."

"So we sit here and wait like victims?"

"Until we come up with a better idea, yes. We do exactly that. And we're not sitting around, doing nothing. We've closed Windows, gained allies. We need to think this through."

Under normal circumstances, yes, he's absolutely right. But Finn doesn't have the time it would take for rational action.

"It's not only the king I'm after. Hell, if we can't do anything to him, so be it." I pick at the loose threads on the blanket. "Have you forgotten Pia? Are we supposed to leave her there? Let her sacrifice herself without even trying to bring her back home?"

He closes the gap between us, and with his hands on my shoulders, he bends so we're eye-to-eye. "Of course not, but going to a world you've never been to won't put you at an advantage. Please, give us more time to figure it out. More time to–"

"I can't." It's killing me to not confess why I made the decision. He and Luca have earned my honesty and my respect.

But so has Finn.

I cup his cheek, running my thumb over his full bottom lip. "Please, Ben."

His face sags with disappointment, and he backs away. After he stares at me for a few seconds, searching for what I refuse to give him, he opens the door. A gush of frigid wind snakes past him and blasts me. "You say you're not your mother." He pauses. "She didn't trust us with the truth, either."

He slams out of the shed, leaving me with my secrets.

Chapter 9

The next morning, Luca, Seamus, and Malcolm ready themselves to leave for New York. Everyone is quiet while some of us clean the kitchen after breakfast and others help pack Luca's Range Rover for the trip. It's an awkward, tense quiet, the kind that makes my stomach pitch.

Not all of us are suffering from this horrid silence. Finn hasn't left his room, and Ben went for a run before the sun came up. It's been two hours since he slammed out the front door, and I can't help throwing worried glances toward the backyard, waiting for him to reappear from the woods.

With a forced smile to Helene and Alexie, who are finishing up the dishes, I set the broom back into the utility closet and head out to the porch, coat and shoes on this time.

Seamus and Malcolm bicker about who's sitting up front while Luca busies himself with tossing their bags in the back. You wouldn't look at this scene and think they're on their way to curtail yet another Fae uprising and illegally acquire much-needed drugs. They act like any typical family getting ready for a road trip. Even Malcolm seems comfortable, laughing at some of the dumb shit Seamus says in his argument as to why dibs is a legally binding way to call front-seat privileges.

I hope we can be that typical family one day. The lot of us bickering about who gets to sit up front.

Including Pia.

And Finn.

My heart dips at the thought of him. We're not Bonded, and it looks like we never will be. I try not to let the rejection sting too sharply. He's entirely too important to his people to tie his life with mine.

Yet, a life without him...

It'll be close to unbearable, I can admit to only myself, but worth it if he's alive and healthy somewhere in the universe.

Luca shoves one last bag into the back of his SUV and turns to me. He takes the six porch steps two at a time, and without a word, he pulls me into his arms. I wrap mine around his waist, basking in how small and safe I feel against his big body. This is my perfect feeling. If I could carry it with me wherever I went, anxiety wouldn't have a prayer.

Luca hadn't given me the cold shoulder last night when I finally found the courage to come inside. As soon as I went into Topher's room and found him in bed, I pierced him with a frown, ready for round two with the other love of my life.

No accusations flew from his mouth. No disappointed looks. Instead, he glanced up from his novel and held out a welcoming arm. I couldn't strip out of my clothes and scramble into bed fast enough. As I rested my cheek against his bare chest, my body as close to his as I could manage, he continued reading. Only, he read aloud in his lilting, deep voice. I fell asleep to the haunting words of Mary Shelley's *Frankenstein*.

"You're not to be a hero, lass," Luca whispers in my ear, bringing me back to the present. "I know you're not going there to start a war. And I have a feeling your reasons involve Finn. Ben would see it, too, if he were not so furious."

Luca sees deeper inside me than anyone else. Of course he'd picked up on Finn's tension last night.

I don't even try to deny it–but I don't give Finn away, either. It pisses me off that he's asked me to be in this position, and it pisses me off more that I agreed to it. "Thank you... for trusting me," I finally tell Luca.

"'Tis not a matter of trust. My faith in you is not even in question." He tightens his embrace. "Whatever it is you need to do, do it, and get the hell out of there. No dawdling about in that bloody world."

"I won't."

I relax further into his chest, my eyes burning with appreciative tears. He doesn't ask me questions. Doesn't demand I explain myself. Yes, my decision confuses him, as it had most people in the living room last night, but he trusts me. Trusts my judgment. I wish Ben did.

"In and out, as quick as possible," I tell him. "Promise."

He pulls back, takes my face between his massive hands, and kisses me slowly. I groan my frustration when the tenderness of his touch leaves my lips. Before he releases my face, he peers into my eyes, his gaze intense. Then, "If you're in trouble, I'll feel it."

"I know."

"And I'll be coming for you. You won't be able to stop us."

"Us?"

"Ben will come."

I hold on to his whiskey-eyed gaze like an anchor. "He's… I don't know if he'll forgive me."

"Give him time."

We don't have the luxury of time.

Luca kisses me once more, hard and desperate. And then he walks away, not looking back as he gets in on the driver's side and starts the engine.

I try to smile as I wave to Malcolm, who waves back after winning the front-seat battle. I then nod to Seamus as he stares at me while gripping the backdoor handle. "Behave, kid," I tell him, my voice a wavering mess no matter how much I try to hide it. "Listen to Luca, and no running off this time. He has my permission to kick your ass."

His violet eyes glow against the frigid gray morning, and my heart lurches. Despite how big he is, his face is the face of a child, and fuck if I'm not putting him in potential danger again.

"Nora... Shit." He lets go of the handle and bounds up the porch stairs, yanking me in for a hug. "What you're doing is fucking crazy, you know?"

"I'll be fine," I say, trying not to allow my voice to hitch anymore as his breaks.

He hugs me tighter. "Don't die, okay? Don't fucking die." He releases me and runs back to the SUV. I don't miss how he uses his sleeve to wipe under his eyes.

I press against my heart as they drive down the long driveway.

Chapter 10

As soon as I get back inside, I take the stairs to Finn's room and tap lightly on the door. Silence answers me.

I knock again.

More silence.

My third knock is a little louder.

Nothing.

I close my eyes, count to ten, and then pound on that fucker. "Open the door."

"Sorry, love, not receiving guests at the moment." His muffled voice is arrogant. Not even a closed door can hide the tone. "If you'd be so kind as to come back at a more convenient time, I would appreciate it."

"You know what…?" I try the knob. Locked. Now, he's being childish. "A locked door ain't gonna keep me out."

"*Ain't* it?"

Oh, yeah, I'm sick of that shit, too.

With one hard shove, I break the lock, and the old door creaks open like one of those doors in a cheesy horror film. No matter. I have extra knobs in the cellar for this occasion. Not the first handle I've broken, and it won't be the last.

Finn stands at the window, his hands pulled behind his back. He doesn't turn at my intrusion. Whatever is going on outside must be a hell of a lot more interesting than me breaking the door and invading his privacy.

His refusal to acknowledge me takes the angry wind from my sails, and I'm left staring at his back, my fidgeting hands bunching the hem of my flannel.

I take a moment to study him while figuring out how to broach the subject. He wears fitted jeans and a dark blue sweater that does a fine job of highlighting all his sculpted back muscles and accentuates the blue undertones of his silver hair. He's no king, and he refuses to claim his royal blood, but right now, I feel like I'm in the presence of nobility. I'm a peasant waiting for her lord to grant the gift of his attention.

I breathe through the fast beats of my heart. This man does this to me every time I'm in the same room with him. This angry, irritated, obsessed mixture of fuckery is so not healthy for me. Add in how the Pull sings in my stomach when he's close, and I'm very nearly useless. I'm drawn to him and terrified of him. It's a heady combination.

I swallow, lift my chin–leave my fucking shirt hem alone–and fist my hands at my sides. "We need to talk."

Finn continues to inspect the happenings outside as if I hadn't said a word.

"Finn. You can't ignore what's going on. Even if you can, *I* can't." I take a step forward, reach out, and *almost* touch his shoulder. I drop my hand to my side.

"And what is going on, exactly?" Finally, he turns to confront me. His face is void of a glamour, as if he wants to punish me with the full force of his appeal.

It works.

My mouth slackens. What would it be like to have sex with a Fae? Rumors abound in Assassin circles of how hot the experience is. How otherworldly. Jesus, I don't know if I'd survive it. My pleasure sensors would probably implode.

To be with him…

It would change me forever. I would never be the same.

So, yeah, maybe it's best we don't Bond.

The thought helps me slam my eyelids shut, and I squeeze them so tightly, my temples ache. "Can you…? Stop, Finn."

He's closer now. I don't need to open my eyes to feel the heat radiating from his body or take in his clean scent. The desire to press my nose to the base of his throat and inhale makes a moan reverberate in the back of my throat. I want to bathe in his scent, let it drown me.

"What is it, love? Can you not handle being near me?"

"I–"

"Because this is exactly what you'll have to look forward to if you cross over to Etherias. Not only from me, but others you encounter who are more… captivating. You'll face beauty that will make you weak. Powerless."

As soon as he utters that last word, the tingle at the back of my skull goes crazy as he lifts the shielding spell. My head gradually numbs, as do my cheeks, my lips. It gets so intense my knees give and the only thing keeping me up is the sudden grip Finn has around my waist.

Sweat soaks the roots of my hair, under my arms, and I gasp for breath. If I had the wherewithal to beg him to stop, I would. The only defense I can muster is to anchor my hands on his shoulders and open my mouth in a voiceless scream.

In seconds, the tingle dissipates and feeling returns to my face. My lungs demand air as I take in heaving mouthfuls of it. I still hold on to Finn, still keep my eyes tightly shut. I feel his palm slide from my waist to cup my cheek, his touch gentle. "Open your eyes, Nora."

His voice is a hypnotic Siren's call, and I do as he commands. Relief turns my body to water, forcing Finn to tighten his grip on my waist. He's back to being tolerably perfect, achingly beautiful without being painfully so. My gods, he doesn't even need to use his Mage strength to bring me to my knees. How the hell am I going to navigate Etherias if every single inhabitant from a farmer to the king's royal Guard can do this to me? If–

Wait…

I lick my dry lips, lift my trembling hands from Finn's shoulders, and take a few steps away from him. I've been around other Fae without their glamours or Finn's spell to tamp down the tingling. Hell, I spent time in a Fae den with naked Fae, their music, and a whole lot of tingling at the back of my skull. None of that ever affected me the way Finn just had.

So, yeah, a little magic played a huge role in this show of his. I don't know whether to be pissed he's tried to steer me wrong or proud that I didn't fall for it.

"I'm going," I say with my treacherously shaking voice. "Come with me."

He watches me, his hands behind his back again and composure slammed into place. Yes, he's regal and intoxicating to be around. But he can't hide the exhaustion on his face, the deep circles under his eyes. After what he pulled, he seems even more drained.

He purses his lips as he studies me. "How much has Callum told you, exactly?"

I shrug, trying for nonchalance. Failing miserably. My body's stiff as a shot of moonshine. "That the iron chains Oberon kept you in have damaged your body. That you need a Healer to…fix you."

He raises a brow, amusement lifting one corner of his mouth. "Fix me? Those were his words?"

"I mean, yeah, basically."

Silence. Then, "Who have you told of my need for fixing?"

I stand straighter. He has no clue what I've gone through to tell him, "No one, like I promised I wouldn't."

"Not Ben or Luca?"

"No, and I'm paying for it."

"I imagine." He turns toward the window again, as if dismissing me. "I'm not going, and neither are you. The Windows are closed."

My frustration builds again. Yes, this is a roadblock. One I have every intention of driving straight through. "How long will you be able to keep shut the ones you do have closed?" My voice carries the same subtle threat as his. "My guess isn't very long.

72

I'm a patient person. I can wait you out if I have to. *Come with me.*"

"You're being foolish. Rash." He doesn't rage, doesn't flip out. His indifference is completely intact–except for his white-knuckled hands clasped behind his back. "Have you considered why I've never mentioned my... sickness, love?"

When I don't answer, he continues. "I've come to care for the people in this house and your Order." He faces me again, and his gray eyes flame with sincerity. "Care for *you*. Something I would admit even without this... connection between us. And I've never shared because I feared precisely what you are attempting now. Helene and Callum are wanted and will surely perish once they step foot through a Window. As for you, with all your strength and ability to heal, it would serve you little in Etherias. None of you would survive that world. And in your fervor to *fix* me, you'd get yourselves killed."

My treacherously fidgeting hands fuck with my shirt hem again. "We'd be okay... if you came with us."

He lets out a slow breath through his mouth. "You're asking me to put myself before you. Before the brave, naïve *children* who are entirely too enthusiastic to risk their lives alongside you."

This is the sincere Finn. The one who comforts and protects. My heart aches seeing his fear for us tightening his face, and I give in to the desire to touch him. It's my turn to wrap my arms around his waist and give him as much of my strength as he's willing to accept.

He's right. This is a fool's mission.

For him, I'll gladly play the fool.

Hesitantly, he unclasps his hands from behind his back and slowly folds me closer to him. When he kisses the top of my head, my heart flutters. Sincere Finn is almost too much to bear. Not even his un-glamoured, beauty-hyped face can affect me as intensely.

"Please," I whisper against his chest. I count the beats of his heart, his slow inhalations.

"We will have to use another Window," he finally says. "Yours is too close to the palace. We'd be dead before we managed three yards into my world."

Relief pours through me, and I hug him tighter. "Okay."

"A Healer isn't easy to find, love. We will have our challenges."

"Callum knows of a Healer."

"Of course he does," he retorts, his tone thick with exasperation. His right hand runs a path up and down my back, leaving a trail of tingling goosebumps behind. "As for Pia... Extracting her from Oberon's grip will be more difficult than finding a proper Healer." He takes a slow breath. "It's likely you'll never see her again."

I swallow all the argumentative words I want to say. We'll get her back, but not this time.

Chapter 11

I spend the rest of the morning with Finn, Callum, and Helene at the kitchen table preparing. Planning. Drinking way too much coffee.

Jessie left for Pittsburgh about an hour ago. She's coming back tomorrow, thankfully. Our Order always comes before whatever we've carved out as our own in the human world. Jessie feels the same. However, being an integral part of a securities firm forces her to make more detailed arrangements to cover for her absence.

Ben, Luca, and I are lucky we own our own businesses. For now, anyway. Who knows if my bakery will survive my long hiatus. Who knows if I'll ever be able to get back to it again. Maybe I should hire someone like Luca has to run his bar. Yet, the only other person who's ever worked with me at Mountainside Bakery is Pia.

My friend's face flashes through my mind, and I press against the pain squeezing my heart. We *will* get her back.

Somehow.

Alexie stands by the kitchen screen door, watching for Ben. I don't complain about the cold she lets in or ask her to close the door and wait for him by the window in the living room, where the view of the woods is just as clear. No need to agitate her.

Whatever cold is blowing in from outside is less biting than the cold she can produce when anxious. As of now, she's pretty content while eating a cinnamon roll as she stares outside, never taking her eyes off the tree line.

As for our next move, we're heading to Canada, to Ontario's Window. Finn closed it a while back, but he's opening it long enough for us to slip through. Thankfully, the Windows he's already closed will remain shut on the other side, but not for long—unless Finn is healed. Our biggest lead is Callum's knowledge that a Healer may or may not live in the village closest to where we're entering the world. It appears these Healer Fae are as rare as unicorns.

Anyway, the Ontario Window leads out somewhere in the middle of nowhere. It's the safest place to land, but pretty far away from where we need to be. It'll take a couple days of hoofing it.

I won't admit to everyone that I'm nervous about traversing a foreign world. But yeah, nerves are having a hell of a time hopping around in my gut. All we can do is prepare ourselves, I reckon. We'll be landing in what Callum calls the Mystic Forest, where there's plenty of water, game, and edible plants. The weather's mild this time of year, too.

The forest's name is a bit cheesy, like something found in a children's novel, and when I say so, Callum patiently explains it's the English translation of an ancient, complex Fae language I might hear while there. When he says the actual name of the forest, it's breathtaking and something I probably wouldn't be able to pronounce correctly. It's the same language Finn and Alexie use for their incantations.

"How long until we find this Healer of yours?" I ask Callum as I turn my mug in slow circles on the table.

"*If* we find her," Finn reminds me with pessimism that grates on my nerves.

"Fine. *If*." My gaze drifts out the window above the sink to hide my irritation. Finn agreed to come. No need to get into it with him, give him an excuse to change his mind.

Callum clears his throat. "Our most pressing issue will not be seeking her out. She has lived in the same place for over two centuries. I highly doubt she's moved on in the couple years since I left Etherias."

I lean back in my chair. "All right, so what's the problem?"

"Where Ontario's Window leads is dangerous. Beings who live in Mystic will not be happy we've come to disturb them."

Well, shit.

"We made it through already, though, with Alexie," Helene says, rapping her knuckles against the scarred tabletop. She nods to Finn and me. "With the two of you, we will be fine."

The Ontario Window is how they came through when they landed here in search of me and my Order. And yup, we filled Helene in on our main purpose for this trip–which absolutely means I can't keep Ben in the dark anymore. Or Luca. Finn's reasoning for not wanting anyone else to know was understandable. But now that he's agreed to go, there's no point in keeping secrets.

All Ben needs to do is come home.

"I spent time exploring Mystic in my youth," Finn says with a secret smile. "I'm actually looking forward to the visit."

Callum scoffs. And then claps a palm over his mouth, his eyes wide with mortification. "I apologize, my–"

"It's fine, boy. If I let you live for prattling on to Nora about my weaknesses, I can forgive your reaction." No malice laces Finn's voice as his face takes on a faraway look. It softens his features, as if whatever he remembers smooths out any stress and exhaustion. "You're right to feel incredulity, Callum. Few have spent an extended amount of time in Mystic and lived to tell about it. Yet..." He lifts a hand, palm up, and a glowing white ball appears, hovering above his fingers. After a few whispered words from Finn, the orb dissipates to snow and drifts to the table in glistening sparkles. "When you have certain talents, the monsters aren't so scary. There was a time, directly after Oberon's unfortunate coup, when Mages hid in Mystic. Not even his Guards would enter those woods."

Callum's cheeks redden. "Of course. I… I remember reading of it in the histories, of how you saved so many. The disease and hunger were unfortunate, yet fascinating material, nonetheless."

Jesus, there's so much of Finn I don't know. I want to hear these stories, but not from Callum or a book. From Finn's mouth, from the true source.

Finn closes his palm, and the glowing snow vanishes. "I'm pleased the misery of my people has entertained you," he says with a raised brow and sardonic grin. "Perhaps you'd like me to regale you with stories of rotting bodies and emaciated children, information you won't find between pages."

Callum's floundering is almost painful to watch. He leans up, his head shaking so vigorously I'm nervous he'll give himself a concussion. "Oh! Oh, no, my lord. I didn't mean to–"

"Callum," I say, covering his white-knuckled fist resting on the tabletop. "Don't let him fuck with you."

His dark eyes shine with contrition as he stares at Finn like a puppy begging forgiveness.

Finn waves a hand in the air and leans back in his seat. "A thousand years of water under the bridge."

Helene covers a grin with her palm, surprising me, while Alexie giggles and mumbles something about how funny her "lord cousin" is. Finn smiles in her direction, and the love flowing from his eyes takes my breath away. I don't know how well he knew her before they met in those Pennsylvania woods months ago, but his love is genuine. I'm almost jealous, which makes me feel like shit.

What would it be like to have a man like Finn love me?

I shake off the feeling. "Okay, so we're good?" I give each person at the table my attention until they nod with agreement, then stand. "Excellent. We leave in two days. That'll give us enough time to gather our supplies and prepare."

And it'll give me enough time to grovel to Ben.

I give a pointed frown at Finn as I say, "Y'all need to rest as much as possible."

Finn inspects his fingernails, acting like I haven't said a word.

"*Rest*, Finn." If I could erase those dark circles under Finn's eyes, I'd do it in a heartbeat.

Finn curls his fingers into fists and narrows his tired gaze at me.

I try for a smile, and it falls from my lips before it has the chance to fully form.

So, Callum can talk about death and mayhem with clinical apathy, but I can't tell the man to rest?

Okay, cool, cool, cool.

Mental note: Don't coddle the thousand-year-old Unseelie Mage in front of an audience.

"He's back! He's back!" Alexie's ecstatic squeal saves me from Finn's uncomfortable staring game. Thank the gods for small favors.

I rip my eyes from his as Alexie runs outside to Ben, who lifts her in his arms as he waltzes out of the woods like he hasn't spent all morning and early afternoon avoiding me.

"Time for a bit of groveling, eh, love?"

I turn to glare at Finn as Helene and Callum leave the room a little too quickly. "Enough," I tell him in a raspy whisper.

"Oh, I've barely begun. Perhaps you should *rest*. Surely, you'll be dispensing some energy while apologizing to your Bonded."

"Why can't you…? I don't know… Turn off that sardonic charm, or whatever you wanna call it?"

"Is that what you really want?" His voice is smooth and lyrical. Not too deep, but deep enough to vibrate through my bones.

"Yes." No. And that alone makes me angry. He's still fucking with me, even though he's made it clear things won't go any further between us.

He stands with a curve to his lips and faces me. He's not as tall as Luca or Ben, but he still has me by a couple of inches. Honestly, he could be a foot shorter and still have the presence to fill a room.

With a graceful sweep of a finger down my cheek, he says, "Maybe I should join you. Help you grovel. It would be fun, don't you think?"

My eyelids become heavy, and my folds instantly get wet with the image of Finn and Ben... and me. "You don't want me. Remember?" I shake my head, lick my dry lips. "You need to stop. Please."

His finger travels to my collarbone, sliding under my shirt and slipping under my bra strap. I close my eyes as my clit throbs and the Pull begs. "I never said I didn't want you." His voice is all regret.

"You've said enough, Finn. All you're doing to me now is making your rejection worse."

His touch leaves my skin in a flash. He averts his gaze and backs away, my words an effective repellent. "Go on, then. Tell Ben how you're saving me from myself. Don't let the man brood too long."

Without responding to his sarcasm–because goddamn, a person can only take so much–I rush toward the stairs, palming my stomach. The Pull begs for him. It hasn't gotten the memo that Finn's not interested. Not in a Bond, anyway. And we can't fuck without the Bond happening, so lose-lose.

"Rest, Finn. I mean it." Oh, my shaky voice isn't helping. "Can't have you fainting in the *Mystic* Forest."

He grins. "Won't you be there to catch me if I fall?"

Yes, yes, I will be.

I turn from him. "I'm going upstairs."

On trembling legs, I run up the steps and don't stop until I'm behind my closed bedroom door.

Chapter 12

I sit on my old bed and strum Ben's guitar. I don't know any notes, no matter how many times Ben has patiently tried to teach me. Maybe I refuse to learn intentionally. It doesn't sound the same when I play it. When Ben plays, it's like the instrument was created for him. He's not the best guitarist, not even close, but he was the first to capture my heart while playing it. The first to make tears come to my eyes when he played and sang for me in his slightly off-key voice. He was the first I felt the Pull with. The first I gave my heart to.

He's the first. Period.

And I feel so far away from him.

I let it happen. After Topher died, I let myself slip away, just like I ran after Mama died. I've wasted so much time being afraid to love him, and now that he's finally mine, I'm creating another chasm.

Shit. Just…shit.

I wait in this room for what feels like hours with my old furniture, handmade quilts passed down from prior generations, and years of memories. Ben knows I'm in here, and he's making me wait. He might make me wait forever.

He might tell me to fuck off.

I try not to dwell on "mights," but if he won't even give me the chance to make things right, any panic-laden "might" in the back of my mind could very well turn into reality.

With a huff, I set the guitar next to the bed by the nightstand, careful not to let it fall. It's older than me and scarred, but it's his most prized possession. Well, that guitar and his ancient truck.

I stand, smooth a hand down my wrinkled flannel, and prepare myself to seek Ben out. Then I hear his footsteps. They are as familiar to me as the nose on my face, and the even, steady tread coming up the stairs absolutely belongs to him. He confirms it by hollering down to Helene and Alexie to get some lunch, that he'll be down soon to join them.

No, no, he won't be going anywhere but inside this bedroom, and if everything goes well, he won't be leaving it until we're both sweaty and aching from a good bout of making up.

Except he detours into the bathroom. A door slams, and a minute later, the shower rushes to life.

I'm left standing in the middle of the bedroom, mouth agape and temper flaring.

Hell. No.

So why am I still standing here, staring at the door with my hands balled into the hem of my shirt? I should storm the bathroom, rip open the curtain, and demand a confrontation.

It's because I'm a fucking coward. All talk and no follow through. He might reject me. He might decide I'm not worth the effort.

I squeeze the bridge of my nose and close my eyes. *Might, might, might*–a dirty word for anyone riddled with anxiety forty percent of the time.

When the shower stops, I straighten, try like hell to leave my damn shirt alone, and keep my arms hanging at my sides. I won't let this space between us grow wider.

The doorknob turns, and I take in a deep breath, forgetting to exhale when Ben walks in, clad in a towel with his dirty clothes balled under his arm. He glistens from his shower, and goosebumps prickle his olive skin. He's beautiful, a renaissance sculpture come to life. All symmetry, all sleek muscle and grace. And he ignores me completely.

I press a hand to my heart. Jesus, this hurts. He acts like I'm not in the middle of the room as he dumps his wad of clothes in the hamper near the door. He acts like I'm not drilling holes into his gorgeous, rippling back as he stands in front of his dresser riffling through his top drawer for underwear.

He acts like that trek in the woods washed me away from his mind.

I force myself to relax with a slow exhalation, force the anxiety to stand the fuck down. Here's the thing: he can act all he wants, but relief spirals through my muscles when I let go of my fear. Why? Because the Bond prevents him from hiding how he actually feels. He's not done with me. He's consumed by me, as I am with him and Luca.

With Finn, too. I don't need a Bond with him to feel it.

Ben's pissed, though. So, so pissed and confused and lost for what to say.

But he's not done with me.

He drops his towel, and my mouth instantly salivates. He's sleek and smooth and hard everywhere. *Everywhere*.

Damn.

His ass had to have been molded by the gods themselves. All muscle and definition. I stifle a growl of disappointment when he yanks on his boxer briefs.

"Stop," he rasps out without turning. His voice is husky despite the anger he wants to spit at me. He can feel my desire. It infects him, his own lust boomeranging back to me.

I lick my lips, shake off the remnants of cowardice, and take the few steps toward him. I don't reach for him, even though my hands beg for his skin. Words must be shared between us first. I'm not my mother, and I won't leave this house having him disagree with me.

"I can't stop, Ben. I miss you."

He finally faces me. His arousal gives him away further, even if his face is set in stone. Yes, his cock presses against the black cotton of his underwear. Oh, and he doesn't have a six-pack. He has eight deep, defined ridges that ripple down his abdomen like Satan's ladder. I'd give my soul to lick every rung.

I've missed more than his conversation. More than the notes of his guitar.

Fuck.

I shouldn't have neglected my men for so long. Grief is a life-sucking thing.

"Miss me, huh?" He crosses his arms over his chest and leans against the old dresser. His face is all tense lines and disbelief. "Funny, 'cause I haven't seen you in this room once since Topher died." He doesn't cover his arousal, and he doesn't come closer.

"You don't think I wanted to come in here?" I smack a finger against my temple. "My head's fucked, Ben! I'm trying to dig myself out of the black. I'm *really* trying. But Topher *is* gone. He's gone, and I want him back. I want him to lead us. I want *him* to fucking make this right. But he's not here, and he never will be."

"I get it. I do. And this is a shitty thing to say, but he wouldn't want you to use his death as an excuse to close yourself off again."

"I know that." Tears fill my eyes, and I wipe them from my cheeks. I didn't want to do this. Didn't want to break and crumble. "Believe me, I've tried to be stronger. But every time I look out the kitchen window, I see Topher die. Every time. For the rest of my life, I'll look out that *fucking* window and watch him fall to the ground with Kellen's sword pierced through his heart. How am I supposed to go on living and pretend I don't see it?"

The hard edges soften on Ben's face, and his rage dissipates, replaced with guilt. Guilt for bringing it up. Guilt for making me feel like shit.

Damn it! I don't want his guilt. I don't. This conversation can't devolve into an episode where he consoles me while I break into a thousand pieces. Where nothing gets resolved, and I leave with him still furious and confused.

He reaches for me then, wraps me up against his warm skin, and smooths back my tangled curls while I fight to get my shit together.

I take a few deep breaths. "I didn't want to do this," I whisper against his chest. "I really didn't. You lost him, too."

His chest lifts with a deep sigh as his fingers untangle from my hair. He releases me and steps back until too much space exists between us. His green eyes are no longer glittering with fury, but he's not ready to stop being mad. Don't blame him. He has a lot to be mad about. "Why are you up here, then?"

My fingers find the hem of my shirt, and I pull on the last button until it's hanging on by a single thread. "I want to explain my decisions. Be completely honest."

He folds his arms across his thick chest again and tilts his head. "The shit explanation you gave last night wasn't *completely* honest?"

I yank at that button until it pulls free and clinks against the worn floor in muted surrender. "Ben…"

"Nora."

He's not going to let me off the hook.

"I had my reasons."

"I'm sure you did." His patronizing tone is as sharp as his narrowed gaze.

"Look, yeah, I'd be pissed in your position. I just needed to make sure I could tell you."

Yuck. That came out wrong.

He laughs a shocked, humorless laugh. "Haven't I proven myself trustworthy? Our Bond not enough of a commitment for you?"

I try to close the gap between us, and he doesn't let me, taking a step backward for every one of my forward steps. Shit. I drop my hands to my sides. "Of course it's enough."

"Then why lie to me?"

Ouch. "Lie" is such an ugly word. "I didn't lie to you. I have every intention of figuring out a way to bring Pia home. Every intention of getting as much info on Etherias as possible, too."

"But that's not all, is it?"

I shake my head.

"Last time I checked, withholding the truth is the same as lying, Nora Jean."

He's got me there. "Yeah, I get it. Believe me."

"Fine. Great." He closes his eyes, collects himself, and then gives me back his emerald stare. "Look, whatever your reasons for evading the truth, what you're planning is foolish. We can figure out a better plan than this one. Give us more time. *With more time*, we'd be able to convince Assassins from other Orders to join us. You gotta agree with me. You're not dumb."

"Under normal circumstances, you'd be right, but we have to leave now," I whisper. Why can't I spit it out already? Easy. Because it still feels like I'm betraying Finn, even though he knows I'm giving his secrets to Ben.

"Why? It makes no sense." Ben runs a frustrated hand through his wet hair, his patience at the end of its razor-thin line. "With so many Windows closed, Oberon hasn't even attempted to get at us. We have the advantage now. You going there half-cocked will erase that."

"It's not like I'm going alone. I'll have Finn. And… and Helene ain't no wilting flower."

He scoffs. "So, the three of you, then? Great plan. Just perfect."

"You don't get it!" Frustration ripples to the surface. Frustration at myself for my stupid desire to keep Finn's secret. "We're out of time, Ben. *Completely* out."

He steps close enough to tip my chin with his forefinger and thumb, forcing me to meet his gaze. "What're you saying?" His voice is soft now, desperately coaxing me. "What aren't you telling me?"

I squeeze my fists so tightly my fingertips go numb. "It's Finn. He's… He can't stay here." *Get it out!* "He's dying." My voice skips on the last word.

Ben's eyes turn to saucers, and his grip on my chin drops with shock. Silent shock that's loud and thundering. Fear and worry and utter disbelief run from Ben's heart to mine. Finn means something to him. He means so much to all of us, even with his caustic tongue. The man is a hero to his people, and after what he's done for us, he's a hero in this house, too.

Ben stumbles to the bed and sits as if in a stupor. "What?" The word barely leaves his mouth as he peers up at me.

With a shaky breath, I sit next to him–and tell him everything Callum confessed to me. Tell him everything Finn grudgingly admitted. With every word I speak, Ben's shock transforms. First to anger when I tell him Finn wanted his predicament kept secret, and on to empathy when I told him why, and finally straight to determination when I tell him about Callum's Healer.

"I don't see any other option, Ben," I say, staring at my hands folded on my lap. "I don't plan to storm the castle, okay? My first goal isn't even to find Pia, as much as I hate to admit it. My priority is saving Finn's life, and he refused to go back on his own. I… I had to use myself going to force him. Finn's irritated, but I won't let him sacrifice himself. I can't."

Ben shifts his weight, moving closer to me. Longing courses through him and envelops me. I'm not even gone yet, and he misses me. "Jesus, what a fucked-up situation," he says, his voice strained.

"Completely fucked up."

Ben places his warm palm on my thigh and massages away the tension there. We lapse into silence for a bit. The only sound invading the room is wet snow hitting the window. It's the comfortable silence I miss. "I could go with you, but…" he finally says.

"Alexie needs protecting," I finish for him, knowing exactly where his thoughts are.

"Right." His hand snakes higher on my thigh, and I'm sorry, but my body reacts when his fingertips graze closer to my core. "But if you're in trouble, I don't give a fuck about anything else. I'm coming for you."

"I'm counting on it."

His grip tightens on my thigh. "Before you leave, I want to know exactly where you'll be, understand? I'll need logistics, starting from our Window."

"We're going through Ontario's. Safer that way."

"Then I want a map drawn from that Window. I want lots of maps, actually, and they'd better include every tree, every goddamn field, got it?"

"Got it." I can't help my smile despite the seriousness of the situation. He and Luca would, of course, be on the same page, wanting to come to me if I needed them. And yeah, if I were in trouble, I'd want my men leading the charge to get me out of it.

Look, I'm no damsel in distress. I'd do the same for them.

Speaking of Luca, I owe him a call. It's best we're all working with the same information.

Leaning closer to Ben, I huff out a relieved sigh. It's like I haven't seen Ben in months. Honestly, I haven't really seen Ben, even though we've been in the same house. "I'll get Callum on drawing some maps tonight."

"You know what?" Ben stands and stalks to the door. He leaves me with my mouth open in confusion as he goes down the hall in his underwear. In moments, he pounds on a door.

I smile when Callum's voice drifts and mingles with Ben's. Their conversation floats into our room. Ben gives specific instructions, and Callum politely accepts the task, even sounding excited.

When Ben storms back into our room, he shuts the door and locks it. "Done."

"Well, all right, then." I'm tingling with happiness. Ben no longer looks at me with disdain and mistrust. Lust coats the green of his eyes, making them shine.

"As for you, Nora Jean," he says, his r's rolling off his tongue like sex and honey. "I got plans for you."

I swallow, my throat dry and my body wanting. "What plans?"

He touches the indentation on my chin. "You're mine, *only* mine, for as long as you're home. Starting now."

Chapter 13

He ambles to the bed, and I take the moment to admire his body, all muscle and defined lines. His face is a masterpiece, too: chiseled jaw, dimpled chin, full lips, and green eyes fringed with dark lashes.

He strokes himself through his boxers, his heavy-lidded eyes never leaving mine. My mouth waters for his cock, and I'm jealous of his hand. I want to smack it away and rip off the black fabric obstructing my view. I want to taste his velvet hardness. When I reach out for him, Ben steps away, still rubbing his cock with a grin tipping the right corner of his mouth.

"Not so fast." His voice is husky sex, his Boston accent thickened with desire.

"Ben…please." I sound drunk, not in control.

He lets out a slight moan, his hand moving a little faster. My body reacts, my folds already saturated. Ready for him. "I heard you with Luca the other night," he rasps. "I felt what you felt when you came around him. I lay in this bed, imagining you writhing under me, moaning my name as your pussy tightened around my cock."

My mouth goes dry. Him knowing, *feeling*, how I feel when Luca touches me only makes me hotter.

Luca will feel the pleasure Ben gives me now.

I reach out, and Ben shakes his head, wagging a slow finger in my face. "It's my turn. My turn to do what I want. My turn to touch you. To fuck you until you can't walk."

An edge colors his voice, and it's both hot and surprising. He means to use my body to take out all his pent-up frustration.

I'm so here for it.

Panting breaths escape through my lips as I nod my consent and slide on the bed until my back is against the headboard. He pleasures himself as he keeps his distance. He assesses me. Tortures me.

"Take off your clothes." His command is brusque, leaving no room for bullshit.

With trembling fingers, I unbutton my shirt, shrugging it off while watching his hand rub, rub, rub his cock. An urgency kicks in as I unsnap my bra, tug off my jeans and underwear. I don't want him to come without me. I want all that hardness slamming into me, swelling inside me.

And I *do* want to watch him come. Watch him bring himself to the brink while his gaze drinks in my naked body.

I want it all.

His lips part, and another moan leaves his mouth when I spread my legs, giving him a full view of my pussy. I then open my folds to show him my clit. It's swollen for him.

I say nothing. Don't beg him to press his hot mouth against me. I torture him as he tortures me. My index finger glides over my clit as our eyes remain locked. I rub myself, licking my lips, beating him at his own game.

He frowns, dropping his hand from his erection, and goes to his dresser. With a quick slam of his top drawer, he comes back to me, a belt in his hand. Before I know what he's doing, Ben pulls me down until I'm flat on my back and has my arms over my head, securing my wrists with his belt. He doesn't tighten it, doesn't make it painful. And it turns me the fuck on. I think I like this aggressive Ben. A flimsy belt won't keep me immobile. One slight tug would rip it apart. But I'll play this game.

I like this game.

"I'll be doing all the touching tonight, Nora Jean. Understand?" He positions his body over mine, his cock stiff against my stomach. When all I do is nod, he says, "Say it."

"I understand." My hips jut upward of their own volition. I can't help it. I can't.

Ben's smile is triumphant and full of promises. "Good."

His face dips to the hollow of my neck, and his tongue licks at the sensitive spot behind my ear. His dark, wet hair brushes my skin as he takes his time exploring with his mouth. The wetness leaves a path of goosebumps in its wake.

He pinches a taut nipple as his lips draw paths over my collarbone. He pinches and rubs, and it sends jolts to my aching pussy. I force myself not to snap the belt to touch him, force myself to play by the rules he's set out. But I can't stop how my hips circle against him, how I try in vain to rub my clit against his body. Any part of his body. He won't let me. Won't give me anything he's not ready to give.

Ben's pleasure game is maddening.

When his mouth latches to my nipple, I'm almost weeping for him to go faster, to make me come and come again and keep me coming until my legs no longer work. "Ben... take off your fucking underwear. I want to feel your dick on my skin. Let me have that, at least."

He chuckles against my nipple, a nipple so taut it could probably punch through glass. But he doesn't rid himself of the barrier. This is his punishment.

His hands are everywhere, his mouth leaving hot, wet trails along my rib cage, my stomach. Sensation, upon sensation, upon sensation, and I can't do a fucking thing except absorb it.

When his lips capture my clit, I rear up with a gasp. There's no licking and tender care. He sucks and sucks, my clit slipping in and out of his mouth. I writhe and groan and scream incoherent things. His hands hold my hips still then. He takes away my ability to move, and all I can do while he gets me off is scream out the pleasure. When I explode, he doesn't stop. I'm weak and sensitive, and I don't think I can take it anymore.

Until he works my clit with expertise, building and building another orgasm, all the while preventing me from moving, from getting closer to his tongue, his devilish mouth.

"Ben! Ben, Ben..." I repeat his name over and over as if it were an incantation, one of Finn's murmured chants. It works because the magic builds again, the pleasure mounting and doubling. My eyes roll back in my head as if I were possessed. When another white-hot climax rips through my body, I think I might die–or at least pass out from the pleasure of it.

Ben growls against my pussy, the sound sending vibrations through my body. He scrambles up, flips me on my stomach, and lifts my hips. I hear his underwear rip away from his body, watch the fabric fall to the floor, tattered and ruined.

And then he slams into me.

Ah! He's so fucking hard. His groans fill me up, awakening my body, priming it for another orgasm. He lifts my hips high in a firm grip as he slams into me from behind. Gods, he's going so deep. So fucking deep as he pounds and pounds. Our skin slaps together, his slick with sweat. There are no slow strokes, just fast and almost brutal.

I can't take it anymore. I need to touch him. With a grunt, I snap the leather as if it were made of cotton and reach down between us, cupping his balls, massaging them as he drives into me. I tighten around him as another orgasm grips me. As I come, he lets out a ferocious groan, yelling my name as he pours himself into me.

When he's spent, he gathers me up as he lies on his side, my back facing his chest, his cock still throbbing its last pulsating tremors inside me. He kisses my temple, his breath ragged and matching the fast tempo of mine. We're both drenched in sweat and cum and unconditional love.

As his breathing slows, he slips from inside me. His trembling arms hug me so tightly, and it's all I can do not to burst from the emotion drowning me.

I swallow, the lump in my throat surprising, and not so surprising at all.

He kisses my temple once more, and says against my skin, "Never let that much time separate us again. Please. Whatever you're feeling, whatever's going through your head, I want to feel it, good or bad. Let me be here for you."

And the tears come, leaving hot tracks down my cheeks. "It's tough for me to…"

…share my grief.

He's quiet for a moment, snow pattering against the window our only music. "All right. Then *I* won't let it happen again. I'll take your pain, Nora Jean. I'll take everything."

Chapter 14

Two days later, Finn, Helene, Callum, and I leave for Ontario. Ben, with Alexie by his side, stays on the porch as they watch us go.

The maps Callum made him are tucked away in his room. Ben spent our last night together poring over them, strategizing with me. We FaceTimed Luca to go over the plans. He filled us in on his mission, too.

New York City is going as well as can be expected. So far, they've collected a good stash of pills from Julius's apartment. They had to take care of a few Fae camped there. No killing, only putting the fear of our Order into them. Luca has a knack for intimidation, what with him being a giant and all. He'll be heading home soon, which makes me happy. I like knowing my family will be safe and together while I'm gone.

Anyway, the drive to Canada is long and uneventful. Finn sleeps most of the way, his exhaustion so obvious during our drive. He only leaves the car during a few of our stops long enough to use the bathroom. I don't say anything, don't bring attention to his physical state. I just drive, with Helene and Callum taking turns when I need an hour or two of sleep myself.

Finally, twenty-four hours from the time we left, we made it to our destination. Finn and I sit with the two sole members of the Ontario Order, a Bonded couple who act as though we're here for an afternoon tea.

As we listen to Angie and Chris, who can't stop chatting, my attention keeps pulling toward Finn. He's cast a glamour to make his exhaustion less apparent, but it's still there, lurking under all his beauty and regal posture.

"So, let me get this straight," Angie says while dipping a chocolate chip cookie into her coffee mug. "You're going to cross to Etherias to save your Pixie friend, eh?"

So polite, so Canadian. Looking at her smiling, trusting face makes guilt warm my cheeks for both lying and using Pia in the lie. I give a quick glance to Helene and Callum. Both are studying their coffee mugs way too intently.

Finn has his haughty smile intact, legs crossed and a finger tracing the rim of his mug. You would never know how weak he's becoming. He hides it well.

"Yeah, yes. Oberon took my friend... before he killed my father. She's an innocent." I force the words from my mouth. It's still difficult to talk about Topher without misery hedging for a spot at the front of my brain.

I startle when Finn's warm hand presses against my back, his fingertips gently grazing over my spine. I close my eyes for a moment, concentrate on how his touch soothes me.

"Why would Oberon take a Pixie? And alive, for that matter?" Angie's voice is gentle, even with curiosity lacing her words.

"We don't know," Finn says when I stare at the Assassin, racking my brain for an answer I don't have. "We mean to find out. I have contacts within the kingdom. One way or another, we'll find our compatriot."

He leaves it at that, lets silence overtake the room without fidgeting or trying to fill it. The only tell he gives is the slight pressure of his fingers against my back. Me? I'm wreaking havoc on my flannel's hem under the table, pulling and balling it until a small rip of fabric renders the quiet in the cabin.

Angie nods in contemplation as she finishes her cookie, while Chris looks at her to make the next move. They may be

Bonded, and their number only consists of the two of them, but she's Leader. What she says will dictate our next move.

When Angie dabs the corners of her mouth with a linen napkin, she finally gives me her attention. She's a person who blends with a crowd, dark hair and light eyes. Someone you wouldn't give a second glance to. Yet, she's fierce. A fighter. She has to be, seeing as her Window is one of the more vulnerable ones. For every being who has sneaked through her Window, ten more didn't. I think when we came up here a month ago with Finn to tell our story she was relieved the Window would finally be locked–and not for the same reasons as we were relieved to close ours. No more trespassers. No more feeling the burden of having to explain to the king's Messenger how she and her Bonded dropped the ball.

"You didn't mention this friend when you came last time, Nora." She tilts her head. "Why now? And why use our Window?"

"Ours runs straight into the kingdom's backyard," I say, keeping my voice steady. That much is absolutely true. I can't tell her the whole truth, can't let her know the magic locking her Window hinges on healing the Fae who is dying. No need to give panic. Yet. "We have a better chance of succeeding if we use your Window." I then gesture to Callum and Helene. "They've used it to cross over, and they know the best paths to take to avoid the King's Guard."

Angie gives a slight frown to Helene. "I'm aware they slipped through. It's fortunate for them I believed your story, Nora." She then narrows her eyes at me. "Why should I believe the story you tell me now?"

Fucking fuck.

Finn stays silent, but yeah, the tension in his fingers against my back coaxes me to stick to my guns.

I clear my throat and lean forward to rest my elbows on the dining room table. Surrounded by cozy things in this cozy cabin, I give her all the sincerity I can muster. "I'm asking you, as a friend, to trust me, Angie. It's important we go and go soon."

She tilts her head, lifts her mug to her lips, and takes a slow sip of coffee. Then, "I think you're out of your fucking mind to go there." Even her cussing is polite, calm. "Chances are, you won't be coming back."

I can't help how my insides turn hollow. "It's a chance I'm willing to take."

"For your Pixie friend?" she says with a quirked brow.

I nod. And for Finn. Especially for him.

She points her gaze at Finn. "And you'll be able to seal the Window again once you've crossed?"

"I will." Finn hesitates, and for a moment, his haughty façade drops. "But it won't be directly. I'll need at least a few minutes before I'm able." The truth is, all the Windows will be vulnerable for a few minutes—except our Window. Alexie's magic is keeping it closed now. Finn and she practiced and practiced the incantation to keep it closed. The girl did it without so much as a sweat. Just like she took the magic off those swords. Have I mentioned she still scares me a little?

She does.

But, yeah, we're banking on a few minutes without magic on the Windows won't be enough time to bring Oberon's army charging through. Gods, I hope we're not wrong.

"Helene, Callum, and I will defend the Window from Etherias's side while Finn recuperates," I say quickly before Angie can say no. "And all we ask is that you and your Bonded be ready on this side. It'll be minutes, two or three tops."

Chris leans in to whisper in Angie's ear. He's as nondescript as she is, and it has probably helped them hunt in the past. When he sits back in his chair, he folds his arms on the table and watches me as if searching for the lie in my words.

For this part of the story, he won't find one.

Finally, Angie gives me a nod. "I don't believe for a minute your purpose is to find a long-lost friend, but I believe whatever reason you need to go there is important enough you're willing to risk your life and the lives of these Fae. When do you want to leave?"

I don't deny her words. No sense in it. I stand, my knees weak with relief. With a slight wave of my hand, I implore Finn, Helene, and Callum to do the same as I say, "I reckon now is as good a time as any."

Chapter 15

We're going through now. I love you both...

I stare at my phone before hitting *send*. It's for Ben and Luca, a group message that feels so far away from what actually flows through my mind. I might never see them again, and all I can do is send a group text. But if I hear their voices, I might unravel. Might change my mind. That'd make Finn happy, wouldn't it? He'd gladly stay behind, let us use him until he's a shell of himself. Until he stops breathing. For what? So, we don't put our lives in danger for him? Like he's not worth it?

Not happening.

I straighten and stuff my phone in my pack. Now's not the time for second guessing.

A blizzard whips around us, freezing me to the bone as we surround Ontario's Window. It's in a rare, open field, a beautiful place. The flora and fauna are so much like home in this small corner of the province. Snow thankfully covers any perpetually dead grass and vegetation around the Window. You can almost imagine it's not here. Maybe someday, none of the Windows will be. Maybe we can all pretend and live as humans live in this world. Pay our bills. Work until our fingers are bent with arthritis. Love and live without the threat of some tyrannical ruler from across worlds deciding we're not worthy of it.

Christ, I'm tired.

I peer up at Finn. He's watching me, his face tight with worry.

"We don't have to do this," he says softly. "We can go back right now. This instant."

"And then what, Finn?" I give a quick glance to Angie and Chris, who are scouting the area, making sure no human hunters are out trying to bag themselves a black bear. "You save and save and save us and the Fae until you die?"

He drills me with his silver stare, searching. "Would that be so terrible?"

What? I want to hit him, and I want to hug him until whatever's killing him is extracted from his body. "Yes!" I hiss out. "Yes, Finn. That would be fucking terrible."

"Why, Nora? Tell me why it would be." His voice is so serious, not one hint of sarcasm marring it.

"Because... Because..." So many reasons! So many, and it's hard to articulate just one. "I told you before. I can't lose you."

"We all die sometime, don't we?" He's so serious and searching, and I have no idea what he needs me to say.

"Finn..."

He drills me with his intensity for a few more seconds that feels like a thousand years and then tears his gaze away. "Let's get on with this fool's mission, shall we?" He tips his chin to Helene and Callum. "Be ready. I've no doubt we'll be dealing with trouble the moment we cross into Mystic." He gives me a concerned frown. "Prepare yourself, Assassin."

I adjust my coat. Fine. I'll let him drop the subject, but I still won't let him die.

"What're we looking for?" I ask anyone willing to answer.

"Anything you might imagine," Callum says, a hint of nerves in his voice. "Mystic is full of beings who will not enjoy our visit."

"That ain't helping me, Callum."

Helene takes off her thick coat, despite the arctic winds rushing across the field. "Be sure to look up, Nora. There are beings we call Devas, small, nasty, winged creatures. They tend

102

to attack with little provocation." She pauses to allow her wings to unfurl from the slats she's cut into one of my old thermals. I'll never get over how impressive she is, how much I want to be a warrior Pixie like her when I grow up. "One or two is not an issue. An entire horde will flay you alive if caught unawares."

What the...? I yank off my coat, too, and stuff it into my bag before pulling out my daggers. "Anything else I should know about?"

"Plenty," Callum says as he prepares, a sword in his left hand. He presses his still-healing right wrist close to his chest. "But let's worry about the Devas for now. They will be most bothersome at this point since it's night there."

"How will I spot them, then?" What am I walking into?

Finn chuckles some, pissing me off. I'm not finding anything funny. "Look for the bright lights, Assassin. You can't miss them."

"Fuck," I mutter as Angie and Chris join us at the Window.

"It's all clear, folks," Angie says, her daggers out and ready. "I don't know why you're doing it, Nora, not the real reason, but watch your back, okay?"

I muster a smile for her. "I will. Thank you." I gesture to Chris, who's carrying a bow. "Both of you."

Deep breath in, I look at Finn. His lips are already moving in a silent chant. He said thirty seconds. Just thirty seconds until he has the power to shut the Windows again. *Please don't let this be a mistake.*

I give Helene a frown, my nervous system on full volume. She smiles at me like I'm a little girl needing reassurance. "All will be well, Nora. I won't let anything happen to you."

"I..." What do you say to that? This Pixie, all of maybe five feet, is reassuring me. "Thank you."

She nods, and then focuses on the Window, daggers out and fierce.

Time stops and speeds up at the same time. It's crazy how fear tingles through my legs, my arms. I breathe, breathe, breathe to relax. At this moment, in the cold and frost of the Ontario wilderness, I'm terrified of the unknown. Devas? Fucking hell.

Finn steps ahead of us once he's done chanting. He rolls his neck, and his shoulders lift with a heavy breath. "I'll go first. The faster I cross, the faster my magic returns. Do hurry after me, though. I'm no fan of vulnerability."

Right. He'll be almost as vulnerable as a human.

And he's doing it for me. He's helping to save his own life because I want it, not him.

I grip my daggers tighter. I'll make sure he doesn't regret it.

When Finn disappears through the Window, Helene and Callum are directly behind him. I take a deep breath and plunge into the unknown.

Chapter 16

I'm not prepared for what greets me. Not even a little bit.

It's pandemonium the moment I leap through the Window. Finn is on his knees in soil so black and rich, it's as if we're standing in a void. Helene is already attacking darts of golden light coming at us, Callum at her back. He fights with courage, but he's floundering.

I don't have time to take in my surroundings, adjust myself to this new world. I rush to stand in front of Finn. He's weak and not able to do more than smack away Devas who zoom in too close. I slash and stab at the flashes of light coming at us. They're relentless, and my strength and speed aren't much help when my targets are quick, flying piranhas.

About twenty get so close their mangled little bodies and grotesque faces almost freeze me with shock. Their shrunken raisin faces with gnarled, twisting noses and wide mouths filled with razor-sharp teeth are what nightmares are made from. Their wings whir in the darkened night as they keep coming and coming and coming. Mewling growls ricochet off trees. The smell they give off, like roadkill on a summer day, makes my eyes water.

I keep swatting at them, and for every ten knocked to the ground, thirty more take their place. Teeth scrape through my thermal, slicing open my skin. My body heals and heals, but they're fierce little fuckers. Growling and vicious and relentless.

I can't take my eyes from my targets, can't see if Helene and Callum are okay. If I do, these things will most assuredly strip the outer layer of skin from my body and then some. My calves press against Finn's heat. I'm so close to him, and I swear to the gods, I will drape myself over his body if I lose the upper hand. The Devas will have to eat through my flesh and bones before touching him.

As I swipe and stab and shove, little cries echo behind me. The swarm around my head lessens as the cries become louder, more urgent. I'm able to take a moment to inspect directly behind me, where dead and decaying tree limbs shroud the Window. Relief springs in my chest, fast and painful. The Window... It burns these creatures away as it does all of nature.

I push Finn closer to it with my legs as I backtrack to the Window's opening. He gets the gist and scoots himself nearer. I spare a glance at him, his pale lips moving in a chant. His magic is back. The magic that's killing him to use.

"Helene! Callum!" I yell as they fend off the little bastards, their clothes riddled with tears from sharp teeth.

Callum turns his head in my direction, his face contorted in concentration.

"Come closer! Hurry!" I'm now swatting the occasional Deva who braves death by Window. My breath comes easier. My body heals without being re-torn.

Callum turns to grip Helene's shoulder and yells for her to move backward.

We huddle together now, Finn standing and by my side. Our backs are to the Window, the hive of angry Devas hovering about five yards away, waiting for us to come back into their territory. It's a classic standoff, a game of chicken. Who's going to break the lines first?

Not us.

"All locks have been restored," Finn says, his voice tired, strained.

He needs rest. Whatever happens, we need to make sure we all rest. After we handle our current situation.

"Why're they burning up at the Window?" I ask whoever's listening while catching my breath and keeping my guard up.

"They're of the earth," Callum says, his breath coming out in heavy pants. "They are more nature than sentient being, alive like the trees are alive."

Well, holy shit.

"I thought we were close enough to the Window to avoid the worst of their attacks," Helene says, her voice regretful. "I miscalculated. For that, I am sorry."

"What's done is done. No need fretting about it." I try to count the Devas waiting for us. My guess is anywhere from a hundred to three times that. Their light blends together as if they make one gigantic monster Deva. "What now?"

Finn waves a hand with a soft chant, and the Devas fall to the ground in a glimmering unit. They make the forest floor glow in golden light, and it's so treacherously peaceful-looking I'm tempted to lie down in it.

"They'll sleep for a time now. Let them live," Finn breathes out, his voice a fraction of its usual timbre. "We're invading their home, not the other way around."

I sheath my daggers, think better of it, and pull them out again before shrugging off my pack. The buggers managed to give the canvas material a few decent slashes, but nothing fell out and nothing appears in danger of it, either. After signaling Helene closer, I pull out peroxide, gauze, and some ointment. "You first," I tell her. With a closer inspection of her wounds, I command her to lift her shirt. A shirt, I might add, that looks as though Freddy Krueger has had his way with it.

"I've only managed a few scratches," she says, doing as I tell her.

"Yeah, well, those few scratches will be a bitch to deal with if they get infected. I can only imagine how filthy those little demons' mouths are." I hunker down to dress her wounds, refrain from blowing on them when I dump peroxide into the gashes. She wouldn't want me to treat her like a child.

After I finish with her, I take care of Callum's wounds. A few scratches on his forearm. I also inspect his right wrist and change his protective covering after again digging through my bag for supplies.

When Callum is all bandaged, I move to Finn.

"Are you okay?" I ask him quietly.

He nods once. "I suppose it depends on how you define 'okay.'"

Without thinking of it, I move under his arm, my shoulder now his support beam. It worries me that he accepts the help, doesn't scoff at it with his usual arrogance.

"We need to make camp first thing," I tell Helene and Callum.

"We can camp near the river," Callum says. "It's not far, perhaps a quarter mile from here. Devas aren't fond of water."

I wave a hand in front of me. "Perfect. Lead the way."

He straightens his spine, giving me a confident look. "It would be my honor."

As he takes the lead, Helene throws me a grateful smile before following behind him.

When they get a few yards ahead, I hold Finn tighter, so tight my fingertips go numb. I want my strength to sap into him, heal him as it heals me. "Please tell me you're going to make it, Finn. Promise me."

His hold on me is almost as tight, and he's so warm next to me. "I promise you will not wake to my stiff corpse tomorrow, Assassin. I still have life in me."

A thought strikes me, one that should have popped into my head a hell of a lot sooner. "What if you stopped holding the Windows closed? Would that–?"

"Not even remotely an option." He moves forward, taking me with him. "Come, let's get this bloody day over with."

I keep my mouth shut and walk with him, force myself to be content with the feeling of his warm body pressed to my side.

It's difficult to see as Callum leads us to the river. At least we're now close enough to hear the trickling of water. Light from two full moons thankfully helps to prevent pitch blackness.

Strange sounds echo through the trees. Like bird calls, except more graceful, lyrical. It's almost hypnotizing, akin to the Fae music pumping through Julius's club in New York. I inhale, absorb the clean, earthy scent. So much better without those little fuckers swarming us. How can they smell so badly when surrounded by an environment that smells so good?

When we finally stop at a small clearing near the bank, we don't waste any time building up a fire and unpacking bed rolls made of super-thin blankets.

I'm the only one toting a backpack, and it's by design. I'm strong enough to carry the load for all of us. We can't be wasting time fighting for our lives while the Fae wrestle with the weight of a pack strapped to their shoulders. Our Deva skirmish is a prime example.

As we all unroll the blankets, the soft smiles on the Fae's faces, even Finn's, tugs at my heart. They love this world. With all the danger waiting for us, even possible death, in this moment they're content.

Once we set up camp, I pull out power bars and toss one to everybody. Next are twelve-ounce canisters of water. "Eat. Drink," I command them. "We'll fill our bottles in the morning." Callum said the river's water is cleaner than anything we'd find in my world. The info made packing easier.

Everyone listens except Finn, who makes a path for his bedroll situated across the fire, opposite of mine. He slumps to his ass, drops the bar and water on the ground next to him, and is on his side with his eyes closed before I silently count to ten.

I won't go over there to check the rise and fall of his chest as if he's an infant. I won't.

Not yet, anyway.

For the moment, Callum, Helene, and I sit by the fire and eat in companionable silence. I watch the flames lick the kindling as I chew on chalky peanut butter. Even the fire burns more vividly here. I can decipher all the hues of orange, white, and blue that flame together. A fire rainbow.

The ground is soft, but not too soft. It's like a pillow. My ass doesn't get numb from sitting on it, with only my thin blanket as a barrier. If I didn't already prefer nature over city life, this place would've converted me. Well, if you take out the Devas... and whatever other fanged creatures we might encounter.

I swallow my last bite and stuff my wrapper into my bag. It takes about thirty seconds flat to down my water before I twist the cap back on and stow that away, too.

Keeping my eyes on Finn's sleeping form, I ask, "Where do we go from here?"

Callum clears his throat and crinkles his empty wrapper, handing it to me to shove into my pack. "We'll be going to Rutsk, the village bordering Mystic." He nods to Helene. "There are places to hide whilst I seek out the Healer. Places with those we can trust to keep us safe."

"*We* will find your Healer, Callum." I shift my knees so I can wrap my arms around them. "I ain't about to let you go off alone."

He smiles a little. "Always protecting people. You make a fine Leader, Nora. I hope you know that."

My cheeks heat under the compliment, one I'm not sure I deserve. "I protect those I care for, and that includes the both of you. Y'all have grown on me."

He and Helene tinkle out laughter as melodious as the echoing birdsong. "Did you ever imagine yourself saying that only months ago?" Helene asks.

I grin. "Ah, before or after we were trying to kill each other?"

"Oh, definitely the former, Assassin." Helene covers another giggle. It's odd seeing her this relaxed. I like it.

"Well, whatever the case, I'm saying it now."

"And we're grateful." Callum stretches his arms over his head with a soft grunt. "If we hurry, we should make it to the village by nightfall tomorrow. But I must get some rest. I fear my eyelids are too heavy to remain open any longer."

I tip my head to him as Helene whispers a sweet goodnight. Like Finn, it doesn't take him long to fall asleep, his chest moving with slow, steady breaths in no time at all.

Helene and I inspect the fire contemplatively, listening to it crack and sizzle against the kindling. We've never really spoken before, not like this, in the quiet of night. Not without a purpose. I can't imagine small talk with her. I think she'd stab me in the eyeball with her dagger if I tried.

But there's so much I still want to know. Inconsequential things that hadn't mattered before. I want to know them because I want to know her not just as the warrior she is, but who she is underneath the armor. I want to know them all.

"Helene?"

"Hmm?" She's so calm now, so at peace with where we are. She wraps her arms around her knees like I do, her head resting on her hands. That soft smile she's worn since building the fire remains on her full lips.

"Tell me how y'all came to know each other. I mean, how did someone like you end up friending Seamus? I reckon his cussing alone wouldn't earn him a seat at your table."

Her smile deepens, her focus remaining on the flames. "We grew up together, mostly. Callum's father was a teacher who taught Callum and I when we were younger. Callum became our village's teacher when his father passed. He taught Seamus and Alexie in a one-room schoolhouse. Let me tell you, Seamus has always been colorful with his words, even before he'd learned new terms across the Window. He was none too happy to be learning his letters with a child of Alexie's age. But his parents made him go."

I laugh softly. "Yeah, I'm sure he didn't like it much."

"He's an intelligent boy, our young Seamus, but reckless. Yet…what he lacks in patience, he makes up for in courage. I will forever be grateful to him and Callum."

Helene's smile dims some, and I stop myself from reaching out to her. I've learned to listen since being with Ben and Luca. Learned to be comfortable in the silent pauses of a hard conversation.

"Angora… um… Alexie's mother, took me in when my parents were named on Oberon's list for not paying their taxes. She felt pity for me, the tiny Pixie girl who had to watch the

King's Guard execute her parents. Angora was... *beautiful,* inside and out. Perfect. She was everything I aspire to be." She wipes a stray tear from her eye. "It is my fault she is dead, Nora. I'm the reason Alexie no longer has a mother."

I give in to the temptation to comfort her, my hand grasping hers. "Whatever you might think, I'm sure–"

"No. It is what I know." Her shoulders lift with a heavy sigh. After a slow exhalation, she continues. "One day, on the way home from the market, I ran into three of Oberon's Guards, not too far from our house. I didn't fear them, really. They patrolled the roads all the time. But these Guards..." Her tears flow now, turning her light blue eyes to liquid diamonds. "They stopped me. I was scared then. Afraid I'd done something to be put on a list." She balls her free hand and presses it against her mouth when a soft cry escapes her lips.

"It's okay, Helene." I squeeze her hand tighter. Rage courses through me. I want to find these Guards, make them pay for the terror on my warrior Pixie's face. For the absolute devastation in her voice. "You don't have to finish."

She sits straighter, her spine so stiff, I worry it might snap. "No, I... No." She takes a cleansing breath. "I wasn't a fighter then, you see. I was as fragile as your friend. A vulnerable Pixie surrounded by trained Seelie. They... They attacked me. All I could do was scream and scream and scream until one of them punched me in the face, breaking my jaw. I thought I would die that day. Then Angora appeared. She was angry and breathtaking, her hair swirling about. I'd never seen... never known..." Helene shakes her head. "With a few words, she shattered them like they were shards of glass."

My gods.

"She'd kept her and Alexie's Mage power secret, even from me. She never uttered a chant, always hid in plain sight. And she let her secrets lay bare to save me."

Alexie's mother was a hero. Like Finn. A family trait, it seems. "Angora sounds as though she was extraordinary."

Helene's tears rip my heart to pieces, but after my words, her smile returns, shaky and fragile. "She was everything." She takes a sip of water, the canister shaking in her trembling grasp. "It didn't take long for word of her powers to reach the kingdom. People in our village were terrified. Not of Angora, but of the king's wrath if they helped us. No one would sell us food or supplies. They shunned us. The only people who helped us were Callum and Seamus. They made sure we had food. Protection. And then one day we saw the Guard marching down the road, the king's banners whipping in the wind." She closes her eyes. "Angora demanded we take Alexie and run. Hide. We...we listened. We had no other choice."

She says nothing for a long while as we both stare at the flames. Jesus, what these Fae have been through. Old guilt trickles in. They risked their lives to find me, and I almost finished what Oberon had started. If it weren't for Finn...

I peer at his sleeping form over the fire. Thank the gods for him.

"I stopped being fragile that day," Helene says after a while. "Stopped being weak. I learned to fight. Learned to help protect those I love. My sewn-together family. It took Oberon two years to find out about Alexie, and when he did, we found a way to get to a Window. We'll *never* give up."

I can't help it then. I pull her into my arms, hug her like my life depends on contact with her body to keep going. "You're absolutely amazing, Helene, and I'm in awe of you."

She hugs me for a moment longer and backs away, wiping her face. "Yes, well... ah... thank you."

I grin. "Any time."

She looks around a bit, acting lost for what to do next.

I let her off the hook. "Get some sleep. I'll take first watch."

She gives me a grateful smile, her face puffy but her courage intact. "Wake me when it's my turn, Assassin." She then scoots her bedroll closer to Callum's and rests with her back to me.

Sighing, I get to my feet and stretch out kinks in my back. After a slight hesitation, I move next to Finn. With my palm against the steady beat of his heart, I listen to the music of the forest.

Chapter 17

I wake to Finn's warm hand against my cheek.

Those strange birdsongs infiltrate my groggy mind, and it's like listening to a woodland symphony. The ground is still as soft as when I fell asleep. No desire nags me to stand to stretch out the kinks usually accompanying a night on the forest floor.

For all the warnings Callum gave about traversing this forest, I reckon it's about as close to perfection here as any place has a right to be. If you don't count the Deva piranhas.

A deep breath fills my nose with Finn's clean scent. It's the only way I can describe it, like the smell of a crisp winter morning after the first snowfall.

My eyelids stay closed as I revel in the sensations of his nearness. His touch–an innocent, light caress–sends heat through my entire body. All other thoughts get pushed away to make room for his callused palm against my skin.

I shift closer. The solid length of Finn's body fits perfectly with mine. As if my parts were cut and shaped to match his. I don't want to open my eyes. Don't want to face the morning light. In this state, without eye contact and harsh reality, I can pretend he's mine and I'm his. Pretend he's not dying and pretend the Pull between us is something we can act upon.

When I finally meet the harshness of the dazzling morning sun, I find Finn's soft gaze on my face. Circles still darken the delicate skin under his eyes, but he seems stronger.

And more intimidating.

This Finn is trickier to meet head-on than arrogant Finn, the one who toys with me, promising contact he never intends on delivering. This Finn makes me believe there's a chance for us.

As if he can hear my thoughts, regret darkens his eyes, even as he smiles down at me. Finn lifts the comfort of his hand from my cheek to smooth tangled hair from my face. "I was curious when you'd stop pretending to sleep."

"Maybe I like being here with you," I tell him. I slide my hand between us and press against his heart.

"Would you like being here with me if there were no Pull between us?"

"Yes." I tilt my head, using more pressure against his chest. "Has it ever happened before? With others?"

"A Pull between an Assassin and Fae? Never. It never has and it never will."

"Uh… I beg to differ." I move my hand to his stomach, to where the Pull dwells, and don't miss how his breath hitches when my palm lingers against the dips and ridges there. "We're living proof."

"You should ask more questions."

I narrow my gaze. Always so evasive. Always impossible. "You could offer the information, you know." He might set me afire, but he's still Fae. Still prone to play and toy like a cat with a mouse.

"Where's the fun in that?"

I give his secret smile a stop-fucking-around stare.

"A man can't resist the wiles of an angry woman, can he?"

"Finn…"

Slowly, he takes my hand from his stomach and guides it to the back of his head.

An indent as familiar as the sun is light marks his scalp. Shock widens my eyes. "What the…? You're…? What are you?"

He keeps his hand over mine at the back of his head, tightening his grip when I try to pull away. By damn, his strength almost matches my own. "I'm a bastard, remember? Whelped by a member of my father's Guard." He pauses. "A woman I've never had the pleasure of meeting."

"Your mama was an Assassin?"

"A Guard, technically, but yes."

"Jesus..." I fiddle with the mark, using my fingertips to measure its size and depth. Same as mine. Same as Ben's and Luca's. "How come you never told me?"

"You never asked." All his sass rushes back into his expression with that bullshit answer.

"You kept it from us deliberately." I push away from him and stand. With a deep stretch, my arms reaching for the sky, I try to hide my surprise and hurt. He doesn't trust me at all. After everything these past few months, he doesn't trust a one of us. "Dick move, Finn. Real dick move."

He adjusts to lie on his back, hands laced behind his head as he studies the vibrant green-and-yellow-leafed treetops. "It doesn't matter, does it, Assassin? It changes nothing." He rejects me again as if it's nothing more than swiping at an annoying fly buzzing around his face.

Fuck, that pisses me off. "It does matter, *Assassin*."

He pins me with his gray eyes. "Why?"

"Because you're part my kind, that's why. It means something."

His eyes turn cold, void of the warmth he'd given so freely not minutes before. "So, I'm more palatable? Worthy of you?"

"*What?*" I put my hands on my hips and glare down at him. "You ain't making a lick of sense, Finn. Not one."

"Ain't I?"

My vision blurs with fury. Leave it to him to lower himself to ad hominem attacks directed at my accent. "Fuck you," I seethe. "I'm the one who wants to Bond with you–even before your little revelation. You're the one denying *me*."

117

He gets to his feet and straightens his thermal as if it were a cravat. "Oh, come now, Assassin. You don't really want that, do you?"

"What the fuck do you mean? Of course I want it! Are you really doing this right now? Turning it on me?"

"I should have never told you." He gives me his back. "My mistake."

I step forward, not nearly finished with this conversation. "You—"

"Ah, look. Our traveling companions have returned with our water." He shifts to frown at me. "Best get on with your mission to save my life." He saunters to Helene and Callum, not giving me the chance to spout off another curse.

Oh, how I want to kick him.

I want to...

I don't know what the fuck I want to do.

Why the hell is he so mad? Why the hell am I? It shouldn't be that much of an issue, but it is. Fate brought him to me. Biology. Whatever. And I'm mad because he's supposed to be mine. It makes sense now. He was meant for me, and I for him. It's not a coincidence. I stopped believing in them long ago.

But I'll never have him. He'll never be mine.

Because *he's* decided not to Bond.

As close as he's gotten with Ben and Luca, he'll never be theirs, either. We'll always have a large, aching Finn-gap in our Bond. Because Finn belongs to Etherias. He's said as much. So why *the fuck* is he dismissing me like it's my decision?

You know what?

He'll be explaining himself. I refuse to hang on to a man's mixed signals with anxiety or agonize over something that a question or two can resolve. Last time I checked, I'd graduated high school a long while back and left my juvenile tendencies with my teen years.

Finn's right about one thing. I need to ask more questions.

And believe me, when I catch him without an audience, he'll be answering them.

Chapter 18

Mystic Forest by day is extraordinary, rivaling the mountains I love. Colors are crisp and vibrant, like Caravaggio himself painted every leaf, every tree. The soil's so dark and soft and fragrant, I'm half-tempted to strip down to nothing and roll around in it.

While Callum leads us closer to Rutsk, Helene acts as my tour guide, pointing out edible plants while warning against others that'll kill a full-grown person with one bite. She waves to tiny fluttering creatures above us, and I think she's a bit touched until one of those creatures flaps their wings in front of my face. Squinting at first, I gasp and clap a hand over my mouth when a tiny Pixie-like creature, with a Pixie face and all, smiles at me.

"What in the name…?" Awe makes my voice airy as I hold out a finger for the thing to perch on. Its translucent wings are splashed with purple and delicate. Unlike Helene's wings. Hers are battle-ready. Fierce and strong.

And is this little lady wearing tiny clothes?

Well, fuck me, yes, she is.

Helene lets out tinkling laughter as the mini-Pixie lands on my index finger. "They're called Heather Pixies," she says. "Fae who tend the forest. Fae your humans always portray Pixies to be in their stories."

I bring the spritely thing closer to my face. She has perfect little features. "Hello, young lady."

The Heather Pixie squeaks a high-pitched retort, her hands firmly on her rounded hips. A-fucking-dorable.

"She can understand me?"

"She only understands Fairy, our ancient language." Helene picks a vibrant orange flower. When she sniffs it, its petals caress her nose as if it sniffs her back. "The king deemed our language too crude. He's adopted languages from your world. English, Spanish, and Mandarin, mostly."

"Why?" I ask, my fascination glued to my new friend.

"He's destroyed a lot of our ways with no explanation. You would have to ask him why."

"Right." Maybe I will ask him, the moment before I plunge a dagger into his throat.

I've not forgotten the promise to myself. I *will* kill that bastard, and that fucking Mage, Talia.

And Kellen.

I'll kill the Haunt slowly. Make him feel the pain he's given me.

A flash of his poisoned blade stabbing my father's heart invades my peace.

I'll make them all pay.

Clearing my throat, and my mind, I say goodbye to the Heather Pixie as she flits away, her inspection of me complete. "We will kill him, Helene. Someday. And when we do, he'll no longer be able to terrorize your people or mine."

She's silent, lifting the flower to her nose again. Then, "Another tyrant will replace him, one hungry for power and willing to do whatever it takes to obtain it. The best we can do is get enough Fae through the Windows and then find a way to seal them forever."

I watch her as we walk, our gait slowing as if her predicted future adds a hundred pounds of stone to our shoulders. She doesn't want to only save a few; she's said as much before. Yet, she's resigning herself to accept the lesser of evils.

All I can do is nod. Forgetting our troubles for a second feels almost treacherous. Good thing it didn't last long.

As Helene sets the flower on the ground–where it literally roots itself in the soil to live another day–my gaze travels to Finn's back. His posture is always on point. Mamaw would have never bitched at him for curling his shoulders. He stands even straighter with his fury. Fury I don't understand.

Exasperating.

What the hell does he got to be mad about, anyway? I should be the one stewing in anger, not him. Part Assassin, for Christ's sake. He's the one keeping secrets.

The walk is uneventful for the next few hours, nice, despite the cold shoulder Finn's freezing me with. Helene resumes giving me info here and there and answers my questions. No humidity weighs down the air, and the sun doesn't torture us with relentless baking. It feels more like one of my grandmother's quilts draped over my shoulders. Soothing.

We eat what we can eat, and it's delicious, especially these red flowers that are everywhere. The blossoms contrast vibrantly with all the green and yellow, like deep rubies embedded in nature. They taste like a mixture of strawberries and cantaloupe, and Callum swears they're loaded with protein. These things would make a great buttercream for devil's food cupcakes. Maybe I'll take some back, and Pia and I could–

My heart sinks, and the red flowers in my hand tumble to the ground with my appetite. How the hell are we going to get her back? How can I leave this world without her?

Yet, I'll have to leave her this time.

Because she gave herself to the king.

And the king wanted her.

Why did he want her?

"Prepare, Nora," Helene whispers behind me, as we reach the middle of a clearing. "Darkness brings nightmares with it."

Shit. I hadn't even noticed how the sun descended, giving way to the rising moons. I pull my daggers from my pack. "What're we preparing for?"

And then the silence creeps up on me. Dead, dead silence that screams across the treetops. No more birdsong. No insects whirring overhead. No Heather Pixies monitoring our trek through their territory.

Shit. Shit.

Callum rushes to my side, his face pale in the waning light. His sword is in his left hand, and it trembles in his grasp. "We are close to Rutsk. It's not a quarter mile north. I had hoped we'd avoid this, but..."

"Avoid what, Callum?" I scope the surrounding landscape, my anxiety itching.

"This parcel of land is territory to Fae almost as powerful as Mages."

"The fuck you trying to tell me? What Fae?" My attention drifts to Finn's silhouette in front of us. He doesn't come to stand in our huddle. No, he's out in the open, his arms at his sides, his fists balled around brilliant silver light.

He can't be using a heaping amount of magic. Who's to say he'll recover this time?

"Shifters," Helene answers, her voice shaky. Now, that puts a fear in my chest. She's afraid, and she's never afraid. Not even when Oberon's soldiers infiltrated my yard. "Seelie Shifters. Wolves."

"You gotta be fucking kidding me. Like, actual werewolves?"

She nods.

"This is something y'all could've given a heads-up about."

Silence answers me. Because I'm right, and they fucking know it.

I glance up, searching for any glowing piranhas. "Them Devas around here?"

Callum's audible swallow sets my teeth on edge. "No. They would not dare come into Shifter territory."

"But we'll dare it, huh?"

"It was the only way," Callum says with regret. "Their territory circles the entire village, and they will not appreciate strangers on their land."

"You Fae and your goddamn secrets," I mutter. I stand straighter, breathing past my building terror. "Come on. We can't be letting Finn use his magic."

As I make my way toward Finn, Callum stammers, starting and stopping sentences.

I turn to him. "What?"

"We can't fight against them without magic."

I charge him, getting so close, he shrinks back. "Why the hell would we try to cross into Rutsk at night, then?"

He shakes his head. "Time does not matter. They occupy these woods, day or night."

"They're more aggressive during the night, when the moons are full," Helene adds, causing Callum to wince as he bravely maintains eye contact with my scowl.

I look up toward the moons. They're wide and round and full.

Of course.

I grip my daggers tighter. "It doesn't matter. I've been fighting battles without magic my whole life and survived them. Even won a few."

"You don't understand!" Callum says. "They're fierce creatures, unforgiving and stronger than all of us."

"Not all of us."

"Nora, please. We must—"

"Enough, Callum, god damnit. We can't keep making Finn carry the burden. He won't survive it. You said so yourself." I turn from him, my angry footfalls carrying me to Finn's side.

"Stand down, Assassin," Finn says without taking his gaze off the tree line. "No need to play the hero. I'll handle these mutts and have us at an inn in time for supper."

My scoff is loud enough to ricochet back to me. "How about you take your own advice, *Assassin*? Let me help this time."

I don't miss how his lips quirk into an almost-smile. No doubt in my mind, he wants to have a battle of words with me.

That'll have to wait till later.

"I'm not leaving your side, and you ain't draining yourself by expelling a bunch of magic." I drop my pack to the ground, pull out one of Luca's dirks, and hand it to Finn. "Here. You got strength. Let's see if you know how to use it."

Finally, he brings his attention to me, his gray eyes bright. Eyes that match the color of the moons perfectly. Slowly, he takes the dirk from my grasp, brushing his fingers against mine. His touch makes the Pull dance in my stomach. "Challenge accepted."

Helene and Callum now stand with us, everyone ready, waiting to see what's scared the forest into silence.

"Do not kill them if you can help it," Finn says softly as rumbling growls invade the quiet. "We are not here to murder those going on about their lives. We are the intruders, don't forget."

Fine. Maiming it is.

Not like Finn needs to give the warning. We all know his rule against killing innocents. Even if those innocents are bent on killing us.

The low rumbles lacing the trees become louder. It's hard to discern from which direction they originate, and my hackles rise while searching every inch of woods.

All of us are vigilant. Waiting. My body's braced, ready for what comes from the woods, but the tension radiating off the rest of my group suffocates the air around us.

"We can do this, y'all. We've fought worse."

"We have." Helene moves to my side, Finn flanking the other. All of us form a line in front of Callum, none of us willing to sacrifice our weakest link to save ourselves.

Howls render the darkened sky. Wolves' language. Warnings. Messages between pack mates.

Jesus H...

Werewolves?

"Again," I hiss-whisper as the howls grow more stressed. "A simple, 'Hey, we might run into Fae Shifters,' would have been a sufficient warning."

"In fairness," Helene answers, "you never warned us to watch for bears."

An incredulous groan slips between my tense lips. "Nope. Not the same."

"Says the super-strong Assassin," she quipped. "Try being a Pixie meeting one of those beasts in the woods. One almost had us for dinner in the Pennsylvania forest. Ben scared it off by doing an unpleasant dance while yelling. It was almost as terrifying as the bear itself."

My lips twitch with a suppressed smile. Oh, I've seen Ben's bear dance before.

Humor evaporates from my body when the first wolf makes its presence known at the edge of the clearing. They come out slowly at first, keep their distance. Two after the lead wolf also make an appearance under the moonlight, and my mouth gapes in shock. They're massive creatures, taller than me, even on four legs. Their eyes shine tawny yellow against the night, and they point those eyes in our direction.

I lift my daggers higher. "I've never seen a black bear that big."

"Ben's dance wouldn't help now, I'm afraid," Callum says.

A smirk twists my lips. Look at Callum making jokes before our death.

Finn closes the space between us until our arms touch. His attention never leaves the animals a hundred yards from where we're standing. "You know what they say about bringing knives to a Shifter fight?"

"No, Finn. Never heard that one. Maybe 'cause y'all forgot to—"

"Yes, yes. But in our defense, you never asked."

I swear I'm gonna beat those words out of his vocabulary. "Not. Now," I say through gritted teeth.

"Very well, then. Best raise your cute daggers a tad higher." He lifts his dirk and situates himself into a fighting stance as the three wolves move forward, followed by four more. "Here they come."

Fuck me.

Two wolves behind the three leaders, equally massive, take off running. They don't come directly at us. No. They run opposite ways along the field, circling behind us. Trapping us. The leaders move forward with stealthy grace, the two behind them following. Their lips are pulled back, sharp teeth white and glinting against the moonlight.

I've spent my life in the woods and have tracked all nature of things, including black bear and bobcats. Never once did I let fear cloud my vision. Yet, as these giant, gorgeous animals draw nearer, so near I can smell fresh blood from a recent kill and see it coat their brown and gray fur in a glossy sheen, fear sends the synapses in my brain into warp speed. Fight-or-flight begs me to run.

We don't have anywhere to go.

All we can do is fight.

Without magic.

Helene moves closer to Callum, her sword up and ready. "They're smart creatures, able to understand us. Perhaps if we plea for leniency…"

Their answering growls tell me all I need to know. "They're not in the mood for pleas."

As soon as the words leave my mouth, a wolf from behind lunges at Callum. Without a thought to my safety, I drop a shoulder and check the beast before its fangs rip out his throat. The wolf yelps, my shove tossing it about five feet away. It lands in a heap, only to get back up on all fours, shaking its head as if shaking off my attack. The thing bares its teeth again, thankfully not attacking a second time.

Because it's his buddy's turn.

The new wolf snarls and gnashes his teeth, his focus locked on Helene. As soon as he lunges, Helene whips up into the sky, fluttering out of his reach. Undeterred, he leaps in the air to take a chunk out of her. He almost gets her before she darts higher.

Finn beats me to it this time and bum-rushes the thing, wrapping his arms around its thick neck and tackling it to the ground. With surprising speed, Finn is off the creature and standing next to me before the wolf regains his footing.

"They're toying with us," Finn says, his voice strained. "We can't win this way, Nora."

126

I don't answer–because, yeah, he's obviously right.

The wolves' circle around us grows tighter. So tight, their hot breath blasts my cheeks. Their bodies block out the rest of the field. I can't see above them. Under them.

God damnit.

"To hell with this." Finn's angry voice barely registers above the chorus of growls. What he says doesn't matter, though.

He raises his hands, chants a few words, and the circle of fur blasts back about fifty yards.

As the wolves lie stunned on the ground, I take off. "Come on!"

We move as a unit, trying in vain to make it to the tree line and to the other side of it. As the wolves recover, they come after us. Finn and I are the only ones with the strength to push them back, and my body is tired from using every single muscle to heave them off us. Not near enough time elapses between each of my defensive maneuvers for my body to recuperate.

Helene flies above us, diving to attack the advancing wolves with superficial slashes of her iron blade. Her sword is no match against their tough skin. Hell, our weapons wouldn't do any real damage even if we wanted them to. Though our blades are iron, their thick fur protects them from the burn.

We keep pushing forward, our movements slow. We might as well be walking through a blizzard at the highest peak of a mountain. For every step we take, the wolves push us back, our shoving and prodding a game to them now. They nip and tear at our clothes, shredding our sleeves and leaving surface gashes on our skin. Callum is helpless behind us, without strength to fend them off or the power to wield his weapon properly.

They're corralling us in the woods so they can kill us under the cover of a thick canopy of green leaves.

Sweat and blood from superficial wounds on my cheeks drench my face. Heaving breaths cause my lungs to feel small and wizened. This is fruitless. Finn's keeping up with me, though. For every wolf I temporarily shove away, he shoves one, too. But they keep coming back. We're house cats to them. Helpless beings who brought knives to a wolf fight.

Yes, magic drains Finn, but this physical exertion isn't doing him any good, either.

"Finn, you were right." I shove another wolf from Callum, who will not deal with this much longer. "We ain't gonna make it."

He grunts as he thrusts a wolf from me before its snapping jaw connects with my shoulder. "Hold them off!"

At my nod, he throws another wolf going after Callum before scaling a tree with speed Ben would envy. No time to admire his agility, I keep pushing at fur and snapping jaws, fetid saliva spraying my face. Callum tries, he really does, to fend off our attackers, but with only one hand and lack of strength, he's losing the battle. Helene attempts to help, yet she's busy avoiding leaping wolves doing their best to take her out of the sky, one almost getting close enough to slice a wing.

We're losing.

My arms tremble with exhaustion, and my legs demand to take me to the ground.

I fight anyway.

Fight and fight and fight.

They'll have to rip out my throat before I give up.

But then... relief.

Slowly, the attacks lessen. Wolves yelp and whine as they fall back, some frozen in place. Others are trapped on the ground as though an invisible weight presses them down. Their cries grow more desperate as Finn's chants become louder, faster, more intense.

When the last wolf falls to the ground in a crippled heap, I heave, bending to rest my hands on my knees. Sweat drips from my face and splashes to the ground. My body aches, and then feels like fire when the healing mends pulled muscles and a fractured wrist. At least three cracked ribs, too.

Once the pain is manageable, I limp to Callum, needing to gauge how hurt he is. When I stumble over a wolf, I freeze.

He's no longer an animal. None of them are. They're Seelie men and women. Most have passed out. Some writhe in pain.

Holy shit.

Naked Seelie are scattered across the forest floor like they'd had some sort of BDSM orgy. Beautiful, battered bodies. But alive.

Shaking my head, I rip my gaze away to make sure Callum is on his feet and still alive. He inspects the faces of every shifter, as does Helene.

"What are y'all doing?" I huff out.

"Memorizing faces." Callum doesn't take the time to look at me while he speaks. "They will search for us. It's best we see them coming."

Great. All we need to add to our list of enemies is a bunch of wolves sniffing us out.

I don't help them with their task.

Finn needs me.

I turn toward the tree he now slumps in, and my heart drops to my feet. He's not moving.

"Finn!" I rush to him as fast as my still-healing body can go. As I reach him, he slips from the tree branch he's perched on like water tipping from a bucket. My arms clasp around him before he hits the ground. He's heavy and saturated with perspiration. As I gently lay him on the dark soil, I touch the back of my hand to his forehead. Cold.

His face is so pale it's tinged with blue.

He's not breathing.

No.

He can't be…

No!

"Finn," I whisper against his cheek. Tears warm my skin as I press harder against him. "Please, Finn. Please…" When he doesn't respond, panic laces my words. "Callum! He's… He's not moving. Help him. Please help him!"

Callum rushes over, his face strained, but his actions calm. I hold Finn in my arms as Callum checks his pulse. "He's alive," Callum says after long seconds with his fingers pressed to Finn's carotid.

"He's not breathing." My voice is a child's voice, desperate. My arms tighten around Finn's still body. I need Callum to tell me everything's okay. I need him to say the words.

Callum places his palm on Finn's chest and seconds *tick, tick* by. Too many seconds. An eternity of time. He then puts his ear to Finn's face, listening. Relief escapes his mouth in a thankful, quick laugh. "He is breathing, Leader. I promise you. It's shallow but breathing all the same."

"Thank you." I bend my ear to Finn's mouth, the panic subsiding enough to wait patiently to feel soft breath touching my earlobe.

"We must go before the Shifters wake."

I nod, rock Finn in my arms, my relief turning my limbs to water. "Helene?"

"Yes, Nora. I'm here." She flutters down next to me, her tiny hand coming to my shoulder in support.

"Will you collect my pack from the field?" I don't look at her, my attention solely belonging to Finn's unconscious face.

"Yes, absolutely."

As she flies off, I nuzzle Finn's neck for one stingy second. A cry bubbles from my throat as his pulse beats against my skin. Still sluggish, but there. Alive.

"Leader?" Callum says with his tempered patience. "Can you carry him?"

"Yes." I'll carry him to the end of this world if I have to. "How far?"

Callum stands. "Less than a mile. The path should be clear from this point."

With a deep breath, I get to my feet, and then bend to lift Finn in a fireman's carry reminiscent of our first meeting. Only this time, I've got more invested in keeping him alive.

My heart depends on him surviving.

As Helene flies back with our supplies, I gesture to Callum. "Get us the fuck out of these woods."

Chapter 19

By the time we make it to the woods' edge, my body is mostly healed. Finn's heavy, so unlike the first time I had to carry him from a forest, but I'd haul him on my shoulders for a hundred more miles without a complaint. His warmth and the way his chest rises and falls against my back give me the strength to do just about anything.

He's still here, all that matters.

Can't say Finn is enjoying the free ride, though. When he wakes the moment we stop to assess the village, he's none too pleased to be hanging over my shoulder.

"I do love a good humiliation, love, but would you kindly set me on my feet?" Finn's weak voice makes my heart sing with happiness. His sardonic words are as strong a balm as Ben's music and Luca's prose.

I do as he asks, setting him gently beside me, my shoulder ready for him to lean on, which he uses without complaint. My hand automatically goes to his cheek as I inspect his color. Still pale.

And still alive.

He covers my hand with his, his exhausted eyes meeting mine. "I'm fine, Nora," he whispers for only me to hear. "Death will have to fight harder to get me."

I press my palm tighter against his cheek. "No more magic." My demand comes out in a shaky plea.

He nods, gently pulls my hand down, and clasps it at his side.

I'm absolutely fine with that.

Callum clears his throat, and I tear my gaze from Finn's to find the Seelie blushing like he caught us having sex. Helene smiles at us, her eyes wistful as she lifts her hand to cover a giggle.

Really, this side of Helene, this relaxed version of her, amazes me. She's more comfortable in this world, even after fighting a bunch of werewolves.

"So, what do you have for us next, boy? Please let it involve a warm bath, hot food, and a soft bed." Finn may barely be recovering, but he still commands the space he's in. It doesn't matter that he uses my shoulder to keep him on his feet.

"Yes, my lord. That's exactly our next step. However,..." He fidgets with the hilt of his sword, now hanging in the scabbard at his waist, as he looks over the distant village. All we can see from where we stand are shadows of buildings and the lights illuminating their windows.

"Out with it, Callum," I say.

"We can't all march into Rutsk as we are. We're dressed wrong, for starters, and you"–he gestures to me–"will have a challenging time blending with Fae. Many of these villagers have never lain eyes upon a Changeling, but I can imagine they've heard stories and none of them good."

Oh, I don't like that. "A Changeling, huh?"

"*Assassin* is only a term used in your world. Fae understand your kind are one and the same, but there are no Assassins here. Changelings... It is rare for them to come back to Etherias once planted in your world."

"Fine. I get it. We're monsters." More terrifying here than Shifters, I'd reckon. "What's the next step, then?"

"I have a contact, an innkeeper of an establishment on the outskirts of the town center. Let me go to her alone, explain our situation. She hates the king as much as the next person, and she will help us, especially after I tell her about Lord Finn."

"*Finn*, Callum." Exasperation gives an edge to Finn's weakened voice. "For the love of all the gods…"

Callum simply nods like always when Finn corrects him. "Right, well, she'll be honored to have a legend in her establishment. I've no doubt she'll help us."

Yeah…after Finn proves he is who Callum claims him to be with magic. Like a show pony.

Not that my Order had him doing any different the last couple months.

There's been so many hoops to jump through, and Finn is always paying the price.

"Go on. Make it quick," I tell Callum. As soon as the order leaves my mouth, he blends with the shadows.

Once Callum is gone from sight, I take a selfish moment to close my eyes and… feel. Finn's heat melts into my body, the weight of him grounding me. A deep breath fills me with his scent, and I even appreciate the smell of sweat and dirt caking his skin and clothes.

He hugs me close, and any animosity he might have still had isn't present in how his fingers massage the hand he holds and how he nuzzles the top of my head. His former anger requires explaining. But not now. Now, I bask in the knowledge that we're still alive, still able to feel.

And we're being rude as fuck.

Reluctantly, I open my eyes to find Helene not even bothered by us. Her attention is fixed on the village, face glowing with excitement. She smiles radiantly, and it's sweet how her wings flutter so much her toes barely touch the ground. She obviously doesn't care that I'm ignoring her to absorb Finn. Her enthusiasm surprises me after hearing her story, though. But who am I to judge? If she's happy to be here, then I'm happy for her.

Finn shifts his weight, and I almost cry out with both relief and disappointment when he's able to stand on his own. My body instantly feels too cold without him. He straightens his clothes–

which is pointless because his thermal and jeans are as tattered as my and Helene's attire–and tips his chin toward the village. "I wouldn't bank on these people being as in awe of my presence as Callum believes. There is a good chance we'll be sleeping in this field for the night."

Helene is shaking her head before he's done speaking, her attention now on us. "Oh, no, you're wrong, my lo–ah... Finn." At least she's catching on. "They will react like we did when Angora told us of you, of her lineage. Callum, Seamus, and I were star-struck, to say the least. Especially Callum. He made it his mission to learn your entire history. He even tried to figure out a way to free you from prison."

Finn chuckles. "My aunt had a soft spot for me, I suppose. She always felt sorry for the bastard kitchen boy."

That's something else I want to know about. If Finn's mother was a Guard, how did he end up in the palace kitchens?

Helene stands straighter and lifts her chin. "Angora loved you. Believed in you. You're the reason we knew to go through the Window to find Nora's Order. You're the reason we're alive today. If you hadn't shared that with her, given her the picture of Miriam and Nora, we would have never known who to trust to help us."

My heart instantly tightens at the mention of my Order. Finn trusted my mother, and by default believed in me. I glance up at him. "When did you tell Angora about my Order?"

He tucks tangled hair behind my ear, his expression soft. Sad. "After the first time I met your mother and Casey. I was with someone on her list one unfortunate night. She showed them mercy when she realized they were innocent. My trust for her formed at that very moment. Your mother and I grew close that first meeting, spending days together, and she learned to trust me, too. She even gave me the picture to find you if anything happened to her. So, of course, I needed to gossip about the honorable Assassin to my aunt in a letter." He makes it sound so flip, like he isn't a man who puts every single other innocent being before himself.

Those who know him feel his loyalty.

Those who've only read about him seem to pine for it.

He is their hope.

It brings me pride–and it brings me misery. For the thousandth time, I'm reminded of how he can never belong to me.

He belongs to all of them. To this world.

But...wait.

I tilt my head, narrowing my eyes at Finn. "So, you knew who I was when I found you in the woods?"

He wipes some crusted mud from the front of his shirt. "I wasn't in any condition to remember faces, but once I was well enough to truly look... Let's say I felt fortunate you're the one who found me."

Fae, man. They're slippery when they want to be.

I can't even be mad. It's not like I asked–which will be his excuse if I call him out further. He's not such a mystery to me now. I know how he plays his hand.

Callum's copper hair glints in the moonlight as he makes his way back to us. When he's close enough, I let out a relieved breath.

He's smiling.

Which means we'll be sleeping in a bed tonight.

Chapter 20

A Seelie woman, Regina, meets us at the back entrance of a quaint inn. She's nice enough, especially after Finn gives her a small show by frosting over the windows and stone face on the lower level of her establishment. That level being a pub. It's not much, but even that little bit of exertion shows on Finn's face as he smiles politely at the small woman, giving her every ounce of his charm. She bats her lashes, fans her face, and she gives me a scowl when I lock my arm around Finn's.

I can't help it. The woman is stunning, and she's pissing me off. The Pull makes irrational thoughts seem perfectly rational.

She mutters something about weird Changeling behavior and then guides us up a set of wooden steps to a block of rooms. Music and muffled voices leak through the floorboards from the pub below, making me nervous. Too many folks in one place, and many won't take kindly to our presence.

I try not to think about that now as Regina shows us to our rooms. She gives us two, one for Finn and Callum, one for Helene and me.

"Will you be wanting supper, Callum?" Regina asks while ogling Finn.

"That would be lovely, Regina. Thank you." Callum isn't his usual timid self here. He walks with his back straight and head high. He fits in this place, like Helene fits.

Like Finn.

I'm the misfit. The odd-looking Changeling.

"Very well. I'll have my boy bring platters." She leans closer to our small group. "Best stay in your rooms this evening. King's men are enjoying a night of drink downstairs."

"The Guard?" Helene asks, her voice taking on an edge.

Regina nods. "And then some."

Finn moves from my possessive touch to clasp Regina's hand gently between both of his. "Thank you for helping us, my dear. You can't know the depth of my gratitude."

She blushes, her pretty, un-glamoured face brightening. "It's my honor, my lord. You've come to help us, and if I can return the favor in any way, I will do it smiling."

None of us correct her, and I'm sure I'm not the only one feeling guilt when she leaves to have food brought to our rooms.

We can't help them. Not all of them.

It's impossible.

Finn gives me a frown before heading to his appointed room, Callum following him in.

I stand in the hall, waiting. Waiting for what, I have no idea.

"Come, Nora." Helene takes me gently by the forearm. "We shouldn't stay out here too long."

Right. Definitely not a smart idea.

Once we're in our room, I take a moment to soak it all in. It's cozy, a mixture of modern and medieval. Two beds with quilts covering them are situated against the back wall, sleeping gowns laid out on each one. A fire flares in a stone hearth that takes up the entire opposite wall, a table and two chairs in front of it. Another wooden table sits under a window with thick glass. Oil lamps light the space, and the smell of wood-smoke gives the small room a cozy feeling. What shocks me is the small bathroom connected to our room. There's a flushing toilet and a wooden tub with running water. A basin with plumbing and a drain, too. Above it is a piece of glass I wouldn't quite call a mirror, but I can make out a blurred reflection when I peer into it.

"What a strange world," I mutter, touching the thick glass. It's smooth and dull. Maybe it's a good thing I can't see myself well. Gods know I don't hold a candle to anyone in this world.

Okay, maybe I'd win a beauty contest against the Devas.

"Are you surprised?" Helene asks from behind me.

I shrug and turn toward her. "Don't know what I am, honestly. This place is everything I thought it might be with so much more." I raise a brow at her. "Seelie werewolves? How come I never heard of them?"

"There are all kinds of Fae here, Nora. Many cannot cross to your world. Even with a glamour, they would never blend in with humans. As for Shifters, they'd never trade this land for another."

I wag a finger at her as I leave the bathroom to set my pack on one of the beds. "Still, next time we're out and about, give me a heads-up on any other beings bent on killing us."

"Deal," she says, humor in her voice. "Would you like to bathe first?"

I watch the flames lick the hearthstone. "You go on. I'm gonna rest a bit, wait for food."

"Very well." She collects one of the sleeping gowns and heads into the bathroom. "I won't be long."

"Take your time," I tell her as she closes the door on me.

Minutes tick by, and I don't move from where I'm standing. The fire keeps my attention as my mind wanders into Finn's room.

I should be in there.

No. I *need* to be there.

With him.

"Fuck," I mutter through a heavy exhalation. Yeah, I might regret this.

I'm in front of Finn's door and knocking softly before I can analyze all the cons of my decision. Callum answers with a soft smile that droops some when he lays eyes on me and not on a platter of food. "Something wrong, Nora?" Concern colors his cheeks. "Is there trouble?"

I try for my best reassuring smile. "No, no. Ain't nothing like that. Um…" I glance over his shoulder at an empty room before meeting his gaze again.

His eyes widen with understanding. "Did you want to speak with Lord Finn?"

I could lie, but why go to all the trouble? "Yeah. Yeah, I'd like that."

"Certainly." His brow crinkles in consternation. "He's bathing now, but–"

"Perfect." I move past him and stand in the middle of a room identical to mine, staring at the closed bathroom door. "Give us a minute?"

"I… Yes, of course. I'll take my supper with Helene, then."

"Sounds great, Callum. Thanks," I say, not taking my attention off the bathroom door. I don't let go of my breath until the door shuts quietly behind him.

The Pull dances inside me, egging me on. All that sits between me and my exasperating Fae is a closed bathroom door.

I tug on the hem of my flannel and worry my bottom lip. He knows I'm out here. The Pull gives me away.

I drop my hands from my dirty shirt.

Fuck it.

I shove into the tiny bathroom without knocking, closing the door behind me. My eyes adjust to the dim glow of the oil lamp on the sink, and I blink a few times before focusing on the wooden tub. Finn's eyes are closed, his head resting on the lip and arms draped over the sides. The heat emanating from the water makes the room a sauna. Sweat already pools at the small of my back.

I can handle the heat.

What I'm having trouble ignoring is the gorgeous man in the tub–who's ignoring me completely. He didn't even twitch when I barged in, and he's acting as though he's still alone while I soak him in.

Yes, I take a stunned moment to admire what the cloudy water doesn't hide. Finn's lean and perfect, his arms and chest a compilation of sinewy muscle. He's not massive like Luca or ripped like Ben. He's gracefully lethal, a dancer's body hiding power behind beauty.

"You're being rude, Assassin," he finally says, interrupting the silence. He doesn't open his eyes to grace me with his attention. He sounds bored. Tired. "It's a trait of yours I don't find endearing."

"We all have to deal with things, don't we?" I lean against the sink, trying not to ogle him. "You have some explaining to do."

"Disagree."

"Disagree all you want. Explain, anyway."

Finn opens his eyes to give me a daring look as his mouth curves in the slightest smile. "I would love to purge my soul. *If* you join me in here."

Oh, the Pull enjoys that idea. My entire body reacts, really. But my brain remains on task. "Why do you do that?"

"Do what?" Innocence I could poke a thousand holes in now shadows his face.

"Try to fluster me whenever I ask questions."

"I fluster you, do I?"

Instantly, my birthmark tingles.

I refuse to take the bait. "Good. Let the camouflage spell wear off. It'll save you energy."

He stares at me for long seconds, his eyes gradually narrowing while a frown replaces his smile. It's my turn to smile now. This is the Finn I want. The one who doesn't hide behind flirtation and flippant remarks.

"You should have told me," I say.

"Told you what?"

"Everything." Everything, *everything*!

He tilts his head as he contemplates me–and then closes his eyes and sinks deeper into the steaming water. Dismissing me. "I'm tired, Nora. Perhaps you can invade my privacy another night–after I've rested from saving your life yet again. I am keeping track, you know."

I stand there, mouth agape. His mercurial moods make it so hard to adjust my own.

He hates me.

He wants me.

He's indifferent toward me.

He cares for me.

It's a rollercoaster that I'm sick of riding.

You know what? Time has long come for me to take charge of the situation. He said he'd talk if I got in that tub with him? Well, then. I could use a bath.

I make as much noise as possible, stripping my belt from my jeans with a sharp *snap*.

Oh, yeah, I've got his attention now.

His eyes burst open as he narrows them at me again. "What are you doing, Assassin?"

I answer him by lifting my shirt over my head. Next goes my bra, falling to the wooden floor in quiet triumph.

His narrowed eyes widen, shock filling his gray gaze as he takes me in. Good. "Nora, let's not–"

Aaaannnddd I unzip my jeans, shimmying out of them with a quick tug over my hips.

His eyes do all his talking now. He wants this… and maybe he's a little scared of it.

I slip off my underwear and move closer to him, my back straight and chin up. I may not be Fae-perfect, but I'm not ashamed of what I have to offer.

Finn's face softens with lust as he watches me. It's like he's never seen a naked woman before. He makes me feel beautiful in this moment, scars, dirt, and all.

"You said you'd talk if I got in there with you." My voice comes out husky and not intentionally so. The way he stares at me… Damn. I feel it as if his hands roam my body. "You're many things, Finn, including a man of your word."

He shakes his head slowly. "You…"

Well, holy shit. I've made him speechless.

I step closer, bend to dip my fingers in the steaming water, and keep my gaze on his. "Can I come in?"

He nods once, and I can't help noticing how the tips of his fingers whiten with a tighter grip on the edge of the tub. Jesus, why does his reaction infuse power in my veins? It's so unexpected, this shock and awe he gives me.

I get in opposite of him, the tub barely large enough for the both of us. Slowly, I sink into the hot water, the scent of lemongrass wafting from the steam. Bath oil that explains the cloudiness and the obstruction of a full view of his body.

Our legs touch, his ankle connecting with my hip. Finn doesn't move, his body stone against mine. *So not* how I thought he'd react. He's always so confident. Cocky.

I sink lower into the water until my boobs hide under the cloudiness. He still doesn't move a muscle.

"So…" I glide a hand over his leg and gently massage his calf muscle. "Why didn't you tell us you were part Assassin?"

He closes his mouth and swallows quickly, his Adam's apple bobbing with the effort. "I've never told anyone."

I feel my eyes widen in surprise. "Are you saying it's a secret?"

His chest moves with a heavy breath, as if he's been holding it this entire time. "I'm saying *I've* never told anyone. Anyone now living, that is. My aunt knew, and it's possible she shared the information with others through the centuries."

"Like whom?"

He gives a small shrug.

"I wish you'd trust me. Trust my Order. You mean something to us, Finn."

He licks his bottom lip, and the action sends liquid pleasure straight to my core. "And now I mean more, since you know my lineage?"

I squeeze his calf tighter. "Your lineage changes nothing."

"I beg to differ." He shifts ever so slightly until our legs barely touch. "The knowledge got you naked and in this bath, didn't it?"

"*You* got me in this tub. I don't give a damn who your mama was. She could've been one of them Devas, and I'd still be in here with you. I've wanted this for a while, Finn. I've wanted *you*."

"Liar," he whispers.

"No."

"Yes."

"Do you want me to prove it?"

He doesn't answer.

Fine. He doesn't have to.

I slide up until I'm straddling his hips, which causes water to slosh over the tub's edge. His skin is hot next to mine, and the tingling at my birthmark radiates through my entire body with the contact. Swallowing, trying to maintain control, I spot a sponge on a holder behind him and lean close until my nipples brush his chest to grasp it. The sharp intake of his breath when my nipples tighten against him sends wet heat straight to my pussy. Jesus, all I have to do is shift my hips, and I'd have him inside me.

I don't give in. Don't force a Bond he doesn't want. Instead, I glide the sponge over his chest.

"Why are you doing this?" he rasps out as I bathe him.

I watch how his nipples tighten when I smooth the coarse material over them. "A wall stands between us. Has since the day I found you." I bend until our lips almost touch. "I mean to tear it down."

"How do you plan to do that?" His breath is a hot wave across my mouth.

"Like this." I settle deeper on his lap and feel his cock stiffen against my aching core. Rocking my hips, I glide my wet folds over him, the gentle friction sending currents of pleasure through me. He's so *fucking* hard.

He lets out a moan filled with surprise and pleasure.

And he still doesn't move to touch me.

I cup his cheek in my hand as I shift over his cock again. His eyelids droop, but I don't miss the shock in his eyes.

It's as if he's never felt…

Oh.

Oh.

"Are you…? Have you ever been with a woman, Finn?" I ask gently. "Been with anyone?"

He shakes his head once. Twice. "Does that turn you off, Assassin? A man not as experienced as your Ben or Luca?" The rancor in his voice gives me pause. It shouldn't surprise me at this point, the way he uses his sharp tongue when feeling backed into a corner.

It will not work this time.

A turn-off? That can't be further from what I feel.

I'll be the first to give him pleasure. To make him come.

I'll be the first, and there's power and a responsibility to make this count.

I smile at his scowl, move against his cock until the scowl disappears behind surprised desire. "Hell, no, it's not a turn-off." I moan as I circle my hips against him again. "It makes me want you more."

He releases a shaky breath. "I don't understand you." His words are a mixture of a groan and confusion.

"You will." For the first time, I softly press my lips to his. Fire shoots straight into my heart. "You can touch me, Finn," I say against his mouth. "Please touch me."

Slowly, he releases his grip on the edge of the tub and brings his hands to my back. His touch is reverent, worshipping. When I move against his cock again, his trembling hands travel to my ass, squeezing with gentle pressure. "We can't…"

I try to smile. "I know."

"And you still want to… touch me even without the promise of a Bond?"

"You're mine, Finn, and I'm yours. I don't care that we can't Bond. I still want you."

The Pull flips wildly inside me, protesting my words. I absolutely want to complete our Bond. But I'll take what he can give. This will have to be enough.

I touch my lips to his again. He's so responsive, his lips soft and seeking against mine. When his tongue darts into my mouth, it's my turn to moan in surprised ecstasy. He may be a virgin, but he knows how to use his mouth, and as his lips and tongue become more urgent, it's all I can do to not melt against him.

Finn's hands continue to explore my body, hesitating at my rib cage before his thumbs flick my nipples. I groan inside his mouth and grind my hips tighter against his cock. Gods, I want him inside me.

Shifting, I rub my clit against his velvet erection, slowly at first. And then faster, my mouth never leaving his. He squeezes my nipples as he moans and moans, his tongue lapping at mine, expertly tongue-fucking my mouth.

I'm so close to coming, so goddamn close.

A sharp yell bleeds from his mouth into mine as hot cum sprays my thighs. I move faster as gracefully as I can in this position until he's spent, his chest heaving.

I lift my mouth from his trembling lips and smile down at him, even though my pussy still hums with need.

It's fine.

I can handle it.

Satisfaction still burns through me. Finn, this powerful Fae who no other person has ever touched, and I gave him his first orgasm.

Well, the first orgasm he didn't give to himself.

My mind shifts to picturing him rubbing his cock until cum spurts to his stomach.

Aaannnd now my pussy throbs with more intensity.

His grin is full of surprise and wonderment. "That was…" He pulls me down for another mind-blowing kiss full of tongue and passion.

Is it possible to die from being so fucking horny? Yeah, I'm thinking it is.

When he releases my mouth, I can't help pressing a hand to his heart, my own matching its thrumming rhythm. The awe shining on his face…

The exhaustion he's been caring with him is barely visible.

"See?" I tell him. "We can still… do things."

"Oh, I want to do all the things, love. Every last one of them."

Except Bond.

I can't let that hurt me.

I won't.

A quick knock on the bedroom door breaks the spell, and the cooling water enveloping us takes over the heat our bodies created together.

Finn easily shifts me to get out of the tub, offering a hand to assist me in doing the same. "Sounds like our supper's arrived."

I take his hand and pause while watching his cock harden again. It's perfect and begging for my mouth.

This no-Bonding thing may actually kill me.

Chapter 21

We eat a meager dinner of soft bread and cheese at the tiny dining table by the fire. It's not bad, and I'm not complaining, seeing as so many people in this world are starving. We do have dessert, which is a custard made with those red flowers we ate in Mystic, and let me tell you, if I eat nothing else but this for my entire life, I'd be content.

Once we've finished, Finn stacks dirty dishes on the tray and places it by the door. He then returns to his chair across from me. They're uncomfortable wooden chairs, but I barely notice while we smile over the rims of our cups like we're in middle school.

A pitcher of mulled wine sits on the table, and we've done a good job depleting its contents. Neither of us bothered to don clothes. I have no desire to put my dirty ones back on, and neither does Finn, apparently. Smart thing would have been to bring my pack in here with me, where I stashed clothes for each of us.

Actually, the smart thing to have done would've been to not come in here in the first place. I'm glad I hadn't bothered with reason.

If I had, I wouldn't be sitting across from a very naked and glorious Finn. I can't explain it, really. He's not ripped muscle, but he's strong. He's not tall, yet he's a formidable presence. And he's... beautiful. Graceful.

It's not only his appearance that draws me. It's his presence, the way he makes a room vibrant. His light is ridiculously bright, and I'm drawn to him like a moth to a flame.

"What are you thinking, Assassin?" He purrs his words, and he's so relaxed and unguarded. I want to weep with the relief it gives me.

I take a sip of wine before answering, savoring the taste of berries on my tongue. "I'm wondering why a man like you has gone over a thousand years without having sex."

He raises a brow, mischief curving his lips upward. "A man like me?"

"You know, perfect, gorgeous. Smart." I take another sip. "Mildly amusing."

He chuckles, a sound so contagious and surprising a giggle escapes my lips.

I'll blame it on the wine.

He slouches in the gawd-awful chair, legs spread and showing me all he has to offer.

He has a lot to offer, let me tell you.

Point is, he doesn't act nervous to be with me like this. He doesn't hide how he admires my body, his gaze stopping unabashedly at my chest or at my own spread legs.

Maybe I sit this way to entice him. Maybe I want him to give in and Bond with me despite the weight of this world on his shoulders.

Maybe.

I reach a foot between the small gap separating us and lightly tap his ankle with my toes. "You fixing to answer me, or...?"

He sighs–and then tears his eyes from my still-throbbing pussy to meet my gaze. "I've never been tempted, you might say." He's quiet as his attention lowers again. The heat in his eyes makes it almost impossible to sit still. I want to squirm. I want to touch myself.

I want him inside me.

"I always assumed perhaps I wasn't capable of lust," he continues. Finn returns his attention to my face. "I had no desire for it. No need. Until I met you. Now, I can't seem to shut it off. Every time I'm close to you, every time I touch you. Any time you're annoyed by me." He grins. "I've spent a lot of time picturing you naked, imagining how you'd taste. How you'd feel. I've also spent a good amount of time envying Ben and Luca, I'll admit." His gaze roams over my tits, making my nipples tight. "You've awakened something in me."

My body heats to combustion, and my heart melts from his words. If I had known all of this...

If I had only known...

"Do...? Um... Is that common for people like you to not be attracted to anyone except the person they have a Pull with? Fae who are part Assassin?"

"I wouldn't know." He takes a long sip of wine, still appreciating my chest. "I've never met anyone like me."

"So, you're the only one?"

"I didn't say that."

"Well..."

He lets out a hefty sigh and slouches deeper into his seat, obviously trying to find a more comfortable position. "And what about you? Did you only feel the flames of ardor awaken when you first met your men?"

I snort-laugh into my cup. "Yeah, no, it doesn't work that way for us."

"Oh?" he says, smiling while smoothing a finger over the rim of his cup. "Pray tell. Give me all the *gory* details."

"Ain't really nothing gory about it." I lean in for the pitcher, pouring myself another cup. When I lift it to Finn, he covers the top of his mug. Setting the pitcher down, I say, "My story's a stereotype, really. Lost my virginity to a human at sixteen, only to have my heart broken after and my mama rushing me to the clinic to get on the pill when I confessed to her."

"Sounds tragic." No sarcasm fills his voice. He actually sounds sad for me.

"Nah, it's life. But when I met Ben…" My heart swells at the thought of him, and I press against my chest for fear of it getting so big it breaks free from my breastplate. "And after he kissed me the first time, touched me. I knew what it felt like to fit with someone. Oh, I had my share of humans when I left home after Mama died, but it was never deeper than the physical release, you know?" I look up from my wine to see compassion soften Finn's features. "Ben is my home, and I finally got my head out of my ass and gave in to it. I felt the same after getting to know Luca and being with him." I pause. "And I feel it now… with you."

"You hated me when we first met."

I shake my head. "I was afraid of you, of how you made me feel. Afraid of the Pull I have for you. I didn't understand it."

"And now you do?"

"I think so. But if I'm being honest, I quit caring about why a while ago. Just knew I wanted it." I look him straight in the eye. "*Want* it."

Finn watches me for what feels like forever. "I want to Bond with you, Nora. I do."

"But you can't?"

He sets his cup on the table and moves to kneel in front of me. His hands travel my thighs as he gives me his undivided attention. It's intense, the way he watches me. It's like his eyes take a piece of me with every second of contact. After a slight hesitation, he leans in to touch his lips to mine. "But I can't," he whispers against my mouth.

I nod—because what else can I do? "Well, then let's get you healed and spend as much time as we can together before the world comes calling again."

He trails a finger over my inner thigh, making my skin prickle with anticipation. "I want you to show me how to please you, Nora."

My heart flips. "I–"

Another knock at the door invades our moment.

Finn releases a frustrated groan and stands. He hesitates, as if remaining still will make the intrusion go away. When another knock echoes through the room, he runs a hand through his silver hair. "You'd think we'd have one night without that pesky world at our doorstep."

"Time has never been a luxury where I'm concerned. Best get used to it."

"I don't think I will, love." He rips a sheet from a bed and drapes it over my naked body before grabbing another to wrap around his waist. When he answers the door, his back is straight and the command he takes of every room is firmly in place. Even with a bedsheet tucked on his narrow hips, he's as regal as any king. No wonder Callum can't stop worshiping him.

Speaking of, the Seelie is our intruder. Callum smiles at Finn, even as his face reddens when he takes in our state of undress. "You look rested, my lord."

"I am, thank you," Finn says with a hint of humor lacing his voice. "What can we do for you?"

"Well…" Callum uses his left hand to fidget with his right wrist. He slips a quick glance in my direction before meeting Finn's amused expression. "We've finished supper, and I thought maybe I could come back–"

"Would you mind terribly if our fearless Leader switches rooms with you tonight, Callum? I feel ever so much safer with her close by to protect me."

I snort out a laugh at the absurdity, and Callum's lips break into an embarrassed smile when he catches the sarcasm in Finn's words. The Seelie nods. "Helene and I have shared many a room during our time together. I do believe she'll tolerate my presence for one more night."

"Excellent! Sleep well, then." As Finn tries to close the door on Callum, the frazzled Seelie places his foot in the way, stopping the door's momentum. "There is one thing I would like to discuss with the both of you, if I may." He winces at Finn's frustrated groan.

I take pity on the man. Holding the sheet around me, I stand and wave him in. "Of course, Callum. What's on your mind?"

Callum gives Finn a timid look before skirting around him. He shuffles to stand in front of me by the fire. His face blushes even more as he tries extremely hard not to take in the sheet cinched around my chest. "Thank you, Leader." He lifts his chin, despite the cherry-red blotches smearing his cheeks. "I wanted to talk to you about tomorrow's plans."

"Okay, shoot."

"Yes, well, I know you wanted to come with me to seek out the Healer, but I do believe that wouldn't be the most prudent action."

I tilt my head, narrowing my gaze at him. "Why not?"

Callum's face is almost combustible red when Finn moves to stand beside me, his arm snaking around my waist. "Well... You see... Ah..."

"No need to tiptoe around me, Callum."

"Right, sorry." He smooths his clean T-shirt–obviously, he's helped himself to his things from my pack–and says, "It will be impossible to remain inconspicuous while traveling with you, Leader. Anyone paying attention will notice your presence."

It never crossed my mind that I would be the one who doesn't fit. I'm so used to doing as I please in my world, blending with humans easily. It's a humbling feeling, really understanding what Fae must do to assimilate there.

"Fair enough," I say after a little thought. "Makes sense."

Relief washes some of the embarrassment from Callum's red cheeks. "Thank you. I've already asked Regina to supply us with attire in case you must leave this room during the day. Our T-shirts and jeans will not go over well, I'm afraid."

I open my mouth to dismiss the poor guy, when Finn says, "Come collect me at dawn, boy. Let's get this done as quickly as possible."

"Yes... Um..." Callum swallows audibly, his throat bobbing. "I think it's best you stay here, as well, my lord. When Angora was outed, rumors of your existence took hold across the villages. We can trust Regina, but few others. All it would take is one person recognizing you from books they've read. If word gets back to the king–"

"You and Helene are wanted, too," Finn says, interrupting him.

154

Callum stands straighter. "Helene and I have allies here. People were afraid to help us before, but no one ever turned us in the two years we spent in hiding before Oberon's Guard inadvertently happened upon us. Nora will anger people, and you…you will create chaos. A legend come to life doesn't happen every day."

Finn stares at him for an uncomfortably long time, but Callum keeps his chin up, never taking his eyes from Finn's.

"Would you lie to me, Callum?" Finn finally says.

Callum lifts his chin even higher, obviously insulted. "Never, my lord."

More staring. Then, "This is what we will do." Finn taps his lip, contemplating Callum for another few seconds. "You and Helene will have until nightfall tomorrow to locate your Healer. If you do not return, we're coming to find you, regardless of the risk."

Callum nods vigorously. "Yes. Absolutely."

"Where will your search lead you?"

Callum rattles off a location so fast I barely catch the words.

Finn has no trouble, though. "I'm familiar with that area." He claps once like a judge bringing down the gavel. "Go, now. Get some rest. See me before you leave in the morning."

Callum gives his goodbyes and almost runs from the room in his hurry to leave. Once Finn shuts the door behind him, he turns to me, a slight grin curving his lips. It makes my blood hum. "It appears we have time to kill."

I grin. "Looks like."

He takes a step toward me. "Whatever shall we do?"

Chapter 22

Finn stands in front of me, his silver hair mussed and the fire's glow bouncing off his chest. He doesn't touch me. He watches me. Memorizes me. His eyes are luminous, round with amazement.

Nerves dance in my stomach. In the bathroom, I wanted to shock him, and when I had in a way I'd never expected, I wanted to leave my mark on him. Make him feel good.

Now, I'm so fucking scared I'm going to screw this up, make him regret what he's willing to give me. Only me.

His chest expands on a deep breath, and then he slowly reaches his hand up to touch my hair. He twists a dark lock around his finger, concentrating on it as if amazed by its texture. "I do want to… please you, Nora." His whisper is full of something I've never heard in his voice. Uncertainty.

Looks like we're both at a loss.

"You *have*. You do. Just by touching me. By *wanting* to touch me."

He gives a small smile, his gaze still on the hair curled around his index finger. "No. I haven't. I want to make you feel the way you made me feel. I want to give that to you."

I lick my dry lips. Swallow. His desire to please me sets fire in my belly and swells my heart. He's so vulnerable now. Trusting.

"Touch me, Finn." With a gentle hand, I cup his cheek, guiding his attention to my face. "Like this."

He presses his cheek into my hand.

"Taste me." I kiss a trail over his collarbone, licking and nipping at his skin, now covered in gooseflesh. "Like this," I whisper.

He slips my hair from his finger to wrap his arms around my waist, bringing me closer. "I want to touch you. Taste you. It's all I've wanted from the moment I opened my eyes in your basement cell."

This shocks me. It really does. And it saturates my folds with wanting. "Then do it now."

He takes a shaky breath and kneads the small of my back.

And doesn't move to do anything else.

Jesus, can my heart swell any bigger?

I tilt my chin and capture his parted lips in a soft, exploring kiss. I take it slow until his mouth relaxes.

His skin against mine makes my body hum, and when he tugs my sheet away, his heat engulfs me. His actions are no longer timid as he kisses me with expertise. Kissing has never been this way, never felt this… *good*. It's like he consumes all of me with his mouth, like his was molded to fit mine exactly right.

He pulls back, frames my face with his elegant fingers. Hunger illuminates his eyes now, his lips swollen and parted, and it leaves me gasping. It leaves me wanting to show him all I can. Give him everything I'm able to give.

I release the sheet from his waist, and it pools at our feet. My hands explore his shoulders, his chest, over his rib cage. Over the ridges and angles of his stomach. I've learned from Luca to take my time. Savor. Stay in the moment for as long as possible.

As I explore, my gaze never leaves his. I want to watch his reaction, see how my touch affects him. When I slide a single finger over his cock, he shudders and his hands tremble on my face. He doesn't close his eyes in his ecstasy. It's mine to enjoy. He gives me what I want without me asking.

I trace his ass with my fingertips, each cheek, and smile when even more gooseflesh puckers his skin. He's subtle muscle everywhere, his skin smooth steel. Perfect as any Fae is perfect.

Perfect as only he is perfect.

Slowly, I kneel in front of him, my neck craned to ensure we don't break eye contact. Nervousness invades his expression.

"I want to take you inside my mouth," I tell him. "I want to taste you."

His tongue darts out to lick his bottom lip, his hands now buried in my hair. At his nod, I kiss the tip of his cock, let my tongue circle its head. He lets out a surprised gasp, his fingertips digging into my scalp.

Oh, gods, that gives me a rush, my body alight with tingling. My folds become so wet.

Still, I take my time.

I lick a quick path from his shaft to tip, and then a slower trail, memorizing the feel of him. Bask in his taste.

His body hums with anticipation, chest heaving, and his eyes are hooded as if my touch has intoxicated him.

And then I take him completely inside my mouth.

His shocked groan is loud, guttural. It thrills me that I've given him this first. No one else has touched him the way I have.

A keen possessiveness takes over me.

Mine.

I worship his body, drinking him in. My tongue is greedy. So are my hands as I work him. His moans fill me. They're so raw, with no filter. His pleasure is my pleasure. It runs through me even without the Bond.

When he explodes in my mouth, the oil lamps flicker. The fire flames brighter in the hearth, crackling and protesting. He yells, pulling my hair with his release, and that makes my pussy throb harder. I drink him in until he's sensitive and spent.

As I get to my feet, my hands everywhere on his body, I can't take my gaze from his face. He's always beautiful. Always perfect. But now, with the flush of discovery on his cheeks and burning his eyes, he's all-consuming.

He *is* mine. With or without our Bond. I'll never let him go.

I kiss his gaping mouth, feel his heavy panting against my lips. Drown in him just as he drowns me. His hands roam my body without hesitation. He's no longer nervous. No longer allows a lack of experience to lead him. His actions are primal. Instinctual.

It's intoxicating.

All I can do is hold on as he lifts me in his arms and carries me to one of the beds. His weight is on me as soon as he sets me down. He whispers words in another language so lovely it doesn't matter what they mean. He's eager, unfiltered, and so reverent of my body. I lace my fingers through his hair, close my eyes, and just... *feel*.

His lips on my neck, nibbling.

His tongue trailing my collarbone.

His hands squeezing my breasts.

His mouth capturing my nipple.

He stops there, whispering in Fairy against my skin.

My body is on fire. It's like every nerve is on the verge of climax, as if the pleasure he gives my nipple circulates to every part of my skin.

He explores lower, kissing and touching. His hands capture my waist as he pushes me higher until his mouth is brushing against my inner thighs. When he nuzzles my curls, kissing me there, taking in my scent, he whispers against me, "Show me how to please you, Nora."

It's a command.

And I do as my Fae commands.

I reach down, spread my lips, circle my wet clit with my index finger. "Here," I rasp out. "Touch me here."

He lets out a possessive sound as he watches me pleasure myself for the barest of seconds before his mouth replaces my finger. Sharp pleasure rushes through me, and I arch my back to get closer to his exploration of my pussy. He's hungry for me. His moans match mine, and they vibrate against my clit. He licks

160

and explores as I open my lips for him. My climax builds and builds and builds until I shatter against his mouth. Finn keeps me still with a firm grip on my hips as he sucks me through to the last vestiges of my orgasm.

Spent, my limbs feeling like water, I pull him up so that I can curl against his chest. His heart races against my cheek as he absently glides a finger over my arm. We're quiet, the crackling fire the only sound permeating the room.

I still crave him inside me. It's so fucking difficult not to beg for it.

"Assassin?" Finn whispers into the silence. "I have a proposal."

I hold him closer, my head nestled against his chest. "What would that be, *Assassin*?"

He chuckles, the sound rumbling against my cheek, making me bite down on a smile. Then he whispers, "Let's do this every day for the rest of our lives."

Chapter 23

The next morning, Helene and Callum leave before the sun rises in the sky.

And they're nowhere to be found when it retreats behind the two moons hours later.

The waiting wasn't so bad initially. During the earlier part of the day, Finn and I made use of our time, exploring each other, talking, laughing. Well, I did most of the laughing.

Look, the man has a wit as sharp as one of Ben's daggers. When I don't let him irritate me, he's hysterical, even if he's making a joke at my expense. I now get why Ben and Luca are always laughing when the three of them huddle together.

But anyway, no, after Helene and Callum dropped off my pack and let us know they were leaving this morning, we didn't think much of their absence. Not until darkness leaked into the room.

"We gotta go after them," I tell Finn as I dress in the clothes Regina brought us earlier. "Something ain't right."

Finn doesn't argue as he dons soft leather breeches and a white tunic similar to my clothes. We might look like we belong in some cheesy pirate film, but the clothes are damn comfortable. The breeches feel like soft butter against my skin.

"Agreed," he says as he laces the front of his shirt a little too aggressively. "Damn it! I shouldn't have agreed to letting them go alone. I wasn't…" Finn lifts his gaze long enough for me to see the guilt all over his handsome face.

He's not the only one feeling it, but I shake my head. "His argument was sound, Finn. Callum was right about us traipsing around in the daylight. We took a gamble."

"That we did." He didn't say the quiet part aloud. The part where we agreed so readily for our own selfish wants. "But I told Callum by nightfall, and here we are."

Exactly. Callum wouldn't go against Finn's orders. Ever. If they were able, he and Helene would've been here, with or without the Healer. I won't let my mind wander to the worst case.

"So, let's focus on that, the problem now, not all the 'what-ifs' and 'should haves' of past decisions." I slip a set of daggers from my pack, sheathing them in the back holster I brought with me. "We'll leave the same way we came in last night. Less chance of any unwanted attention."

Finn sighs and closes his eyes for a moment, as if pushing his guilt to the back of his mind. He then tucks his own weapons, a set of dirks he borrowed from Luca's collection, into his waistband. "Let's go, then."

I nod and go to the door. "No magic. You got strength at your disposal if we find ourselves in trouble. Use it."

"I do enjoy it when you're demanding. Perhaps I'll listen one of these days."

I stifle a groan as I open the door and check the hall. He's literally always ready with a smart-ass comment–unless I catch him unawares. Like I had while he bathed last night.

Damn. I'll play that memory in my head for the rest of my life. My stomach flutters even now when I picture the shock and adoration on his face.

Giving myself a mental shake, I wave for Finn to follow when I'm satisfied the hall is empty. Faraway music from the tavern below wisps up through the floorboards, and the smell of roasting meat makes hunger rage inside me. Regina sent up more bread and cheese today when she delivered our clothes, but it didn't exactly fill me up. I'm not complaining. Nothing tastes better than a free meal. I'll have to find a way to pay Regina back for her kindness.

When we make it outside, Finn takes my hand, stopping me. "It's best I take the lead from here, love. We wouldn't want to get lost during our rescue attempt, would we?"

He's right, of course. I have no clue where I am or where I'm going. It's not easy for me to hand over the reins, though. I'm not lying when I say I'm protective of Finn, especially now. I want my body to shield his. I want my strength to be our first defense. I want his magic to take a fucking hike until we can heal him. He's using enough as it is to keep the Windows closed.

I signal for him to take the lead. Words of caution stay in the back of my throat, burning it. He doesn't like when I coddle him, but, Jesus Christ, that's all I want to do.

He guides us in the shadows, stopping when Fae stumble out of the tavern below the inn. We keep our backs against the stone wall, not even breathing until they're halfway down the cobblestone street and swallowed by darkness. I take Callum's advice to keep a low profile. No need for anyone to see me or Finn. All it'd take is one loud, curious person to spot us, and then we'd more than likely be fucked.

We step away from the inn and attempt to take to the edge of Mystic Forest when an extra rush of tingling attacks my birthmark.

Adrenaline takes over, and I push Finn to the ground behind a stone well about ten yards from Regina's. My blood pumps so fast it makes my lips throb and my fingertips numb. I don't move, don't make a sound.

And neither does Finn when I point to the regal Seelie waltzing into the inn.

Even here, surrounded by beautiful Fae, he stands out like a ray of sun in the dead of night.

Allister. Our Order's Messenger.

Fucking shit.

He's alone, walking as he always does when strolling across our backyard, like he has all the leisure time in the world. Like he owns every piece of ground he steps on.

His presence sends shivers down my spine.

Why is he here?

When Allister opens the inn door, momentarily exposing a slash of light and music before disappearing inside, I let go of Finn's shirt. I don't even remember grabbing it, but my fingers are stiff and sore from gripping the fabric so tightly.

"I take it you know the Messenger," Finn says, his voice strained.

"He's ours."

"It's odd to see one so far from the palace." He says it as if he's easing into what he really means. Which is: "It appears Oberon's Trackers are out in full force."

"Appears that way, don't it?" I have no idea how they'd find out so quickly. We told no one outside our Order and Ontario's of our plans to come here.

Finn takes my hand, squeezing it reassuringly as he meets my gaze. "I will not let him come anywhere near you."

"No magic. Not even for me." I kiss him quickly on the mouth and stand when no other Fae roam about.

Finn doesn't respond when he stands, and I don't expect him to. I can demand all I want, but he doesn't have to listen. And he won't if it comes down to my life. He's proven that he'd put himself in danger for me a few times, and I hate that he has. Hate that I've needed him to.

He signals for me to follow as we rush to the edge of the forest. We go at a steady jog through a mowed field, one eye on whatever lurks in Mystic and one at the happenings going on in the village. I don't know how far we've gone, but the bustle of the town with its nighttime revelers, distant music, and busy cobblestone walkers dwindles to scatterings of thatched-roofed homes, some with orange glows of light shining through glassless windows.

This place is so odd. With only magical Windows separating it from a modern world, Etherias seems mostly frozen in some medieval time.

And when we venture toward the homes, stray animals that resemble foxes come up to us with meekly wagging tails,

166

searching for handouts. Thin ribs push against their dull coats. I wish I would've brought the leftover bread still in our room. I wish I could take these animals back home with me, save them from this existence.

"The people don't fare much better, love," Finn whispers as he leads us deeper into the cluster of homes.

So many places in my own world suffer from poverty. Pockets of my beloved mountains contain folks who struggle every day. No one deserves this sort of life. Not at home, and not in this world.

Up close, most of these houses–if you can call the shacks houses–are in serious need of repair. Caved-in roofs. Dilapidated walls. By the smell, this part of the village doesn't have the luxury of indoor plumbing like at the inn. It's desolate. My heart dips as if in mourning when I spot a Seelie woman through the window of a shitty hut. She tries to comfort a crying toddler, who repeats in his sweet, desperate voice, "Hungry, Mama. Hungry."

"Jesus, Finn." The toddler forces me to stop in my tracks and stare at him through the window, willing food to appear from nowhere. "Is it like this everywhere?"

He takes my hand. "Worse even."

My attention snaps to his eyes, which are filled with the same grief attacking my soul. Evil lives everywhere, but this is reprehensible. Lushness and magic fill Etherias. It wouldn't be too challenging to feed all these people in this very small world. "Oberon has power. Resources. Access to another *fucking* world. How can he let his people starve?"

"He does far more than starve them." Anger now coats Finn's words. He doesn't hide behind sarcastic wit, not when he speaks of those he's spent a lifetime trying to help. "We try to get as many as we can through the Windows, get them hidden in your world. Even in some of the worst parts there, at least a little aid is available. Humanity is quite a beautiful thing at times, believe it or not." He swipes at invisible dirt on his sleeves with frustration. "But the monster always finds the runaways and makes them suffer under the blade of an Assassin."

167

I flinch at his words. There's no malice or accusation aimed at me, but they hurt all the same.

Something awakens in me as I watch the Seelie woman try in vain to soothe her hungry baby. Something visceral. Instinctive. These people deserve so much more. No matter what, we need to figure out a way to help them. If not during this mission, then another. We need to come back. Assassins have played a part in their misery. We owe it to them to at least attempt to set things right. Gods know how we'd do it, but I'm aiming to figure it out.

If we can stay off Allister's radar, that is. Damn, the roadblocks keep piling up.

"Come," Finn whispers, tugging gently on my hand. "We're almost there."

I swallow past the lump forming in my throat and let him guide me to the far end of the village.

We stop before reaching a cluster of trees with branches that resemble the limbs of a withered, aged woman. The gnarled, thin limbs curl toward a small hut set back so half of it sits in the shadowy clutches of Mystic. It's no bigger than Topher's woodshop, and not anywhere near as nice as the building my father would carve his toys in. Gaping slat walls expose the inside to all elements, and like the surrounding huts, no glass fills the windows. It's inhabitable.

The sight of it sends warning chills down my spine. My birthmark doesn't help detect any Fae in there, seeing as it's in a constant state of tingling without Finn's magic. I need to get closer, scout the surrounding area. Except something about the place...

I don't want to take another step toward it.

"What...?" Words die on my tongue. I don't know what to ask. How to explain.

All I know is we shouldn't be here.

Finn secures my elbow, his touch firm. Unafraid. "It's a spell, love. Some sort of protective charm preventing us from getting closer."

"Unseelie magic?" I whisper. I fucking hate my trembling voice and numb lips. Scared of a rundown shack? Really?

Finn shakes his head. "It's the Healer's magic. These wretched people tend not to like others bothering them. This spell is rather strong. Good news, I suppose. If she's willing to help cure me, perhaps she'll actually be sturdy enough to do it."

I look up to find disgust twisting his full lips. "Listen, I don't care how miserable the old woman is, we're going to accept her offered help or force her to give it if she ain't willing."

"We don't have to do this the hard way. I can counter the spell."

"No." I pull my daggers from my holster. "I can handle a little fear." Even as I say it, my body trembles as if my nervous system has commanded it into fight-or-flight. It doesn't matter that my brain knows otherwise. I force my feet to move forward, no matter how loud my body screams, *flight, flight, flight*.

Finn snatches my elbow again, this time with that strength he hides. It surprises me enough to stop. "It's more than a *little* fear. The closer you get to her home, the worse it will become. Fear is paralyzing. It makes people do rash things. She may be old, but all it'd take is a moment of hesitation and she could plunge a knife into your heart. Mine, too. If you prefer I don't use magic, then at least listen to what I'm telling you."

His anger makes me lower my weapons. "Fine." I yank my arm from his grip. "I'm listening."

"Finally." He straightens and tugs at his shirtsleeves in frustration. "We search for Callum and Helene. Maybe they're close, trying to figure out a way around the spell."

"Then what?"

"Then hopefully we find them, get them to safety, and then you can have a go at the Healer—with me at your back to ensure she doesn't take a blade to your throat."

Rational minds do prevail. Occasionally.

"All right, then. Let's go on a fairy hunt." I give the shack a wide berth on my way into Mystic. Even here, surrounded by all the magic Etherias offers, I'm comfortable with my ability to track anything. Thankfully, no Devas fly around, ready to eat our

169

faces off as we search. With light from the two moons, it's easy to spot broken branches, footprints–and a massive amount of large paw prints. Narrow paths made by the animals owning these prints surround us. I don't need to ask Finn to confirm what I already know.

Fae Shifters. And it seems we're encroaching on their territory. Again.

Fuck.

I press on, making an arced path of my own behind the Healer's shack. No sign of Helene or Callum. I don't know whether to be relieved or worried. Our best chance of finding them now is going directly to the Healer.

I signal for Finn to follow me out of the woods and back to the rundown cottage. Fear trickles in again, leaking into my muscles. I want to run as far away as possible, never set eyes on it again.

It's a funny thing, knowing this fear is an illusion, yet still fighting against it.

With a few hand signals, I let Finn know our next move. We sidle up to the lone glassless window. I'm sweating now, the kind of cold sweat that makes my teeth chatter and knees quake. My arms shake, too, making it tough to hold my weapons steady. I squeeze my eyelids shut. *It's not real!*

Finn touches my arm, his hand warm. I open my eyes to his silver gaze. It's full of confidence. Confidence that seeps into me as I slow my breathing and concentrate on steadying the grip on my weapons. Finally, I nod to him and turn, taking my first peek inside the hut. It's pitch black, and all I can make out on the right side is a tiny bed supporting a shadowy figure covered in a thin blanket. The Healer.

She doesn't move, not even when I tap against the dry-rotted windowsill.

"We have to go inside," I whisper to Finn. Even at a whisper, being this close, maybe fifteen feet away from the woman, you'd think it would startle her enough to at least twitch.

Nothing.

Finn takes my elbow and guides us to the door. He gives it a slight push, and it opens with no issues. No locks. No barricades. The Healer seems to depend solely on her spell. It almost worked.

I take the lead once we're inside, Finn at my back with his weapons out. As he watches the door, I take trembling steps toward the figure in the bed. The one-room cottage smells musty, unused. The stench only adds to the fear. *Don't be afraid. It's not real. Not real. Not real…*

I swallow, my throat dry and scratchy, when I'm looming over the woman. A thin blanket covers her waiflike body from head to toe–and she's still not moved or made a sound. I lower, keep my daggers ready. The blanket doesn't move with her breathing, either.

Oh, no.

My stomach sinks like a stone in water.

No!

Gingerly, I use a dagger to pull back the coverlet from the Healer's face. My breath catches in a raspy hiss, and I jump away. As revulsion attacks me, I want to sink to my knees, sob and sob and sob. The Healer can't save Finn.

All that's left of her is bone and the spell surrounding us.

The sweet, bitter punch of death and decay doesn't mingle with the musty odor, as if she's been this way for years without one Fae from the village knowing. Who knows how long she's been dead and rotting in here alone with her spell still intact and keeping others away.

I turn to Finn, who's watching me with regret. He tries to smile, but my tears erase from his lips. Instead, he takes me into his arms and whispers those Fairy words I don't understand.

"What do we do now?" I say into his chest. "This *can't* be the end."

"Nora–"

Howls cut him off, stiffening his body. I lift my face, open my mouth to ask why, when he subtly shakes his head and puts a finger to his lips. The Healer's spell didn't faze him. And her decaying body didn't break him.

But the howls tighten his face and darken his eyes.

He bends to whisper in my ear, "We must leave. Now."

Genuine fear now mixes with the spell as the howls grow louder. Closer.

All those paths in the woods. All those fucking paw prints.

My heart dips into my stomach. *Helene and Callum.*

What if…?

Please, no…

I rush to the door, my hands sweating so much, I can't keep a good grip on my daggers. As I peer outside, I bite back a scream.

It's too late. We're not going anywhere.

A Seelie, dressed only in breeches with his muscled chest gleaming in the moonlight, stands feet from the Healer's cottage. His feral smile chills my blood. "Hello, Changeling."

Chapter 24

We're surrounded in seconds. At least ten Seelie Shifters, some in wolf form, some half-dressed like the obvious alpha Fae in front of us. All Seelie in Fae-form are as muscled and strong as their alpha, both women and men. The massive wolves growl, their coats twitching as if excited to pounce.

None make a move toward us.

"I hoped we'd meet again," the alpha says, his voice deep. Low. "I was skeptical the *great* Unseelie Mage, protector of all Fae-kind, existed at all." Sarcasm drips from every word. "Now, here you are, in the flesh."

"I'm just another unwilling subject to a king we all despise." Finn steps forward. "But do not forget, I let you and your entire pack live."

"You did." The alpha cocks his head. "You also brought a Changeling to our world. A murderer. We can't abide such treachery from our great *savior*."

Oh, shit.

Finn doesn't answer. Instead, he stands at my side, protecting me. My legs tremble, and fear still coats my skin. This Healer's spell will end up leaving me vulnerable to these fuckers. It'll end up killing me. Still, none of the Shifters come closer. Maybe the spell is keeping them away.

"However, I'm not one to let passions override logic, lucky for you. Let's barter," the alpha tells Finn, his voice full of false indifference. He signals behind him, and two Shifter men emerge from the darkness—each gripping a captive by the neck in the crook of their muscled arms.

Helene and Callum.

Helene's left cheek is purple and swollen, but she doesn't cower. Her chin juts out, despite the choke hold on her neck. Callum is lost in his terror, his eyes wide with it. A trickle of blood trails down from his hairline to his temple.

These Shifters, who are as strong as I am, put their hands—or paws—on two Fae not able to protect themselves.

Fear doesn't mean a damn thing now. Not even a Healer's spell can overcome the rage jetting through my veins. I lift my iron daggers, ready to open throats. "Let them go."

The alpha lifts a hand to me. "Shut. Up."

Hell, no.

I rush forward, only to be surrounded by three wolves. They're so close, their fur tickles my arms, and their hot breath lifts the ends of my sweaty hair as they growl. It takes everything in me not to plunge my blades into their chests, take them out and suffer the consequences. One nips at me, and I press my iron weapon to its muzzle. The smell of burning flesh renders the air immediately as it howls in pain. The cries signal the other two wolves to move in on me, ready to take a chunk out of my throat.

"Stop! Just stop this now." Desperation saturates Finn's voice as he moves closer to me, not giving a shit about the wolves gnashing their teeth at him. "If you hurt her, I'll kill you all. I swear it."

"Seems our own sworn protector lies in bed with the very beasts Oberon pays to mow our people down. Kill us, you say?" The alpha is no longer calm. His voice is a razor slicing the air around us. He points to Callum. "Your friend already told us why you're here. He thought he could appeal to our... How did he say it? Oh. Right. Our better nature. You're iron-touched, in need of a Healer. Your own magic is killing you. So go ahead, use your magic on us, *Lord*. Let's see who comes out of this battle alive."

Callum cries out, struggling against his captor. "I'm sorry, my lord. I'm *so sorry*."

Finn smiles at him and tamps the air with a trembling hand. "It's fine, boy."

But it's not okay. We're fucked. No matter what. No matter the outcome. We lose.

"Enough." The alpha crosses his arms over his chest as the wolf I burned meanders to his side, its large front paw swiping at his mangled snout. "The only way these traitor Fae live another day is if you redeem yourself, *Lord Finn*, with a simple barter."

Finn steps closer to him, his arms out. "Me for my friends, Shifter. Let's be done with this wretched game. I'm all yours."

I open my mouth in protest, ready to shove these fucking animals out of my way to get to Finn. To stop him.

The alpha's bitter laughter stops me in my tracks. "We don't want you, *Lord* Finn. You've still *so many* prophecies to fulfill." He pauses. "Give us the Changeling."

Finn stares at him for a few long seconds, his jaw tight and fists now clenched at his sides. His shoulders lift in a sigh then as he turns his head to give me one of his smiles. It's sad and resigned and scares the hell out of me.

I shake my head at him, ready to fight until my last breath.

"Forgive me, love," he says quietly, resolutely.

Then all hell breaks loose.

Finn's mouth moves in silent words, and soon after, fear from the spell evaporates from my body, replaced with the more familiar desire to fight. To win. Without skipping a beat, I shove a wolf standing near me at least twenty yards, adrenaline aiding my strength. When the other tries for my throat, I kick out its front legs. The audible crack of bone permeates the air as the Shifter squeals and transforms back into a naked and injured Seelie woman. She curls into the fetal position, her legs bent and unnaturally twisted.

I don't stick around to finish the job. My focus is completely on my people as I charge toward Helene and Callum.

Finn's magic beats me to them. He wriggles his fingers at their captors until the Seelie Shifters writhe in pain on the ground. After a sharp command from the alpha, the rest shift into their wolf forms and rush us, the alpha taking the lead.

Exactly like in the woods, even with all their strength and agility, they're not stronger nor faster than Finn's whispered words and moving hands. The alpha is last to fall, just as he raises his massive paw to slash open my stomach. His nails barely scrape my billowing white shirt, leaving behind two thin holes in the fabric.

Ending as fast as it began, the Shifters lay helpless on the earth beneath us. All have transformed back to their Seelie form.

Finn straightens his shirt and peers down at the vulnerable alpha while Helene and Callum hurry to my side. As we gather behind him, Finn kneels next to the Shifter, and quietly says, "We've spared your lives for a second time, me and my *murdering* Changeling." He places an almost gentle hand to the Fae's bare shoulder. "If we ever cross paths again, I suggest you remember this night."

Finn then stands with all the stateliness of a king and walks toward the darkened edge of Mystic Forest with his hands clasped behind his back and not one glance over his shoulder to see if we follow.

He's regal and in control—until he collapses in the middle of the field.

Chapter 25

We make it back to the town square in what feels like hours later. Barely any Fae roam the cobblestone streets, and those who do are so deep in their drink, they don't pay us any mind. Good thing, seeing how Finn's limp body is slung over my shoulder.

Callum and Helene lead the way to Regina's and up the back stairs. None of us talk. All of us are more than likely thinking the same thing.

We've failed.

Thankfully, the tavern below us is dark and quiet. No more tinkling music. No savory smells of roasting meat and spilled ale. No Allister lurking about, waiting for the moment to catch me or Finn unawares. I don't care if he spots us at this point. My entire being is drowning in misery and failure. The thought of Finn dying because he had to come to the rescue yet again…

I'm killing him in the attempt to save him.

I don't say a word, my brain screaming and panic itching to take the driver's seat. Finn hasn't moved, his breathing shallow and labored. When we get to the room, I place him gently on the bed and strip off his shoes. Helene and Callum stand behind me as I try so fucking hard not to let any sobs free. It's bad enough tears run unchecked down my cheeks. They don't interrupt the quiet while I smooth sweaty hair from Finn's forehead and press my palm against his heart to assure myself it still beats. It thankfully does, though faintly. My constant pressure against his chest is compulsory. Like, if I stop touching him, stop checking, his heart will quit, and he'll leave me.

I don't know what to do.

Please, tell me what to do!

"Nora," Helene says softly. She's by my side, her tiny hand covering mine on Finn's chest. "Let him rest. He is alive. That's enough for now."

"For now? What happens the next time, Helene? And the next?" I say, my voice hitching. This feeling of despair has become such a close friend of mine during these past few months. A toxic friend.

Helene doesn't give me anymore reassuring words. Neither does Callum.

Gods, I want them to.

I need them to.

Fucking fuck, fuck, fuck!

I straighten, force myself to lift my hand from Finn's beating heart, and wipe the tears from my cheeks as I face Helene and Callum. "What's next?"

Callum gives me all his hopelessness in the way his eyes fill. In my own misery, I almost forgot how much he cares for Finn. I can't bring myself to comfort him. Not when I need answers to fly from his mouth.

He doesn't give me any. "I... I don't know, Leader. I... The Healer was the only one who..." He won't finish a sentence. He won't give me what I need to keep on fighting.

I glance down at my side, where Helene keeps a comforting hand on my limp arm. Sympathy fills her eyes. Sympathy and no answers.

I close my eyes against the words I know need to come from my mouth. I don't want to say them. Don't want to give them life. On this failed trip, I'm going to lose Finn.

But I need to get Helene and Callum to safety. If I succeed at anything, I must succeed at that. "We're going back home," I tell them finally, my eyes still closed and fists clenched at my sides. "We need to get back to Alexie." *And Ben and Luca...* "Finn won't... He can't keep the Windows closed much longer, not like this."

Both nod, neither saying another word. What can they say? I'm right, and they know it.

I turn to Finn, dismissing them as I sit on the edge of the bed, my hand automatically seeking his beating heart. *Still alive.* It has to be enough. It's all I have. "I'll stay in here with him, if y'all don't mind." My voice is flat. Defeated. "Go on, now. Get some rest. Best not leave your room until I come get you, after Finn is strong enough to leave. We spotted my Messenger tonight when–"

My eyes widen, and I rush to my feet. Hope, a tiny spark, ignites in my chest. "Callum? You said the king has a Healer, right?"

Callum wipes at his cheek, confusion now warring with his grief. "Well, yes, but to get to her would take a miracle. We'd never make it past the King's Guard alive."

My chest heaves with adrenaline now. Despair will have to fuck off for a while longer. "You know what? I think I might have me a miracle."

Chapter 26

What I'm doing is dangerous. Foolish. It probably doesn't have a chance in hell of working. I'm perfectly aware of it. Callum has said as much all last night until I kicked him out of the room. He hasn't stopped all day today, either, while we planned and Finn slept.

Allister wants me?

Perfect. I'm all his.

For a price.

"This is illogical, Leader," Callum says for the hundredth time in less than twenty-four hours. "Even *if* one of Oberon's Messengers would be foolish enough to help you, how can he possibly find the king's Healer without the king himself knowing about it?"

"Your guess is as good as mine," I say, repeating the same answer I've given him every time he's asked. "It ain't gonna hurt nothing to try."

I try to end the conversation there and turn my back on him as I braid my hair and tuck my shirt into my breeches.

Callum laughs at my response this time, an incredulous sound. "How very wrong you are. And might I remind you that exposing yourself in the tavern will leave you vulnerable. What if a Shifter happens upon you? You are strong, Leader. We all know it. But you cannot handle an entire room of Fae bent on seeking some sort of retribution against a Changeling."

I turn to him then as I sheath my daggers. "Assassin," I correct him.

"Not here. Here, you are a murderer of innocent Fae. Nothing more."

"I'm going down there, Callum," I say, my voice gentle but stern. "Nothing you can say will convince me otherwise. Best you stop wasting your breath."

He stares and stares at me with his desperation, his fingers tapping relentlessly against his thigh. If this staring contest is his last-ditch effort, I'm afraid he's going to leave this room disappointed. The only person I've ever lost a staring contest to was Topher.

Finally, Callum huffs out a frustrated groan, averts his gaze, and storms to the unoccupied bed, where he tossed a cloak this morning. "At least put this on to cover your features. Perhaps you'll make it out of there alive–if the Messenger doesn't have you killed. Which is entirely possible."

Oh, this spicy Callum is different. I'd like to get to know this side of him sometime when we're not so close to losing our lives.

"Thank you," I say, taking it from him. I fold it over my arm and turn to Helene, who stands by the window. With a quick glance at Finn's sleeping form, I say to her, "Take care of him for me, okay?"

Meaning, if I end up dead, and when Finn's strong enough to move, convince him to leave this world. Go to Ben and Luca. If his life is to end, best he be surrounded by people who consider him family.

Yes, we talked about contingency plans. Callum's words haven't gone unheeded. Again, I'm well aware of the risk I'm taking.

Helene nods, her chin up and sword dangling at her side in a loose grip. "I will not fail you." She sucks in her bottom lip. Then, "Come back to us, Nora. I do not want to go home to your men without you. They won't take kindly to it."

Compassion fills her subtle wink–and concern for my safety. But unlike Callum, she hasn't tried to talk me out of anything. Frankly, if it were Alexie's life on the line–Seamus's or Callum's, too–she'd do the same damn thing.

"Yeah, I wouldn't envy you. They might be a hair upset." I give her one last reassuring grin. "Keep the door locked."

I then go to Finn, who's scarcely moved in his sleep. His pale face pulls at my heart. I don't need the Bond to die for him. It's still surprising how much that surprises me.

I bend to kiss his forehead, which is thankfully cool to the touch. "I won't let you die," I whisper. My eyes squeeze shut against a fresh wave of despair. I can't let it win. Not until I've exhausted all possibilities. When I open my eyes, I find myself staring into his silver gaze. Excitement rushes through me. He's lucid for the first time since last night. "Hey, stranger."

"What are you planning, Assassin?" he says, voice hoarse. Weak.

I kiss his forehead once more, smiling at his leery exasperation. It makes me so blindly happy. He's alive, still with me. We still have options.

I straighten and give him a wider smile that he frowns at. "I'm doing exactly what you would do if it were me lying on that bed. Whatever it takes."

∞ ∞ ∞

I enter the tavern through the front door. It'd be reckless to come into the bustling pub using the main staircase, which leads to the rooms above. If I'm caught, or bested in a fight, the last thing I want is an angry mob barging upstairs to find Helene, Callum, and Finn.

And no need to get Regina in hot water. Gods know what an angry horde of Fae might do to a "traitor" who let a Changeling hide in her place of business.

For the record, I hate being called that. Hate. It.

The vibe in the pub is entirely different from what I'm accustomed to. It's not low key like McDougal's, Luca's bar in the Poconos, or a honey trap like the one we busted up in New York City. Like the village, it's a picture from a history book or a glimpse of a movie set in medieval times.

Wooden benches, tables, and a scarred wooden bar are the only furniture. The succulent smell of roasting meat mingles with stale spirits. An Unseelie plays some sort of string instrument and walks around the Fae hunched over their mugs. Some laughter tinkles in the air from tables next to the far wall, and hushed conversations whisper around me, but there's an air of misery to the place.

It makes me nervous, this tension. From my experience, the best ways to temporarily rid yourself of tension are fucking and fighting. All it will take is one curious person to wonder why I'm wearing a cloak with a hood. They won't want to fuck me when they see what I am.

The good news is I'm not the only one masking myself. Others wear the same type of lightweight cloak I do. Not many, but enough to not instantly draw suspicion.

Small favors and all that.

I keep my shoulders back and stride to the bar like I belong here. On my way, I search the tables and bar stools for Allister. My heart dips to the pit of my stomach when he's nowhere in the place.

I'm not about to give up. He had to have been here for me or Finn last night; I know it. Let's hope he keeps coming.

When I make it to the bar, I pull out a stool and slide onto it, resting my elbows on the scarred wood. Thankfully, Regina tends bar, and when she comes over to get my order, the tired frown marring her face vanishes. She stares at me slack-jawed, her pretty eyes wide as saucers.

"Could I get some of that mulled wine?" I ask her quietly, making sure not to raise my voice above the minstrel playing his music behind me.

Regina slams her mouth shut and narrows her eyes as she leans in closely. So close I can smell her sweat from a busy night's work. "You shouldn't be in here," she hisses so only I can hear.

I ignore her reprimand, and whisper, "The Messenger who came here last night, he come here often?"

Her anger and shock from my presence turns into something different. Much different. Her pretty face becomes a blank slate as she straightens. "I'll get your wine, but then you must leave."

"Regina–"

She lifts a hand in my face and leans in again. "Do you want to get me killed, Changeling?"

I wince. "No. Of course not."

She steps back, again not answering my question, and moves to the row of wooden barrels behind her. Taking a mug from a rack, she opens a tap to a barrel, pours red liquid until it sloshes over the rim, and slams it on the bar in front of me. "Quickly, Changeling," she whispers, and then moves on to the next patron, her face now the tired mask with which she initially greeted me.

I sip on my wine, this one not as good as the bottle Finn and I shared a couple of nights ago. It's bitter and tart, and my lips pucker with every sip. The buzz it gives feels good, however. Helps me relax, even though relaxing is the last thing I should do in this place.

I do plan to stay for only a bit. And if Allister is a no-show, I'll be coming back tomorrow night to do the same.

By the time I reach the bottom of my mug, the pub's energy has heightened. The tinkling laughter transforms to guffaws, and the minstrel sings above those who sing with him, loud and off-key. Enough alcohol can make a person forget their misery for a while.

Heat from more bodies filling the place stifles me, and the cloak's warmth, despite the light material, saturates my hair with sweat and makes my shirt cling to my back. With drunkenness comes boldness, and it won't be long until someone stumbles up to me and gives my face a good, hard look.

When Regina narrows her eyes in my direction, I nod, understanding exactly what her face is screaming: *Get out!*

I pat the nonexistent pockets of my breeches with a contrite shrug, miming my lack of funds, and I swear if she could, she'd physically kick my ass out of here.

No need. I'm leaving.

She wins.

For tonight.

Little does she know, we'll be doing this song and dance again tomorrow.

I push my stool out, move to get on my feet, and freeze when I hear an all-too familiar lyrical voice behind me. "Leaving so soon?"

Chapter 27

I don't move, my ass half on the stool. And I don't look behind me. I don't need to. Allister's voice is as familiar as my own.

This is it. The moment that decides the length of my life.

"Join me for a drink, Assassin?" His voice is so melodious, so deceptively polite. If he were to slit my throat with his next breath, I'm positive he would do it with a genuine, polite apology.

"Yes. I'd like that," I whisper. I clasp the bar so tightly the tips of my fingers go numb.

"Excellent." He sidles closer to me and waves a delicate hand in the air. "Barkeep? Two mugs of your best ale. We'll take our respite at the far corner table, if that's satisfactory?"

Regina's face pales. When she finally gives a slight nod, Allister touches my elbow. "Come, Nora. I believe we have much to discuss."

Like a child, I follow without argument. It doesn't matter that I'm stronger, able to heal from most things. Allister demands respect just by being in the same room.

Once we're seated away from most patrons, Allister folds his hands on the wooden tabletop and peers directly into my eyes. "Take down your hood. No one will see you from where we sit."

Again, I listen, my hands slowly reaching up to do his bidding.

"Lovely," he says. "You've always been so lovely, young Nora. Strength masked in beauty. You were your mother's pride."

I keep my hands clasped on my lap, keep emotion off my face as best I can. "It looks like Trackers already know I'm here," I say, my voice shockingly calm, even.

"They do, yes."

"Surprised you don't have the Guard coming down on my head already."

Allister sips his ale. He takes his time, closing his eyes on a long drink. His Adam's apple ripples in his throat as he slowly swallows. When he opens his eyes and sets his mug down, he leans in, again folding his hands on the table. "I imagine my presence here–alone–gives you pause. But... are you truly surprised?"

Fuck. Yes.

When I continue to stare at him, not offering an answer, he says, "Do you really believe I hadn't known your Order hid Finn? Alexie and her compatriots, too?" He tilts his head. "How do you think you were able to keep it secret for so long? How do you think Oberon still believes our rightful queen is somewhere wandering your world outside of your territory?"

I feel my eyes widen. It takes everything inside me not to call him out, scream at him, accuse him of lying. Instead, I bite the inside of my cheek until the rusty taste of blood coats my tongue.

Allister gives the room a casual scan before hitting me with the biggest questions of all: "How do you think Finn was able to miraculously escape Oberon's prison? How *do you think* he was able to waltz through the Window–to your land–without a soul here knowing it?"

Again, I don't answer.

"Me, Nora. He's alive and well because of me."

"Liar," I whisper. Shock won't let me stay silent now.

"You know I am not, if you truly stop to think about it. Everything you've done, I know about and keep it from Oberon for as long as I am able." He pauses, chuckling at some thought in his head. "I did not know of your Scotsman landing at your doorstep, however. Trackers had not foreseen that. Perhaps because they no longer look for Highlanders." He drums his fingers on the table.

I don't dare grill him, demand he answer all the questions racing through my mind. Saving Finn's life is my priority.

I clear my throat, sit straighter. Try like hell to focus on what I need from him. "Finn's iron-touched. He's dying."

My change of subject forces him back, as if my words had the power to physically shove him. He narrows his eyes at me. "I am aware, Nora."

"Not surprising. You know everything, right?" I bite back any more acerbic words. "Look, nothing else you say means shit to me. He needs a Healer, and the only one we know of who's still alive is Oberon's."

Surprise rounds his hazel eyes, but he says nothing, waiting for me to continue.

So, I get to it. "You're here for a reason, Allister. If it's not to kill me, it's for something else, correct?"

He gives a subtle nod, his face again composed.

"Fine. You help Finn, and I'll help you. You're a person who gets things done? Find a way to give us access to Oberon's Healer."

He watches me, stares into my soul while the pub's noise surrounds us. "What I want is dangerous. For that reason, I will give you what you ask for and more."

"You have nothing else I want."

"Oh, I beg to differ."

I wave for him to answer, to stop dragging shit out.

He gives a smile I don't trust at all. "I can give your friend back to you."

"What?" I meant the word to sound like a demand, but it's filled with all the shock and hope and confusion rattling through my body.

"Pia. I can help you free her from Oberon–*if* you agree to help me."

My heart twists and fills, and I blink a few times to force the tears filling my eyes to dry up. I swallow, *swallow, swallow* the lump in my throat that formed as soon as Allister said her name.

Pia.

My best friend whom I never believed I'd actually see again.

My best friend who sacrificed herself while attempting to save Topher's life.

My best friend who so obviously kept her truth from me since the day I met her.

"Why did he want her?" My voice is small, desperate. He's caught me off-guard. Broken my focus. I don't know if I want the answer, and yet, the question has been burning in the back of my mind since that day. *Why?*

Compassion softens Allister's features, making him appear less regal, less unapproachable. Like the years hadn't stolen his empathy, as I'd always assumed. "It's…complicated. The simple answer is our king's fascinated by Assassins, how they have more than one lover."

I hate the term "lover." It's an oversimplification of the Bond. Bond means family. It means forever. It means sacrifice. It's not something so pithy as having the luxury of multiple sex partners. But I don't correct him. It's not important right now.

"He's taken on many men and women during his reign," he continues, "and… he has a fondness for Pixies."

No. No fucking way. "Are you saying Pia and Oberon are–?"

"I'm saying he has a fondness for Pixies. Your friend can explain the rest. It's not my place." He concentrates on his folded hands. "I *will* say her showing up at your bakery was no coincidence, either."

Betrayal runs through me as hot as lava. "What the fuck does that even mean?"

"It means she needed protection, and I swore to her she could trust you."

Noise like screaming static ricochets through my brain, mixing with the tingle from being surrounded by so many Fae. Allister used me to keep one of Oberon's scorned *lovers* hidden?

Pia used me?

I want to storm off, tell Allister to go fuck himself. But... Finn. I can't. I won't.

And as much as her duplicity stings, I can't leave Pia here. My father cared for her. Trusted her. Whatever her story, she sacrificed herself for him.

She's still my friend.

I've always been on your side, Nora. Remember that.

Her last words to me enter my thoughts. I want her explanation, and yes, I want to hear it from her, not Allister.

I brush away treacherous tears escaping down my cheeks. "What do you want from me?"

His shoulders rise with a hefty sigh, and for the first time in my presence, exhaustion sags his face. "We are on the same side, Nora. If this conversation has not made that clear, I'm now telling you outright. I haven't had the luxury of being as bold with my rebellion as your Order has been–as Finn has been–but I've spent decades doing what I can to right Oberon's wrongs against my people." He rubs his jaw, and says quieter, "Right my own wrongs."

Can't say I trust him fully, or at all, but I have zero options left on the table. Zero. "What do you *want* from me?" I repeat, trying to keep my voice steady.

He opens his mouth. Closes it. Inspects his hands again as if they hold all this world's secrets. "I admire Finn, you know. It pained me to see him in iron, wasting away in the dungeons."

"Allister. What do you want?"

"Finn's magic on the Windows is waning. I've done my best to keep it quiet, but I cannot do so much longer."

"Which is why we need Oberon's Healer." If his magic is fading, he's closer to death than I want to admit to myself.

Allister nods. "Yes, but we need to warn your Order. Alexie must be protected at all costs."

"How do you propose we do that?"

191

"Send Helene and Callum back through the Window in Mystic. Finn will have to take his magic off it completely, but it's a chance we must take while he heals."

I'm shaking my head before he's even done speaking. "They can't go. For one, they'll never make it through the forest without me and Finn. We got ourselves a pack of Shifters fixing to kill us first chance they get. And *two*," I say as he lifts a hand to interrupt, "if they do get through the Window, they'll need help to convince two very tired Assassins to see them home to West Virginia. I will not leave them unprotected."

Allister smiles now, and it grates on my nerves. Nothing I said was remotely funny. "As for your first obstacle, I'll take care of Gavin and his pack. He's an honorable Fae."

I snort. "Honorable, huh? Gavin's the alpha?"

Allister nods.

"He done tried to kill us twice already."

"Yes, well, he despises Oberon as much as we do. I assure you that hatred supersedes whatever he feels for you."

I'm still not wholly convinced Allister is on the up-and-up, but again, zero options. "I reckon he hates my kind as much as you claim he hates the king."

"He'll put his... distaste for you aside to help weaken the king's grasp on our people. No doubt remains in my mind about it. I will also personally see to Helene and Callum's safe arrival and speak with Ontario's Order. Trust me."

I wag a finger at him. "See, now, that's the million-dollar statement. You're the king's man, always have been." I stab my wagging finger at his face. "You want me to take you at your word, after all these years?"

"I do." He grins, and it's not his plastic grin that chills me to the bone. It's genuine. Excited. It sparks excitement in me, too. "I've done what was needed to help my people, and staying in the king's good graces has proved fruitful. *And* I'm risking my life to speak with Assassins who will want nothing more than to slit my throat, and yet, I'm willing."

"Why don't you go alone, then? Leave Helene and Callum out of it."

"Insurance policy, young Nora. I can't very well waltz into a viper den these days without wholly expecting my head being detached from my body. Their presence will ensure your people will at least listen to what I have to say before exacting an undeserved sentence."

"Undeserved?"

"Absolutely undeserved, yes."

When I say nothing–because, honestly, I'm having trouble coming to terms with the notion that I'm seriously contemplating forming an alliance with a *fucking* Messenger–Allister's smile fades and authentic emotion heightens the beauty of his face. "I need you as much as you need me. Please, Nora. *Please.* I took a risk trusting *you* with what I've told no one in my centuries of life. And my being here without the Guard, without another soul to assist me in case you decide to kill me–which you are most capable of doing–should tell you all you need to know."

He's correct–on the surface. This could also be a trap. But Finn doesn't have the time for me to figure it out. "I'll talk to Helene and Callum," I finally say. "If they're willing, so am I." I lean in. "But hear me when I tell you that if anything–*anything*– happens to them, I will kill you. I got a list, and I have no problem adding your name to it."

Allister's genuine grin returns. "Fair trade, Assassin. Fair trade, indeed."

"Perfect. Why don't you tell me what you really need from me, then?"

That grin deepens. "I need your assistance in ridding the kingdom of some Trackers."

Oh, I like this idea. "Some?"

"*All*, Nora. Every last one of them. It is the first step in taking down Oberon for good."

"Fine." I lift my hood to hide my features. "Give me an hour to speak with Helene and Callum, and then meet us outside, by the well."

"It will be my pleasure." The gleam of a fight shines in his hazel eyes. "That'll also give me time to speak with Gavin."

"Do what you have to. You take my people home, and when you come back, you get us access to the Healer. We'll take care of the Trackers after." I take a deep breath. "As for Pia, I'll leave that to you to figure out."

Okay, maybe I don't like his fucking smile.

"What?" I say through clenched teeth.

"I'll be gone four days. When I get back, we take care of the Trackers."

"Absolutely not. Finn gets healed first. End of story."

"Oh, I agree." He winks at me. Fucking winks. "So heal him."

"What?"

"He's meant to Bond with you." He waves a flippant hand at my widened eyes. "Yes, I know that, as well. Don't look so surprised."

I reach for the hem of my borrowed cloak, pulling at loose threads. "Excuse me if I'm having a hard time with you knowing everything."

"You are quite excused." He raises a brow. "Bond with him, and your power to heal will mix with his own small capability he inherited from his mother. His minute ability has kept him alive this long, frankly."

"I don't–"

"Why do you think I made sure he escaped, only to end up in your backyard?"

"I…" Well, holy shit.

"You have the means to heal him, Nora. So do it."

194

Chapter 28

I go back to my room, my head full of colliding emotions. Excitement. Relief. Frustration.

After everything, *all* we've been through to keep Finn alive, could it really be as easy as Bonding?

Could it really be that fucking hard?

His people need him, and he needs me in order to continue helping them. And yes, *I* need him. I do. So do Ben and Luca. He's part of us. He *belongs* with us. We'll figure out a way for him to still help his people while being connected to us.

When I get to our room's door, I hesitate before entering. Take a deep, cleansing breath.

Do *I* trust Allister?

The jury's still out.

The bigger question is, do we have any other viable options?

Nope. The answer to that is still zero.

"All right, Nora," I whisper to myself, "get the fuck in there and spread the goddamn joy."

Another deep breath, and I knock using three long raps against the door and two short, what we'd decided on before I went downstairs.

Helene whips the door open seconds later, her cherubic warrior face wild with barely masked concern. "Well?" she demands before I have the door shut behind me.

"I ain't dead, and neither is Allister." I give her a reassuring smile. "It's fine, Helene. More than fine. I reckon we've found our pot of gold at the end of a long-ass rainbow."

"What rainbow? What gold?" She flutters into my personal space. "Nora? I don't understand."

I suppress an urge to laugh, my giddiness on the verge of combustion, when Callum says in his calm, amused voice, "It's a metaphor, Helene. It means our Leader has had a spot of good luck."

More than a spot, but I won't elaborate. Not yet.

"You're lucky to be alive, Assassin." Finn's weakened voice is harsh, angry. "What you've done is foolish. To risk everything to meet a bloody Messenger, of all people..."

Callum and Helene grow quiet, and they part as if they're Moses's Red Sea to reveal Finn propped up on the bed and livid as he glares at me. His complexion is pale, and I bite back a worried gasp. He's still so weak.

Well, I'll be fixing that. All he has to do is lie there. I'll take care of the rest. My body hums at the very thought of him inside me. Finally. Not only because of the pleasure it will bring both of us, but because he'll heal, become whole again.

And he'll be part of me, and I him. He'll truly be mine.

"Could y'all give Finn and me a moment?"

Callum nods, placing a gentle hand at the small of Helene's back. "We'll take our supper in the other room. Regina will have it sent up soon."

Yeah, if she's not too pissed at me and starves us as punishment. "Ah, good. That's good. One more thing," I start as the two get to the door. "I'm gonna need y'all to pack your things. Take out my and Finn's stuff from my bag. I'll be over to explain shortly."

Questions travel across their faces, but they don't ask them now. I'm still Leader, and they're still an adopted part of my

Order. I will give them a choice, mind you, but I'm fixing to be persuasive.

"We'll be waiting, Nora," Helene says, and flutters out, Callum close behind her.

When they're gone, the room instantly feels smaller. Hotter. Could be due to Finn's eyes shooting fireballs in my direction. Thank the gods he wasn't so lucid a couple of hours ago. I probably wouldn't have gotten out of the room.

"I do enjoy your metaphors." Finn's clipped words aren't at all filled with his patronizing sarcasm I've grown to depend on. "Let me counter it with a popular saying from your world I find appropriate for this particular moment."

I strip off the cloak and toss it on the empty bed, forcing myself to maintain eye contact. "Out with it, then. No need to leave me in suspense."

He doesn't answer right away, instead conveying all his rage through slitted silver eyes. Then in an artificially polite tone, he says, "Correct me if I get it wrong, but it goes something like this: Fuck around and find out. Are you familiar?"

I laugh then. Because he's so pissed. Because his worry for my safety is bright and burning on his face. Because if I don't laugh, I might end up screaming until the windowpanes break. "Oh, yeah, I'm familiar with that one. Seamus says it all the–"

"Nora!" he barks out. He tries to lean forward, but gravity and exhaustion push him back against the headboard. "You could've gotten yourself killed."

"But I didn't."

"You're a silly girl who believes herself invincible."

I saunter to his bedside with a slow grin curving my lips. "You damn well know I ain't no girl, Finn. I believe I've shown you already."

Some color plumes on his cheeks, and it lightens my heart. We're not too late. He'll live. After tonight, he'll no longer be sick. No longer be iron-touched. His magic, something we've increasingly depended on, won't kill him. "Your bawdy words aren't as impressive as you may think," he mutters.

When I reach his side, I bend to kiss him softly on his scowling mouth. "I can save you," I whisper against his lips.

He says nothing. Instead, his expression freezes in a mask of nothingness. A handsome blank page.

I sit next to him and take his hand. My smile is so wide, it hurts my cheeks. "Did you hear me?"

"I did." That's it. All he gives me.

My smile fades some, but his odd mood won't deter me. Reckon I need to explain myself with more clarity. I squeeze his hand tighter. "No, I mean *I* can save you. Me. Without a damn Healer. Allister said a Bond would–"

"No." His face is still a pale blank sheet. No anger. No mistrust. No happiness. Nothing.

I feel my smile fade as my grip slackens on his hand. "Finn, I... I understand your people need you, and I get how a Bond could complicate things, but–"

"No, Nora." He slips his hand from mine. A frown paints his mouth, and resignation dulls his eyes. "I'm sorry. I can't."

I search his face as my heart rips into pieces. The Pull tightens in my already swirling stomach.

Something clicks in my brain then. Something wretched and angry. Something that makes betrayal small in comparison.

Finn doesn't show any surprise at my revelation. No shock. He didn't ask questions or accuse Allister of feeding me false information. His only reaction is nothing with a dash of resignation. He's cold. Detached. Giving an empty apology told through pursed lips.

I stand, my entire body numb. I can't feel my lips, can't feel how my words vibrate against them when I say, "You knew."

He doesn't say a word. At least he has the decency to look me in the eye when he's ripping my heart out.

Misery floods my limbs, thawing out the shocked numbness. I want it back. I don't want to feel how much Finn doesn't care. He never was worried about me, was he? He was only worried Allister would uncover his secrets.

"You... I let you touch me. I *trusted* you." I slap an errant tear off my cheek, hating its existence. Hating this moment.

"You let me come here, let *Helene and Callum* come here, knowing that... that..." Damn it! My voice is too shaky. "Say something!"

"It appears you already have things figured out, Nora." His voice is flat, no longer beautiful and lilting. It burns my ears.

"You bastard." My words whisper out in a raspy breath but scream inside my head. *Bastard, bastard, bastard!*

He flinches at the curse. That's what gets a reaction from him. *That's* what makes him feel something.

I stumble backward, feeling dirty and sick. He decided I was good enough to have some fun with, not worthy of anything else. "Why didn't you tell me?" *Tell me, tell me, tell me!*

He swallows, his throat rippling with it. "You never asked."

He should have slapped me.

It would've hurt less.

The fight leaves my body in a whimper. He's no different from any other Unseelie man. He used me, lied to me, tricked me. Pretended he'd waited his entire life for me. For what? To get off in my mouth?

I'm a fool. A joke.

I clear the agony from my throat, swallow against it until I'm close to choking on it. Shaking my head, I force my feet to move to the door and grapple behind me for the knob. I can't do this anymore. I can't.

"Allister is taking Helene and Callum back through the Window," I tell him before opening the door. His expression is blank again. He really doesn't give one fuck about them or me or anyone. "They need to warn my Order, make sure Alexie is protected." *My* Order, not his. Never, ever his. Never again. "Your magic on the Windows is fading, but I'm sure you know that."

Not one word to defend himself spews from his mouth. Finn only gives his blank stare. It's so much louder than anything he could ever say.

I open the door and face him one last time. "Yeah, you knew your magic was fading. Of course you did." A laugh escapes my mouth. A loud, empty sound. "You know what's fucked up?

You'd rather risk countless lives of your people and mine than Bond with me. Am I that horrible? Do I repulse you that much?"

His blank-stare response will live in my nightmares.

"You *used* me, Finn. You made me think you cared and just took what you wanted."

Still nothing from him.

Say something!

He doesn't.

"It was never about your people. If it were, you would have..." *Bonded with me to save yourself!* "What kind of game have you been playing?"

He scoffs at that. And nothing else.

I now let the tears fall freely. "I need you to take the rest of your magic off the Window in Mystic. At least find enough compassion for us to do that."

"I'll take it off," he says evenly, apathetically.

I yank open the door, and before I slam it on him and this room, I give him one last promise: "I'll never bother you again."

Chapter 29

Callum and Helene didn't put up much argument when I told them everything Allister said. Especially when I got to the part about the Windows. Alexie may be keeping our Window closed, but there were plenty close enough to us that if Finn's magic dissolves completely, Oberon would have easy access to everyone back home. All it took was telling them Alexie and Seamus were in danger. They're family, after all. Forced together by circumstance and cemented together with love.

It could also be they didn't want to argue with a woman who had to pause every thirty seconds to blink back tears and swallow whimpering cries. I tried to keep it together for them, to be the Leader they needed.

I hadn't done a great job of it.

Now, we wait in the inky darkness by the well for Allister. I hold my bag for Callum, who will carry it on their trip back. Even without my and Finn's gear, it still weighs about twenty pounds, but they need the supplies. I can't let them go into Mystic unarmed and without basic resources.

Helene picks at her dirt-encrusted fingernails as she stands in front of me, while Callum sits at my side on the lip of the well. His furtive glances in my direction are drenched in sympathy I can't face.

At least we're relatively alone. Nary a soul lingers outside this late, but we still do our best to remain inconspicuous.

A tremulous sigh escapes my lips after yet another one of the Seelie's glances. I didn't tell them about my ability to heal Finn and his refusal. They're obviously aware that something's wrong, but I won't fill in the gaps. Not now. I don't think I can keep it together enough even if I wanted to. They'd been too polite to ask what upset me after witnessing my almost-breakdown, thank the gods.

The desire to go back with them burns hot through my veins. But I can't. I know I can't. Not when my friend is still under Oberon's thumb.

I don't know what I feel about Pia now, but I cling to her last words to me and draw from years of loyalty and the friendship she's shown me. She deserves the chance to explain, and Allister has promised to make it possible for her to do so.

And Finn?

I close my eyes against tears before they can escape the corner of my eye and alert Callum.

Finn made his choices.

"Nora," Helene whispers. When I glance at her, she tips her chin toward the tree line. "Your Messenger?"

I nod, standing to greet him. My body feels eighty years old. Gravity sits heavily on my shoulders, and the one thing I want most is to hide under blankets and escape into oblivion. Like I had after Topher died. I want that deep, dark place again. I want the void that sucks me in and gives me nothing but blackness.

Four days. I'll have four days to succumb to the temptation, and then I get to work. Finn doesn't want to help his people or mine? Fine. Fuck him.

My hand goes to my chest. I hate how pain burns my heart.

As Allister approaches, I don't notice the figure behind him. Not until Helene lets out a gasp. She pulls her weapon, brandishes it as if the two are already in front of us.

"Who is…?" Words stick in my throat when I finally see what's upset Helene. Actually, *who* upset her.

Moonlight strikes the two Fae approaching, revealing my Messenger and the alpha. The goddamn Shifter we'd fought barely twenty-four hours ago.

"You want us to trust your Messenger still?" Callum asks, disbelief sharp in his voice. "After he consorts with that Shifter? Do you have any idea what that animal and his pack put Helene and me through?"

No, not really. I'm ashamed to admit I was too worried about Finn and how to save him to even ask. Helene did say they weren't beaten or abused, except for one female Shifter who clocked her and bloodied Callum's temple a bit. The alpha put a stop to the abuse before it ever got started, according to Helene. But I suppose being strung up by a pack of Seelie who can shift into massive wolves is enough of a scare for anybody.

"I told you Allister went to speak with him, didn't I? And it's just the alpha. Not all of them."

"He meant to kill us," Callum says through gritted teeth.

"No, he had every chance to kill you two and didn't. Think on that for a spell," I say as I draw my daggers. No need to leave us vulnerable, just in case. "And let's not forget I tried to kill y'all not too long ago, and look what happened? Things change, sometimes for the better."

"That does not comfort me, Leader." Callum's words bite at me, which is so unusual for him. But I'm glad about it. There's little room for gentleness during war.

Helene flanks my left side, ready to tear in if need be. As much as I enjoy Callum's more aggressive words, I forever depend on the power of Helene's actions. She doesn't need words to show her strength. It radiates from her tiny body.

Allister's gait is the same nonchalant pace I've come to expect. He doesn't hurry or stumble. It's as if not a worry in his world or mine rests on his slight shoulders. His copper hair flares even in the soft moon-glow, and his tan breeches and green tunic are impeccable. The sack he always brings to my home is slung over his shoulder.

Even learning what I now know about him, his appearance sends apprehension rippling down my spine. The man has an intimidating aura around him.

When he reaches us, Allister politely bows his head, greeting Helene and Callum as if they're part of the king's court. The alpha–Gavin, Allister called him at the pub–stays at Allister's side, fully dressed in the standard tan breeches and white shirt many Fae here wear. A glower twists his full lips, and if his eyes narrowed any more, they'd be closed. But he doesn't open his mouth or make a move on us. He's obedient. A dog at his master's side.

"Why'd you bring him here?" I ask. My focus is on Allister, but I'm acutely aware of Gavin's presence. One shady move, and I'm going for his throat.

Allister gives me his warmest smile as if I've complimented his shirt. "Gavin had a change of heart after our chat. He wishes to make amends."

A low growl ripples from the Shifter's throat, but he doesn't say a thing to correct Allister.

"With all due respect, Messenger," Callum says, his voice carrying a surprising haughtiness, "the man is growling at us. Is that how Shifters form truces these days?"

I mean, the question's a valid one.

Allister continues to smile as he adjusts his gaze to Callum. "You're quite right. Please forgive his poor manners. Gavin? Do you have anything to say to these fine people?"

"You invaded our land." Gavin's fists clench and unclench at his sides.

Allister *tsks*, delicately wagging his index finger.

Gavin purses his lips, drills holes in my head with his scowl, and relaxes his mouth to say, "Allister explained to my pack what happened to your Order and what you mean to do about it. We want the same thing, and for that, I offer a truce. My pack will not harm your people–as long as you harm no undeserving Fae in this world."

And there it is, the emotion I want from him. He's a protector, and he cares for his people. He tried to kill us because he assumed we were a threat. Granted, I had been a threat to his kind not too long ago, and so I get it.

But still...

"Yes, yes, very good." Allister presses a fatherly hand on Gavin's shoulder. "Now that we have that cleared up, let's get on the trail. Gavin has kindly offered to ensure our safe passage to the Window. He knows of a shorter, safer route."

"And you trust him? *Truly* believe he won't hurt my people?" My voice is low, almost as guttural as Gavin's. We're like two dogs pissing in each other's corners.

Gavin takes a step forward, stopping when Helene lifts her sword. He closes his eyes, and then opens them to give her surprising compassion. "I would never harm an innocent Fae."

Helene doesn't say anything–and her sword remains drawn, the tip touching the white fabric of Gavin's shirt, directly below his heart.

"We do not have time for anymore unnecessary violence." Allister lowers Helene's sword with a gentle hand to her wrist. He then pins me with a pleading frown. "I trust him as much as I trust you, Nora."

"So, not much, then."

"Oh, quite the contrary." Allister chuckles as if I made a joke and gestures to my bag. "Their cargo, I assume?"

Hesitating, with a quick frown at Helene, I hand over all the supplies they have. Food, water, extra weapons, sleep rolls. Everything. *Please don't let this be a mistake!*

Allister slips the pack into his magic sack, and the thing seems to digest it. The sack doesn't bulge or appear heavier.

"Very well, then," Allister says, clapping his hands once. "Come, young ones. The sooner we leave, the sooner I can return."

I hug Helene, and then Callum, holding onto them for longer than what might be appropriate. My gut says this is right, that I can trust Allister. It still doesn't make it any easier. "Be safe, y'all. Stay by Allister... and Gavin." My tongue hurts from forcing out his name. "Tell Ben and Luca that..." *That I love them and need them and miss them and can't be here for another*

205

minute without them next to me! "Tell them I'll be home as soon as I can."

Helene nods, and Callum, his face pale, gives a slight bow. "Please, Leader," Callum starts, "whatever happens from here on out, trust yourself above all others."

"I will." I have to. I have no choice.

Gavin mumbles for them to follow him as he turns on his heel and marches down to the tree line. Allister stays back, watching the trio like a proud father watching his children finally getting along. "Be ready, Nora," he says while still eyeing them. "You've four days to rest and prepare. What I ask of you will not be easy."

I watch my friends with him, my hands balled in the cloak's fabric. "I'll be ready."

"As will Finn?"

His name creates an instant reaction. My chest tightens and misery saps the strength from my words. "He ain't coming with us."

Allister tips my chin after a few quiet seconds and peers so intently at my face, I fight the urge to sob and tell him everything. "Why?"

I don't even try to wrench my chin from his grip. It's so gentle, so reminiscent of Topher.

Jesus fuck, I'm broken.

"It seems he don't want nothing to do with me. A Bond's not possible."

"He'll die."

I close my eyes on the tears stinging them.

"Nora," Allister says quietly. Tenderly. "I am sorry for your pain, but... *find* a way. You must. If we do not have Finn to help us, we will fail."

206

Chapter 30

Time stops existing. A day passes, maybe two. I don't really know. I sleep, stare out the window, and sleep some more. I only leave the bed when my body demands to use the bathroom.

Grief wanted me, and I gave in to it. Let it have its way with me. We're a comfortable fit by now, and it has forgiven me for rejecting it these past weeks. It loves me, caresses my heart, my limbs. Hypnotizes me. It has tamed the Pull in my stomach, made that part of me submit to it like an abused dog.

You're not good enough. Not good, not good, not good...

Why does it hurt so much? Why?

I've ignored the Pull before, pretended it hadn't existed with Ben after Mama died. Why can't I now?

Easy answer. Because I'm the one being rejected. That epiphany makes the despair worse. This is what I put Ben through, what I made him suffer when I turned my back on him.

I don't deserve him.

I don't deserve Luca.

And Finn made it clear I don't deserve him, either.

Every conversation I've had with Finn plays and replays in my head. Over and over and over, his lies bleed into my ears. *Oh, God.* How could I have believed him? How could I have fallen for all that charm and bullshit? A virgin? He's waited his entire life... for me?

Bullshit, bullshit, bullshit!

I lie in bed now, twisting the sheets in my fist and pressing them against my mouth as I scream and scream and scream into them. These thoughts! These fucking, fucking thoughts. I scream until my voice breaks and my throat is raw. Tears saturate the fabric.

When the screaming abates, exhaustion settles over me.

Good.

Sleep is better. Easier.

And the thoughts don't follow me into oblivion.

∞ ∞ ∞

I jerk awake at someone knocking on the door. For a moment, my memory's dim, and I'm... okay. And then the thoughts rush in as if they'd been waiting impatiently behind a screen door for the moment I wake. I cover my ears to block out the thoughts and another bout of knocking.

Sleep, sleep, sleep...

If I will it into existence, maybe sleep will envelop me again, give me another few more hours of reprieve.

Another knock.

"Changeling?" Regina asks, her voice hissing through the only barrier between me and everyone else. "You must open the door. 'Tis been more than two days since you've eaten."

Eaten? I press a shaky hand to my stomach. It gurgles in protest. *Oh...*

Shit.

I move to get up, but my legs are tangled in the sweat-stained sheets. I topple to the floor with a loud thud, my limbs tingling as blood rushes through them. It's been days since I've really moved, and if it weren't for my ability to heal preternaturally fast, I've no doubt my muscles would've atrophied.

"Are you hurt, Changeling? Shall I get Lord Finn to–?"

208

"No!" My voice is hoarse from lack of use, and I hope like hell she heard me. "No, Regina," I say louder. "I... I'm coming."

It takes massive effort to fight through the muck of depression to untangle the sheet from my legs, stand, and hobble to the door. Regina awaits me with a tray of bread, cheese, and some of that red-flower custard. A frown scrunches her pretty face.

I start to lift my hands to accept the proffered tray, a word of thanks on my tongue, when I notice a stack of trays on the floor to the right. All with the same offerings as the tray Regina holds.

All that food wasted when so many in this world are starving. Instead of taking the fresh tray, I bend to collect one from the floor pile. "I'll take this one. Give the fresh food to someone who needs it." I chance a glimpse at my frowning host. "I'm so sorry, Regina."

Her face softens, the irritated frown transforming into one of concern. "Are you ill?" She takes one hand from the tray to feel my forehead, my cheeks.

An actual smile struggles to curve my lips. "Changeling, remember? I rarely get sick."

"Yes, well..." She removes her hand from my cheek, but not until she gives it a light pat. The woman looks a decade younger than me, but she acts like an older woman, one who's seen a lot of difficult years and has lived to tell about it. "A bath would do wonders for you, dear. Take advantage of the plumbing. It is rare in these parts."

The smile threatening my lips curves deeper. "Dear," not "Changeling." Maybe the woman's forming a soft spot for me. "I'll do that. Thank you."

She gives a curt nod and blinks as if trying to mask her concern. "I'll have some fresh clothes sent up. Leave those in the hall. Best to have them burned." She crinkles her nose at my disheveled clothes with sweat stains under the arms and probably a clash of foul odors that waft around me.

"I'll, ah... Yeah, I'll do that."

"Right, then. Eat, get some color back in your cheeks. You look like death itself."

When she leaves, I force myself to stay away from the beds and sit in front of the cold hearth. Hunger pangs don't attack me, but I feel the weakness from not eating. I stare at the tray I placed on the table for a few moments, assess the old bread and cheese. Grief itches to take the lead again, whispers in my brain that I don't deserve food. Don't need it.

Dormant willpower struggles to shove the bad thoughts into a dark corner of my mind. I can't keep going like this. Allister will be back soon, and I need to be ready.

I press on my stomach, ignore Finn's grieving Pull, and concentrate on the Bond with Luca and Ben. They're alive and thriving. Missing me as I miss them. I focus on absorbing their love, try to heal my brokenness with it.

I need to eat.

I need to get myself the fuck together.

Because I need to get back to them. They've felt my despair these past two days, and now they'll feel my burgeoning desire to heal. I hope it gives them some peace of mind.

Slowly at first, I dig into the day-old food. The bread is stale, and the cheese is hard, but the custard tastes as heavenly as the other times I've eaten it. The nutrients from the dish also help awaken my lethargic body.

After polishing off every morsel, I strip the bed and myself, tossing all the smelly shit into the hall. I can't help glancing at Finn's closed door before slamming mine shut and marching straight to the tub.

As water dumps into the wooden basin, I sit on the commode and watch the steam rise in the air. The water needs to be hot. Scorching. I want it to melt off all the sweat and stink and ugly thoughts.

When the water reaches to almost the top, I shut it off and gingerly dip into the heat. My skin reddens instantly as it burns. I hiss through gritted teeth but keep immersing myself until my body adapts and welcomes the heat. Plucking a bar of soap from the holder, I scrub until my body and hair glisten and the scent of lemongrass fills my nose.

When I leave the tub, I dress in one of the long white nightgowns Regina had put in here when we first arrived. The other, Helene's, was balled up on the floor in the bathroom. That went out in the hall with the rest of the dirty laundry.

The nightgown makes me feel like a child, but who cares? I'm clean and fed. I take a second to appreciate those small feats.

After a few tries, I get the fire roaring in the hearth and take the time to detangle my hair while the fire works to dry it. I'm good. For now, I'm as good as I can be. Maybe if–

A soft knock interrupts the sounds of the crackling fire.

I set my brush on the table and stand to get the door. Honestly, if I would've remembered this gown, I'd have told Regina not to bother with fresh clothes. I can stay in this until Allister comes back. Besides, the clothes I wore here have already been washed, mended, and delivered. She really didn't–

When I open the door, all thoughts about clothes and Regina evaporate from my mind.

"What do you want?" I try to make my voice uncaring. It betrays me. All the progress I've made within the last couple of hours vanishes.

Finn stares down at me in surprise, as if he hadn't expected me to answer the door. "Regina is worried about you."

All I can do is stare at him. That's what he has to say after ripping out my heart?

He clears his throat. "This is not what I intended, Nora. None of it."

It's then I notice the tortured look on his face. No apathy tonight. No blank stares and wordless replies. He's wrecked. Exhaustion sags his cheeks, the dark circles under his eyes a mottled purple.

My broken heart demands I soothe his demons and calm his sorrows.

My broken mind can't take any more of his rejection.

My grip on the door tightens so much the wood creaks under my palm. "*Not what you intended*? What do you want me to say to that? Sorry it didn't work out in your favor?"

211

He reaches for me, and I stumble backward in my rush to avoid him. "Don't touch me," I hiss.

His gray eyes fill with real pain. Or maybe it's not real. Maybe he's using his Fae wiles to get his dick in my mouth one more time. "We need to talk about this."

I feel my heart again shatter inside my chest. "No need to say anything, Finn. You've already confirmed everything I need to know. You don't want to live? Fine. I can't make you." My voice gets higher with every word as my face burns with anger and misery. "You know, I should thank you. No, really. Could you imagine if you actually Bonded with me? Oh, the *torture* it would've been for you. I'd have had to feel your regret every day."

He pulls a frustrated hand through his tangled silver hair and mutters a curse in that melodic language under his breath. Concentrating on the floor, he says, "You're wrong, love. About all of it. I... I've handled everything poorly."

I swipe at the tears now pouring from my eyes. I can't stop them. Can't demand they wait until he leaves. The pain is too raw, too new. "You don't need to *handle* me, Finn. I know all I need to. You do you, okay? Just leave me the fuck alone."

He catches the door when I try to slam it on him, his focus still cast on the floor. "Nora! This... I've more to say. A lot more–if you'd hear me out."

"Like what, Finn?" I whisper through my tears. "What more could you possibly have to tell me?"

Finn lifts his gaze to mine, his silver orbs shining with his own tears. It shocks me enough to take a step forward. To almost pull him into my arms.

Fuck!

No.

He doesn't deserve it.

He doesn't.

He swallows, his throat bobbing, and gives me a tremulous, contrite smile. "How about I start with the truth?"

"You're wrong. You're so *fucking* wrong about everything."

"Perhaps. But I'm not wrong for refusing our Bond."

This is his truth? It cuts so much worse than the lies.

"Get out, Finn," I whisper, defeated. "Just get out."

"I can't. Not until you know everything."

I take a deep, cleansing breath. "You have three minutes left."

"Then I shall be quick." His sad smile forces me to retake my seat. I can't look at him anymore. Not without already missing him.

He's choosing death over me.

He's choosing death over everyone.

Finn allows silence to fill the space between us again, and when the quiet becomes so loud I contemplate flinging the table across the room, he repeats, "It has never been about my people or myself." He pauses. "It has always been about you."

I bite the inside of my cheek until I taste blood. Is this how he thinks to let me down gently? Because it feels like he's pushed me off a cliff.

"I've never really spoken of my mother, have I?" At my silence, he continues. "Of course I haven't. I've never spoken of her to anyone."

I find a loose thread on my nightgown sleeve and pull until it snaps off. Then I find another.

"She died giving birth to me. I... I killed her, you see." He laughs, a hollow sound. "She wanted me, even refused potions from my father's Healer to rid herself of her burden. I honestly don't know why she refused. It would've saved her, allowed her to live a long and fruitful life. But...she bet against the house, you might say." He lets out a long exhalation. "Her gamble caused her death and a life in the kitchens for me. Not that I minded. The servants were always kind. Why, my wet nurse was the head cook." Nostalgia mixes with his grief at that. "To say she favored me above the others is an understatement."

His story wrenches at my soul. His pain becomes my pain, despite my broken heart.

The sound of his bare feet padding across the room makes me hold my breath, and when he sits across from me in the other chair, I sit on my hands to prevent myself from reaching out for him.

Finn leans forward, his forearms resting on his knees, his gaze on his folded hands. "My father spoke of my mother often when we'd find ourselves alone. They had no Pull, no Bond, but he loved her. Cherished the ground she walked upon." His focus shifts to the hearth, and he studies how the fire licks the dry logs. "He spoke to me of my birth only once when he was quite inebriated." He's quiet for a moment as he contemplates the hearth. "My father said it was horrendous, a nightmare. My magic… It was so strong, even then, and it…"

He closes his eyes, clenches his fists, and it takes everything in me not to comfort him.

"She was gone before my feet left her body," he finally continues. "My mother turned to shards of ice for refusing to rid herself of me when she had the chance."

I can't take his pain anymore. "Finn…" I stand and move toward him, but he stops me with a hand up and a gentle smile.

"Please, I must finish. If you touch me…"

I sit, do as he asks. Yet, all I want to do is hug him. Jesus, what he's lived with, what he's had to endure.

He keeps his gaze on mine now, and his luminous silver pools are full of raw, unfiltered emotion. The man behind the façade sits across from me now. The man I've been searching for since the day I found him in the woods. The man I've only ever caught glimpses of in unguarded moments.

"I let you believe what you needed to believe, and I'm sorry for that." He pauses for a moment. "I truly wanted to find Callum's Healer. I'm not one to sacrifice my life for many things. Yet, there is one thing I would gladly sacrifice it for with a smile on my face."

"What is it?" Tears flow unchecked. I don't have the energy or desire to keep them in.

"I'm not lying when I said refusing to Bond with you was *never* about my people," he says for the third time. "A Bond

216

would not have changed my mission. Having your Order as my own would've helped."

"Then make me understand."

He kneels in front of me and takes my hands in his. "A Bond would connect us the way I was connected to my mother. A part of me would become a part of you. Your body would endure the same torture as hers had. What if I kill you, Nora? I could live with just about anything else in this world or yours, but I can't live with that. I'd rather die."

My heart swells and bleeds as I slip a hand from his grasp to cup his cheek. "You don't know that for sure."

"I do."

"No, you don't. You're assuming. That's all you're doing."

"Even the slightest assumption is enough to solidify my decision. It may not sound rational to you, but I knew you would want to sacrifice yourself, try anyway. I… I believed not telling you would save you pain."

A small, sad smile plays at the corners of my mouth. "There you go, assuming things…"

"My assumptions have kept me alive for a thousand years," he says softly.

"I think you're wrong about the Bond, Finn." I slide my thumb over his bottom lip. "You know, I never believed in fate, not really. I always considered the Pull a biological thing, something sewn into my kind's DNA." I brush his lips with mine. "Not anymore. We're meant for each other. Made for each other. I was born for you, and… you've spent your entire life waiting for me. Right?"

He nods slowly. "Yes."

"You've truly never been with anyone else?"

He presses his cheek in my hand with a slight smile. "Wasn't it glaringly obvious?"

A deeper smile sneaks to my lips, too. "Not even a little bit."

"I'm a natural, then."

I snort through all my tears and runny nose. Gods, I must look like a swollen sea creature. "It appears you are. No one can kiss like you can, I should add."

Years seem to fall from his face the longer we speak. "I'm a virgin, but not from the lack of trying. I've had my dalliances, as innocent as they were." He raises a perfectly arched silver brow. "I suppose you should let Ben and Luca know of my superior skill. It's only fair."

A sharp laugh escapes my mouth. "You can tell them at your own risk." My smile fades as I search his eyes. "I can't let you die, Finn."

He covers the hand I still have pressed to his cheek. "No one lives forever, my love." He lifts my hand to kiss my palm. "I will die a contented man, now that I've met you. Touched you."

"You could have me and live. And another thing. I'm no martyr. Never have been. I wouldn't be sacrificing myself because fate is real. I know it in my very soul. *You* are the one who doesn't have to sacrifice yourself for an unproven fear."

"Your death is not worth my life, and I will not test it, proven or otherwise."

Stubborn Fae!

I leave the chair, face him on my knees, and bring his trembling hand to my heart. "What if you're absolutely wrong? What if the Bond works exactly the way it's meant to?"

Chapter 32

He shakes his head, a quiet denial whispering from his mouth.

No. This isn't working for me anymore.

I take his face in my hands and kiss him. His lips are stiff, his arms firmly at his sides. Even now, he's trying to protect me from his unfounded fears.

Fine. I can trust our connection enough for the both of us.

My knees ache against the stone floor, but I stay there, move closer, press my lips tighter against Finn's. A moan bleeds from my mouth to his when he finally relents.

His arms circle my waist as he takes our kiss deeper, exploring my mouth, using his tongue expertly. He's a man starved. Starved for me, and my god, that makes my need for him escalate.

I let him take what he wants.

And he wants everything.

Until I slip my fingers under the hem of his wrinkled shirt.

As if my touch snaps him back into denial, he grips my shoulders and jerks me from him. His chest heaves, and his lips are swollen from mine. "Gods, Nora," he rasps out. His fingers tremble against my arms. "I haven't changed my mind. I won't risk it."

I tangle my fingers in the front of his shirt, clinging to the fabric as if it held answers. "You want me, Finn. I know you do."

"Yes! You are all I've ever wanted, and I will not lose you because of it."

"I can *heal* you."

"And I can kill you in the process." He releases me and stands so fast I need to catch myself before face-planting the stone floor. The nightgown tangles around my legs in my attempt to get up to confront him. Fight with him. Convince him.

I cuss while kicking at the hem, fucking pissed now. "Sonofabitch!"

Finn, ever the gentleman, rakes a frustrated hand through his hair before helping me to my feet. He doesn't stay close, opting for his spot by the window, far away from me. His hands grip either side of the windowsill so tightly the sound of splintering wood crackles in the room.

I stand still by the hearth, pulling at loose threads on this obnoxiously virginal gown, and watch his back heave with deep, slow breaths. How do we get past this? How? Because damnit, I need him. And he needs me.

Elation sparks at my nerve endings. Grief isn't forgotten. It couldn't be after the last couple of days. But these new revelations, Finn's confession of all his fears... I shouldn't be so happy. His pain *shouldn't* make me so happy. Yet, it does.

No, not his pain, that's not quite right.

I'm happy for the reason behind it. It proves Finn never used me, never wanted to discard me. Yes, he may have lied to me, but his lies don't come close to what I thought they were. He lied by omission. Lied because he believes our Bond will not only save him but cause my demise. He lied because he'd rather die this slow, agonizing death than put me at potential risk.

He lied because he... cares for me. Maybe more than cares for me.

And when my heart ripped into pieces after he'd rejected me, I've come to realize that *I* feel more. So much more.

I can't let him sacrifice himself for an unfounded fear.

I won't.

Without taking my eyes off his back, I unlace the gown and let it fall to the floor in a flouncy white puddle at my feet.

Goosebumps attack my skin, and my nipples harden. I'm not cold. The hearth has warmed the room. My body reacts in anticipation. I think of how his hands felt on my skin that first time in the tub. How his touch started tentatively until he squeezed and explored while I rubbed against his cock.

I remember how his tongue felt on my clit. How he touched me exactly the way I'd shown him. How he moaned as I came against his mouth.

"Finn," I whisper, stepping out of my gown and moving toward him. "Please. Touch me." Another step. "Let me touch you."

When I'm close enough, I press my body against his back, revel in how the rough fabric of his shirt rubs against my taut nipples. I kiss between his shoulder blades and wrap my arms around his waist. He doesn't pull away or stiffen.

Good. Progress.

My hands again slip underneath his shirt, and I tentatively explore the slender muscles and smooth skin of his stomach. My lips press into his back for another kiss.

"Nora…"

"You say you have trouble trusting people. Well, I'm not *any* person. I trust you, Finn, and I trust our connection. Please… trust it, too."

Finn's still for so long, the confidence drains from my body. I'm about to release him, come to terms with his decision, when he finally turns to face me. He opens his mouth to speak, but inhales sharply as he takes in my naked body. His eyes drink me in, his pupils dilating with pleasure. "You're so bloody perfect." His voice is warm, coating my skin with his admiration.

He makes me feel so wanted. His gaze is bare and raw and worshipping.

Emotion runs thick in my throat, and I have trouble finding the convincing words he needs to hear.

But then he reaches out to me.

His attention stays on his hand as he presses his palm between my breasts. He cups my left one, his thumb grazing over my erect nipple. A surprised moan escapes me. I dare not move. Don't say a word. I don't want to break this spell. Don't want my voice reminding him of his fears.

"I love your soft skin," he whispers. "Your rosebud nipples." He pinches it then, a light touch that sends desire straight to my core. "I would dream about you, picture you naked and wanting me. I would imagine how you felt when I entered you." He lets out a slow breath. "I want to know how that feels...with you. *Only* with you."

I close my mouth, swallow against my dry throat. Still, no words tumble from my lips, but I press closer to his touch. My need for him is instinctual. The Pull inside me no longer mourns. It burns with anticipation.

His touch leaves my breast to follow the curve of my collarbones. He bends to place tender kisses on the sensitive skin of my neck, nipping lightly at my jawline and licking a soothing path afterward, his tongue warm and wet. His mouth is hot against my skin as he then navigates to the spot under my ear. He cups the back of my neck, bringing me closer as he traces tiny circles with his tongue before sucking gently.

I close my eyes, and my mouth opens in pleasure. He could spend hours just touching my neck. The sensation of it travels through my entire body. I feel myself grow wet and swollen for him.

He can't stop. I swear I'll die if he does.

Please don't stop!

"I can't get enough of your smell," he says against my ear before a deep inhalation. "It's uniquely yours. You smell like fire and passion." He again nuzzles the spot below my ear. "Nora is my favorite smell."

My knees tremble, and I slump against him. His other arm snakes around me, sliding to my ass and squeezing. My birthmark tingles, making me dizzy. I'm drunk off his words, his touch.

Don't. Stop.

With his mouth still pressed against my neck, he moves his hand from my ass to lift my thigh. His fingers are quick and sure now as they flutter over my wet folds until he reaches my taut clit. He circles it with the tip of his fingers, shooting pleasure that's almost painful through my entire body.

I cry out my shock, and he captures the sound with a kiss. His tongue licks the inside of my mouth as his finger circles, circles, circles my clit. I lace my fingers in his silky hair, bringing his lips closer. My hips gyrate against his fingers as he works me until I'm *this* close to exploding.

When he pulls back and slips his touch from my pussy, a frustrated groan bubbles in the back of my throat.

He smiles down at me, his magic fingers now capturing my face as he peers into my eyes. "I love touching you. Tasting you."

I'm still afraid to say anything. So, I trace the dark circles under his eyes, the only visible tell he's not okay. His beauty can't hide it.

His smile falters, and as if to erase the reality of our situation, he kisses me deep and long. "What if your body can't handle my magic?" he says against my lips. "What if I *do* kill you? What if I kill Ben and Luca once we're connected?"

I press a hand to his heart, pull back, and smile at him with confidence I feel in my very bones. "You can't kill us, Finn. You can only make us stronger. Like we'll do for you. Trust this. Let go of your fears."

He traces a thumb over my bottom lip, his eyes drawn to it. "And if I can't?"

I sigh. "Well, I guess we'll storm Oberon's castle and abduct his Healer."

"You would do something so foolish, wouldn't you?"

I grin at him, even though hints of misery snake into my heart. "You bet your ass, I would. I won't let you die."

He stares and stares and stares at me, pursing his lips, tilting his head in contemplation.

Then:

"So... let me get this straight." In a surprisingly swift motion, he hooks an arm behind my knees, lifts me as if I weigh nothing, and carries me to the bed I hadn't stripped of sheets. When he gently lays me down, he straightens. As he discards his

223

shirt, he says, "You would risk your life anyway, just to make sure I'm still around to annoy you?"

Elation blooms inside me as I take in his impish smile and the way he tosses his shirt across the room like the cumbersome barrier it is. Relief is a palpable thing. A healing thing. "That's absolutely right, I'm afraid. Either way, I'm fixing to get your stubborn ass healed."

"Well, then," he says as he strips off his breeches. I can't get over how gorgeous he is. All slender muscles and tanned skin. "I suppose the most prudent solution is to enjoy ourselves while you risk your life."

I want to squeal my excitement. Cry out my relief. I settle for a smile that hurts my cheeks as he finally comes to me.

He covers me with his body, and the weight of him fills my heart to bursting. No restrictions stand between us. No lies or unspoken truths or false hopes. We're heat and skin and a million nerve-endings.

He cups my face in his hands and soaks me in. He looks at me as if I'm the only person in this world.

No.

He looks at me as if I'm *his* only person in this world.

I lift my head to meet his lips with mine. Our kiss is gentle. Exploring. My hands roam his back, memorize every ridge, every angle. The touch of his skin makes my fingertips tingle. He's all magic. Every part of him.

Finn lifts his mouth from mine. He smooths hair from my face as he opens his mouth. "I want to please you, but..." He doesn't finish his sentence as he searches my face.

He doesn't have to.

I nudge him until he's on his back, and I straddle his hips. Grinning down at him, I rub my pussy over his cock and delight in how he bucks against me, a breath hissing through his even white teeth. I love how his hands grip my ass to make sure I don't go anywhere.

"I want to please you, too, Finn," I whisper, groaning from the heat of his erection against my core. "Tell me what you want."

224

He bites his bottom lip and arches his back when I slide across him again.

"Is this what you want?" I do it again and again, my eyelids heavy with pleasure. I'm careful, stop when I feel his body tense. Continue when he relaxes. I want him to come inside me. I want the formation of our Bond to be intense.

"Nora…" Finn's touch glides to my hips and tightens, stopping my slow movements. "I want to taste you. That's… That's what I want. I want to bury my face against you."

My clit pulsates, begging for his tongue. It's Pavlovian how I respond to his words.

"Yeah?"

He licks his bottom lip. Nods once.

Well, all right, then.

I move over the length of his hardness once more before I move to sit on his face. His hands instantly come up to my ass as he pulls me close, his tongue seeking and drinking me in. I arch my back, reach between us, and pull my lips apart to give him better access. He growls against me, breathing in my scent, and then the tip of his tongue laps rapidly against my clit. I moan, my eyes wide with pleasure, the pure shock of it coursing through me. I ride his mouth now, pressing close as wave after wave of pure sensation envelops me.

When he covers my clit with his lips and sucks and sucks, I'm undone. I scream out my orgasm, my hips circling, my fingers spreading myself wider, all to get closer, closer, *closer*.

When I float back down to this world, I sag against him for seconds before moving to straddle his hips again. His face glistens from my orgasm, and I bend to kiss some of it away, tasting myself. He's ravenous for me, his tongue darting in my mouth with the same enthusiasm he gave my pussy.

"Now, Finn," I say against his mouth. I move so that his tip is at my opening. Gods! He feels so fucking good. "Please."

He stiffens under me, his hands on my waist, stopping me before I take him all in. I tilt my head, study his expression. Worry clouds his passion. "You can't get pregnant, Nora. If you do–"

I tap a finger to his mouth and smile down at him. "Been on birth control since I was sixteen, remember? No babies, Finn. Not until I say so."

He searches my face. "If anything happens to you…"

I cup his cheek, give him a light kiss on his temple. "Nothing will happen except you healing." I kiss him once more in the same place. "And the tiny aside that we'll be Bonded for the rest of our lives."

His hands move up my back, and he holds me so close and with such care, tears again sting my eyes. "I've never wanted anything more in my life, Nora Waters."

"I'm glad, Finn… um…" I sit up to peer into his gray eyes. "What's your last name, anyway?"

He grins and tucks hair behind my ear. "I am Finnigan Ulster, bastard son of *the* Louie Ulster the Fifth. Lovely to meet you."

Laughter tinkles out of me. "Well, it is mighty nice to make your acquaintance, Finnigan Ulster, bastard son of *the* Louie Ulster the Fifth."

And then I move until his cock sinks into me. Our Bond is instant. Powerful. The pleasure of him inside my body is so acute, it stuns me. It's not only physical pleasure. This is… different. His life becomes my life, as mine becomes his. I see his earliest memory, him as a child, running through large kitchens and laughing as an Unseelie woman chases him with a spoon.

A flash of white bursts behind my eyes then, and I see him at his most vulnerable, his most powerful. I see him wasting away in Oberon's prison. I see his surprise and feel his willpower when he was freed. I feel his pain as he lay in my woods, broken and wishing for death.

Wow… I feel what he felt for me when he was in the cell in our basement. Even then, he… Jesus, he never lied to me. Ever.

My heart swells with so much pain and joy and love and fear.

Is this his magic?

"Nora!" Panic riddles Finn's voice as he switches our positions. I open my eyes when he withdraws from my body to find his worried gray orbs searching my face. "Are you okay? You stopped moving. Stopped breathing…"

"I'm…" I rake my fingers through his tangled hair, memorize every inch of his face. All the sarcasm he's tossed my way, all the taunting and irritation he's given me… It was all to hide how much he loves me.

Oh. Wow.

He… *loves* me.

It might sound crazy, but he's loved me from the moment he woke in that basement cell.

Tears leak from my eyes, and I don't even try to stop them. I'm so full. So complete. "Can you feel it, Finn? Our connection?"

His face relaxes instantly, relief drumming through his brain. I can feel that, too. "Yes, love. I feel everything."

I reach between us, feel the velvet skin of his erection. His eyelids droop as he shifts to drive into me. Stars burst behind my eyes, and my body vibrates with his guttural moan as he moves, once, twice, three times. His actions are jerky, unpracticed.

And so pure and perfect and mine.

I circle my hips, get us into a rhythm. He pumps and pumps into me, and I keep my eyes open to watch his pleasure as I *feel* his pleasure. Yes! I feel his *and* mine. I want to live in this moment forever. Stay here and feel him, touch him, taste him.

Magic.

He's magic.

As his orgasm builds, it triggers mine. I arch my back to get closer. *Ahh!* Pleasure, more intense than anything I've ever felt, builds and builds. I… I can't… "Finn!"

I explode when he does.

And then everything goes black.

Chapter 33

I come to with Finn at my side, tapping my cheek and calling my name. His voice is distant at first, and more urgent as I regain my bearings.

Fear doesn't course through him, only concern.

Holy hell, I feel him as if we're the same person.

I blink a few times, take some deep breaths, and want him inside me again. "Hi," I say, touching his cheek.

"Glad you could join me." His smile is soft and full of the love he has for me.

"Sorry. Never blacked out from an orgasm before."

"I'll take that as a… good thing?"

"I would." I cuddle to his side, my body vibrating with foreign energy that runs like ice through my muscles. It doesn't hurt. It's comfort.

Finn smooths a finger up and down my shoulder. "That was perfection."

"It was." I smile against his chest, drowning in the awe coming from deep inside his soul. "And I'm still here to agree with you."

His finger stops its gentle course against my skin. "Forgive me, Nora. Please forgive me."

I lift my head to face the regret in his eyes. It ricochets through him, entwining with his love for me. The love he has borders on obsession. It makes me so fucking happy. "I can feel the love you have for me," I start, my voice soft. "I've never... Everything you've done for my Order, it's because–"

"It's because I love you more than breathing. It's because since the first time I set eyes on you, I knew my life was yours." He lifts his roaming finger to trace my jaw. "*Because* I love you, I was terrified to Bond with you. An egregious error I plan to spend an eternity making up for. I hate any pain I've caused you. I wanted to come to you immediately after you left my room. Unfortunately, my body had other plans. As soon as I had the strength..."

Truth rings loudly in his words. He'll never be able to lie to me, just like Ben and Luca can't lie to me. Like I can't lie to any of them. Our Bond... It's complete now.

I let go of a breath, one I've held my entire life. I'm finally whole. With Finn, I'm finally who I am supposed to be. He was the last missing piece. "I love you, Finn. Jesus, I do."

He smiles then and taps the end of my nose. "I know that now. It flows through you, and it makes me believe I can move mountains. It's bloody beautiful to hear you say it, however." He shakes his head. "I never imagined a Bond could feel like this, not in my wildest dreams. And you feel it with three of us. I envy you that."

I tilt my head. "I won't deny that I'm pretty damn lucky."

He chuckles and pulls me closer.

This, with Finn, *is* different, though. Could be the magic he's shared with me. It could be anything.

I lean back to study his face. The dark circles are gone. "So, you're...good now?"

I know he's cured, for the most part. Iron doesn't taint his blood or shackle his magic in disease. It'll take a while to mend fully, but he'll mend. That's key. But like he said, it's nice hearing certain things. An extra layer of reassurance.

He pulls me back to him, and we settle deep under the covers. As he nuzzles the top of my head, he whispers, "I have never felt so complete in my thousand years of life."

I kiss his chest, letting my lips linger on his skin. "All it took was a little trust."

"Indeed." He pulls me closer. "You are a miracle, Nora Waters. My miracle."

Chapter 34

"Again, darling, like I'm a child, please explain why you'd trust one of Oberon's Messengers enough to *bargain* with him."

I sit across from Finn in front of the hearth, fully dressed and glaring at him. A tray of the usual food Regina sends up sits on the table between us, barely touched.

We've spent the better part of last night and today exploring each other's bodies in bed, on the floor, in the tub. Finn asked questions, which I found endearing, and he put my advice to good use, which makes me wet as I think about it.

Damn it.

I resume my glare. Not the time.

"What other choice do we have?" I lift a hand with a frustrated wave. "And he wasn't lying about my ability to cure you, or how the magic has weakened on the Windows. That's gotta count for something."

Finn goes silent again. It's the quiet he's given me a few times tonight, right before he spouts off with some more nonsense. I knew this conversation was coming. Knew I'd have to explain exactly what we'd be doing soon–like in a few hours, if Allister keeps to his schedule. I held it off as long as possible. But time doesn't wait for anyone.

"We could leave," he says for the hundredth time. "We could go home and figure out a proper way to weaken the king with help from our Order. I've already secured the Windows, and

Alexie's keeping our Window shut tightly–I sense her magic on it. We can take *more time*."

As pissed as we both are, it melts all the soft parts inside me the way he refers to my home as his, my Order as "ours."

"The last thing we need is to piss off Allister. We need help wherever we can find it. We also have a chance to get Pia, and as many questions that run through my head about her, I owe it to try to bring her home, where she belongs."

I've spent the last couple hours telling Finn everything Allister told me. I let him know about the Trackers, how Allister claimed to have freed Finn–hell, how Allister seems to know everything. He's playing chess, and we're the pieces he's been moving across the board for decades–a fair point Finn has made once or twice.

Finn leans forward, his face serious, exasperated. "Apart from Pia, if I'm understanding this ridiculousness, we are to traipse on into the kingdom, find *every single* Tracker under Oberon's command, and kill them?"

Yeah, that part of the plan sounds crazy, but… "Allister's confident we're capable of it."

He shakes his head at me as if I were a naïve, stubborn teenager. "Are you hearing yourself, love?"

"Christ, Finn! What do you want me to say? I mean, help me out here. What do you know about the Trackers?"

"Nothing. Absolutely nothing." He leans back in his chair, his frustration with me screaming through the Bond. "Oberon's snitches came long after my time in the kingdom. I always assumed his Haunts performed double duty."

I'm quiet for several seconds while trying to swallow the emotion instantly forming in my throat. "Haunts like Kellen, you mean."

Empathy clouds Finn's eyes. "Yes," he says, his voice full of compassion. "Like Kellen. He's the one who let Oberon know of my whereabouts, after all."

"Well, then, I'm willing to kill the fuckers with a smile on my face." I'll never get Topher back, but I can make his murderer pay.

234

"Do you really believe we are capable of the task? We will not leave the kingdom alive if only the two of us start a battle with them."

"I'm willing to try."

He scoffs and now shakes his head in disbelief. "You are the most *impossible* creature."

"So you keep telling me."

My temper's high, as is Finn's, but things are different now. We can be argumentative, bitchy with each other. Angry. That part of our relationship won't change. What *is* different is how I feel his love for me exploding inside him. It blankets every inch of my skin, and it's so damn hard to maintain my glare. I want to keep fighting with him. Keep trying to convince him.

And I want to touch him. Taste him. Feel him inside me and lose myself in the sensation of his building orgasm, which sets mine off instantly. Seriously, it's like coming twice in rapid succession. Talk about the perfect stress reliever.

His pupils dilate as he watches me. Oh, yes. He feels what I'm feeling and knows exactly what I'm thinking. Our Bond makes it impossible to hide. "Stop it, Assassin." His voice is husky, even with his thin hold on anger.

"I can't help it." I float off my chair as if on a cloud and go to him. When I straddle his hips, his erection fits perfectly between my thighs. "You're a drug, Finn. How am I supposed to not touch you all the time?"

He purses his lips, tries in vain to keep the anger in his eyes, and gives up on a long sigh. He releases his grip on the chair's armrests to wrap his arms around my waist. "You do not play fair."

"No, I don't. Can't, really."

He then kisses me until I'm no longer able to think about anything except ripping off his clothes and exploring his body again.

You know what?

I scramble for the hem of his shirt, hissing when my fingers connect with warm skin. He's doing the same, unbuttoning my flannel with his elegant, nimble fingers.

We have time. Yeah, we'll–

A soft knock blares through the room, invading our bubble.

"Fuck," I whisper against Finn's mouth.

He chuckles, nibbling on my bottom lip. "I do enjoy your way with words, love. And I would very much like to fuck you again, but"–another aggravating knock–"duty calls."

"So, you're with me? We're doing this?"

"Do I have a choice?"

"There's always a choice."

"But is the alternative being that you're still going if I say no?"

"Yes."

He lets out a long exhalation. "Then answer the door and let's get this craziness over with."

I kiss him one last time and push off his lap, buttoning my shirt on the way to the door. When I swing it open, I'm met with Regina's frantic stare.

"What is it?" Instantly, I'm in protection mode.

"It's the Messenger from the other night." She fidgets with the front tie on her apron as she gives Finn a furtive glance. "He knows you're here and wishes to speak with you."

I hesitate before placing a reassuring hand on her shoulder, giving a gentle squeeze. "It's all right, Regina. We've been expecting him." I ignore Finn's incredulous repeat of "We?" and smile down at the Seelie woman. "Tell him to meet us at the well."

She nods and steps to leave.

"Wait," I say quickly. When she turns back to me, I smile. "Thank you, for everything. We would've never survived this world without your kindness, and I plan to repay you."

She lifts her chin and straightens her posture. "If you want to repay me, Changeling, save my people."

My smile fades and words escape me. What she's asking is impossible, and I don't have the heart to tell her.

Thankfully, she doesn't wait around for a reply.

Chapter 35

We wait at the well for far too long.

Allister was in the pub not fifteen minutes ago, only a short walk away. He should've been here before us.

He's nowhere in sight.

Finn sits on the cold stone lip of the well, arms crossed over his chest in irritation, while I stand beside him scanning the darkness.

Distant sounds of music and the occasional bawdy laugh drifts from the village. The sounds mingle with the trill and hum of night creatures. I let the noise fill the tense space between me and Finn. It's better than dealing with the apprehension he feeds our Bond.

His narrowed gaze bores into my profile; I don't need to face him to feel it burning me. And he doesn't need to express his "I told you so" bullshit, either. It screams along with the crickets and nightbirds.

"How long should we wait, love?" Finn finally says. "Until he has the Guard good and ready to trounce us?"

I close my eyes against the dread his words create in my gut. I trusted Helene and Callum's safety with Allister. What if I sent them to their death? I hug the pillowcase filled with everything we have in this world until a dagger's sharp edge cuts through the fabric and my flannel to bite my skin. My tongue presses against the roof of my mouth, and it's all I can do not to scream and scream and scream into the night.

Oh, fuck. *Fuck!*

"What if you're right, Finn? What if I fell into an obvious trap?"

"Wait, no, none of that." Finn's arms wrap around me from behind, and the contact shakes loose some of the panic tightening my chest. "Don't listen to my blathering."

"You could be right."

"I'm not." He takes the pillowcase from my limp hands, tosses it to the ground, and then he holds me closer. "I trust your instincts. I do. You've been right thus far, haven't you? The man wouldn't have told you how to save me if he wanted us all dead." He pauses, drawing a circle on the back of my hand with his thumb. "I have a tendency to vomit words with no meaning, especially now, while I'm outside waiting for a Messenger when I'd rather be deep inside you."

A shocked laugh escapes me when I turn to face him. His tongue never ceases to surprise me, not when he's using it to toss out acerbic words or licking me in places I want him to explore again and again.

I brush silver strands of hair from his eyes. I'll never tire of studying his face. His perfection differs from any other Fae's. It comes not only from his physical attributes. It comes from his flaws and his wit and his keen desire to save everyone at the expense of himself.

I smooth a finger under his eye. Not a smudge of exhaustion mars his skin. "I can't believe you're mine."

He kisses me softly on one cheek, and then the other, before touching my lips. "And I never believed you could love me."

I open my mouth to deny his words. To tell him how crazy they are, how utterly ridiculous. But…it surprises me how fast and strong I fell and how easy it was to give him my heart when I had no idea there were any pieces left to give. Those nights without him, believing he lied and deceived and threw me away, made me realize how deep he's burrowed into my soul.

And maybe that's what it took to fully realize how much I need him.

"I love you, Finnegan." His full name feels like silk on my tongue.

When the words leave my mouth, his smile is brilliant morning sun, and his eyes are silver moonlit pools. He takes my face between his fingertips and kisses me. Savors and worships me. With barely a breath between our lips, he says, "If it's not too much trouble, I'd like you to repeat those words to me every hour of every day."

I smile against his mouth. "I don't think that will be a problem."

"Then we have a deal." He kisses me once more, long and possessive.

Then both of us go still.

Shock fills my body. I pull back from Finn, my gaze wildly searching his face for confirmation. For proof that what I'm feeling is real, not a figment of my desperate mind. His mouth curves in a smile filled with resignation.

Resigned is not how I feel once shock gives way to sensation. I feel color and sound and the elated pounding of my heart.

Finn places a chaste kiss on my forehead. "It appears your Messenger brought the cavalry."

My happiness is so large it widens my eyes and steals my voice. I just stare at him. Stare and stare and still pray I'm not dreaming.

Finn looks over my shoulder, his smile deepening as he tips his chin. "Go. They'll not want me to keep you to myself."

His voice activates my body. I squeeze Finn's hand before turning to run toward the woods.

To Ben and Luca.

Ben takes off as soon as he catches sight of me, and I'm in his arms in seconds. He lifts me from the ground, his fingers tangling in my hair, and whispers his love and fear as his kisses rain down on anywhere he can find contact with my skin.

He's real.

He's here.

My lips capture his, and instantly, I'm home. He's comfort and familiar.

He's here.

After Ben sets me down, he pulls away to touch the dimple on my chin. "Knew you couldn't stay out of trouble for long."

My smile hurts, and my heart soars. "It tends to follow me."

"Aye, it does, lass. And I promised we'd come when it found you," Luca says, his voice rough with emotion.

Elation waves over me yet again when I look over Ben's shoulder to find my giant smiling while gripping the strap of his pack. Relief coats his face, just as it coats every muscle in my body.

I move from Ben to meet Luca, who takes my face in gentle hands and places a soft, lingering kiss on my mouth. It's filled with longing and makes me ache with its sweetness. His huge body envelops mine, blocking out this world and all its dangers. My favorite feeling.

He lifts his mouth to study my face, absorbing it as if it's been years since seeing me and not a week. "Did you really think you could infiltrate the kingdom and not have us coming to your aid?"

"I thought…" I don't know what I thought, and it doesn't matter anymore.

Ben's warm hand covers the small of my back, Luca's hands still cupping my face. Our shared Bond sings with the contact.

"Come on," Ben says. "Let's go welcome Finn into the fold. Officially, this time."

Excitement bubbles in my veins. This will be the first time all of us are together, Bonded and a family. All are happy. All relish the shared power we give each other.

Except, Finn's Bond has a small sliver of apprehension running through it. Our Bond is different, a connection we have separate from Ben and Luca. I only pick up feelings and emotions from them. With Finn, I feel those things, as well as read his thoughts, and he's not ready to share me.

We walk toward Finn, my men on either side of me, both with an arm slung over my shoulders. My arms are secure on their waists, and it gives me strength. We can do whatever it is Allister expects from us. We can do anything.

Ben is the first to break free, going straight to Finn and pulling him in. It's one of those manly, who-can-clap-a-back-harder hugs, and it makes me smile wider. Especially because a strong portion of Finn's anxiety melts away. He may not want to share me now, but he sure as hell is ecstatic Ben and Luca are here. We won't be going on our foolish mission alone.

"Glad you're alive, brother." Ben gives Finn one last clap on the back before stepping away. "But next time you make Nora feel like shit, I'm gonna have to fuck you up."

I open my mouth to defend Finn, but he handles himself. "It was a horrendous error, my friend. I've more than made up for it."

Ben scratches at his hair, his gaze pointing to his shoes. "Yeah, man, felt that, too. Um... damn. Good job."

I roll my eyes as Luca gives Finn a rough hug of his own. I don't hear the soft words they say to each other, but the relief rushing from Finn and Luca is all that matters.

After a smile at Luca and Ben, I go to Finn and tuck myself under his arm. I'm not ready to be away from him yet, either.

His appreciation saturates me as he brings me close, clearing his throat in surprise because I chose him in this moment. "Well, then, now it's a party."

"I'm looking forward to the fun," Ben says, hiking his pack higher on his shoulder. "This thing, it's almost over. I can feel it."

"Perhaps." Luca takes in our surroundings. "But we cannot get the festivities started without Allister. Where the hell has the man gone?"

Ben shakes his head, peering at the tree line. "Said he had to find some transportation."

What? I have so many questions. What the hell happened when Allister went to our home? And how the hell did Ben manage to leave Alexie without a battle?

Before I can ask a damn thing, Finn shoves me behind him, his hands filling with white light. His voice is a sneer as he says, "What in the pits of hell…?"

I glance over his shoulder and feel my body tighten.

Shit.

Chapter 36

I may have forgotten to tell Finn a few minor details.

In my defense, more pressing matters needed tending to.

I move to Finn's side and touch his biceps, trying to send calm to his nervous system. Failing. "It's fine. He's on our side."

Finn scoffs. "You can't possibly be serious."

"What? You don't know about Gavin?" Ben thumbs behind his shoulder at the Shifter and Allister as they make their way from the forest's edge. "He's not bad, man."

Finn's magic glows more intensely in his clenched palms.

"Not helping," I grit out to Ben before giving Finn a quick rundown of Gavin's presence.

"Oh, for the love of…" Finn's exasperation with me and this situation bleeds from him and flows through our Bond. At least the magic churning in his fists snuffs out. "Let's try not to forget pertinent bits of information, darling. I almost took the man's head off."

"A bloody waste that would've been," Luca says as he collects my pillowcase from the ground and stuffs its contents into his pack. "He's an asset. Have you seen the man change into a wolf?"

"A time or two," Finn deadpans with a slight glower at me.

Yeah, I deserve that speck of irritation.

I reach for Finn's hand, and even with his irritation, he takes it, his thumb tracing a gentle path over mine.

When Allister and Gavin are close enough, the Messenger acknowledges Ben, Luca, and me with a slight tip of his chin before giving all his attention to Finn. Allister can't hide his admiration for my man. It heightens the color in his face, makes his eyes flame brighter with awe.

Gavin, on the other hand, keeps his fists tight against his sides and a scowl on his handsome face. I enjoy his consistency. The Fae won't bend for anyone. Gotta admire that.

"Thanks for bringing Luca and Ben back with you," I tell Allister, and really mean it.

The Messenger rips his gaze from Finn to acknowledge me. "Yes, well, your giant threatened to take my head. He's quite convincing."

I give Luca a smile, and he returns it with a wink.

Allister refocuses on Finn. "It's good to see you well again, my lord. I had hoped our Nora could convince you of the benefits you'd receive from an Assassin's Bond."

"I am no one's lord, Messenger," Finn says, voice low. His magic brews inside him, begging to hurt Allister. It's like a breathing entity, a serpent, now whole and well and slithering through his body.

No wonder Alexie has such a hard time controlling herself.

"That is where you are wrong," Allister says to Finn with absolute respect, bringing my attention back to the conversation. "You may be a bastard, but you are still a king's son. And you have sacrificed for your people. Oberon has never sacrificed a thing in his life."

Allister waits another moment for a reply he doesn't get and then gestures into the darkness toward the forest. "Come. We've horses to take us on our journey."

"How long's this journey?" Ben asks, not moving from his spot. None of us move. We're a united front.

"The kingdom is no more than an hour's ride if we are quick." Allister points to the Shifter. "And Gavin has offered to be our scout. He will make sure we do not encounter any surprises."

"How kind of him," Finn quips. "He's made me feel so very safe in his presence the couple of times we've met."

Gavin stalks toward Finn, a low growl rumbling in his throat. Ben, Luca, and I close in beside our Unseelie.

Gavin isn't intimidated in the slightest. "I owe you nothing, Mage, yet I'm here protecting you and your Changelings." He then turns his back on all of us and strides toward the tree line, Allister following him with a small smile on his lips and his hands tucked behind his back.

My men and I still don't move, watching the two ahead of us.

"The wolf has balls," Luca says, rocking on his heels.

"Sure does," Ben agrees. "Saw them myself when he shifted to deal with those toxic fireflies when we first came through the Window. Nasty little fuckers."

I don't ask if Ben means he saw Gavin's balls figuratively or literally. Knowing him, he probably means both. "Gavin went through the Window with Allister?" I ask instead. "He went to our home?"

Ben shakes his head. "He met us after we came through. Son of a bitch came to our rescue like a goddamn Avenger."

"How noble of him," Finn says, his voice bored.

"It was." Luca nods at the two disappearing under the veil of darkness. "Time to go."

Respect for Gavin buds inside my chest. He didn't have to meet Allister when he came back. But he did, and he helped them.

The same grudging respect blossoms in Finn, but he doesn't vocalize it.

As a unit, we walk to the edge of Mystic, all of us checking our surroundings, making sure no Fae is caught unawares by our presence. Five horses await us.

Gavin strips off his clothes and shifts into his wolf. It's quick and graceful, and he's as magnificent in wolf-form as he is in Fae. He huffs out a grunt before taking off ahead of us.

I turn to Allister, my eyes wide with wonderment. Finn's magic is amazing, but so is Gavin's.

Allister gestures to the horses, a companionable smile on his lips. "Shall we follow him?"

Chapter 37

I haven't been on a horse in years, and even when I rode–those three times–I wasn't any good at it. After riding for an hour at a fast clip, I slip like water from the saddle when we stop at a rather large manor within eyesight of the kingdom. A kingdom that expands beyond the horizon, filled with stone buildings and twinkling lights. It's vast and foreboding.

The manor is a stone structure similar to what I can see of the stone buildings in the kingdom. There is a quaintness to it, despite its size. Ivy grows up and along the sides, and the thatched roof doesn't look like it'd keep occupants dry during a rainstorm. But it's pretty, an orange glow illuminating the front windows. It's nothing like the poverty we saw in Rutsk.

Gavin is waiting for us on the front step. We passed a few unconscious, and maybe dead, Guards along the way. His handiwork, no doubt. He's in his Fae-form and naked as the day he was born.

Yes, I have three very gorgeous men surrounding me who are mine, but I'm not blind. The man is beautiful, scowling and all.

"You're slow," he says, standing like his impressive man parts aren't swaying in the breeze. "I almost went looking for you."

Slow? What the fuck does he consider fast?

I rub my sore ass and ignore him, focusing on Allister, who strides toward the cottage like he owns it. "Where are we?"

With flare, Allister opens the door as Finn, Ben, and Luca come to my side, Ben the only one rubbing his ass like I am. "Welcome to my humble home. We'll be safe here."

Welp, I guess he does own it.

We settle inside, and Allister quickly sets about building a fire in the hearth. The décor is plain, simple. There's a long wooden table and chairs arranged by the hearth, and a wooden cupboard butts against the far-right wall. A set of stairs to the left leads to a wide hallway and some closed doors. And thankfully, an open door near the bottom of the staircase reveals a modest bathroom.

This isn't at all how I pictured Allister living. I always thought he lived like royalty. Then again, compared to how many Fae in Rutsk live, he does.

Once the fire roars, Allister strides to a wooden cupboard. As if he remembers we're here, he glances up from gathering dried fruit and meat and points to the chairs. "Sit, sit. We've much to discuss." Excitement riddles his voice, and his face is animated.

He's nothing like the suave Fae I've come to know. The Fae who strolls and takes his time. Tonight, his movements are hurried. He's excited. I never thought he had a large enough emotional range to include excitement.

Finn places a hand at the small of my back, guiding me to a chair. Ben takes the seat to my left, Finn to my right.

Instead of sitting, Luca takes the stairs two at a time and comes down seconds later with a blanket in his hands. He tosses it to Gavin, who still stands by the door like a sentinel–a naked sentinel. "If you don't mind, wolf."

Gavin actually gives a flash of a grin as he catches the blanket and wraps it around his waist. "Jealous, Changeling?"

"Oh, quite," Finn answers for all of them with no ounce of anger. He places a possessive hand on the back of my chair.

"Nora already enjoys the view of our genitals. Three strapping men are enough for her consumption, if you don't mind."

I shake my head to hide a grin as Ben outright laughs while Gavin tightens the knot on his covering. He claims the seat opposite of us. "If I had any interest at all in anyone in this room, it wouldn't be in the Changeling." His suggestive stare points to Finn's full lips.

Well, damn.

It's my turn to set a possessive hand on Finn's leg. He chuckles when I squeeze his thigh. "Mine," I tell the Shifter.

"Whatever." Gavin then focuses on Allister as the Messenger sets a platter of food on the table, along with some wooden plates.

"Lovely to see everyone getting along." Allister sits at the head of the table as Luca takes a seat next to Finn. Our host gestures to the food. "Please. Help yourselves."

My stomach growls in appreciation. I glance around the table, my eyes stopping on Ben, who tips his chin toward the platter, and says, "Ladies first."

"Don't mind if I do." I dive in, snatching a plate and piling it high.

I barely taste what I'm eating as everyone else loads up. Well, Finn, Ben, Luca, and I load a plate. Gavin pulls the rest of the heaping platter in front of him and digs in with gusto.

As we eat, Allister looks on at all of us like a proud father admiring his offspring. He says nothing while the five of us have our fill.

After a while, Finn sits back in his chair, patting his flat stomach, as I wipe my mouth with the sleeve of my flannel. Ben swings an arm around my shoulders, always making sure I'm close, while Luca has a whispered conversation with Finn.

"Have anything to drink, Messenger?" Gavin asks, while polishing off the last remnants of food on his platter with admirable speed.

"Yes, of course. How rude of me." Allister gets up and rushes to the cupboard. He pulls out a small wooden barrel and pitcher, filling the pitcher with the barrel's contents. With the

249

pitcher and cups in hand, he rejoins us, pouring everyone some of the red liquid.

I nod my thanks and down the berry wine in a few gulps. The alcohol instantly makes my head fuzzy and warm.

"Now that everyone is satiated," Allister begins, "let's talk."

Finn sighs and sets his cup on the table. "This plan of yours, to kill the entire Tracker population, is a bit overzealous, don't you think?" He waves a hand at Ben, Luca, and me. "Their strength is something. My magic is something. Gavin's ability to turn into a cute dog is *really* something." Finn's lips twitch at Gavin's low growl. "But our talents will not be enough. We will be in the mouth of the monster, Oberon's full Guard detail there to defend what's his."

Allister chuckles, not at all bothered by Finn speaking to him like an imbecile. He might even enjoy it a little. "Your combined talents are more than enough, I assure you."

I lean up, pinning Allister with my skepticism. "Are Oberon's Trackers his Haunts?"

A secret smile shadows the Messenger's face. "Absolutely not."

Disappointment slithers inside me. It would've been nice to kill Kellen sooner than planned.

"All right, then," Luca says, resting his forearms on the table. He's wearing a black T-shirt that showcases his muscled chest and the tattoos running up his arms. Intimidating to most, hot as hell to me. "How many of these Trackers are we talking about? Fifty? More? You said we'd be killing them all, correct?"

"No, I said we would rid Oberon of their presence. I never mentioned killing anyone."

Finn shakes his head. "As fun as semantics are, we still can't *rid* Oberon of a horde of Trackers alone."

"I never mentioned a horde, either." Allister leans back, lacing his hands over his middle, clearly enjoying himself.

"How many?" Ben asks, his frown deepening at Allister's obvious delight.

Allister gives everyone at the table another secret smile and then focuses on me. "Four."

Finn laughs then. A loud, surprising laugh that chills me to the bone. He may sound flip, but his anger and brewing magic flood all of us Bonded to him. I swear if he weren't laughing, he'd be going after the Messenger's head.

"I'm aware of how ridiculous it sounds, but it's true. There are only four Trackers left in this world, hidden deep in the bowels of the prisons." He stares into the fire, his amusement evaporating. "They're… humans."

I stand so fast my chair tips back. "What in the actual fuck are you talking about?"

Gavin doesn't react at all. His handsome face is stone, his dark eyes pointed to the ceiling. The only tell he's as angry as me is the way the veins in his neck pulsate with fury. Finn isn't so quick to anger, and neither are Ben and Luca. Not outwardly. But I feel it coursing through them just the same.

What kind of game has Oberon been playing? Humans? What the fuck?

"Nora, please sit," Allister says, his voice calm. "I have a simple explanation if you'd be so kind as to indulge me for a few moments."

Luca stands to upright my chair and then tugs gently on my hand. "Come, Nora. Let's hear what the man has to say before we murder him."

The threat elicits an audible swallow from Allister. Good.

I sit and give all my derision to the Messenger. The fucker has three minutes. "I'm listening."

He takes a deep breath that raises his shoulders–and then gives a doozy.

Trackers are humans with the gift of Sight. To be more precise, they're the humans whose ancestors came here during the Great Change–when Assassins were switched with human children. Oberon discovered a few of those children could see the future. See the present and past, too. They had some magical connection to the world Oberon ripped away from them.

When Oberon's Mage, Talia, discovered this odd power centuries ago, she cultivated it, made sure the few with the Sight were bred together like studs and broodmares. Some were born with the Sight, most weren't. Through the generations, she helped those "blessed" hone their skills to See the Fae and Assassin population in my world. To monitor us like lab rats in a maze.

And after all these years of breeding and inbreeding and treating these humans like cattle performing a service, only four are left. Three are well into their lives and frail. One is barely sixteen–the human who has found a way to keep most of her visions secret, except for telling Allister. She's the reason the Messenger knows so much about all of us. She couldn't keep Helene, Alexie, Seamus, and Callum's escape secret because the other Seers drew on their whereabouts on demand of the king. That's when all hell broke loose.

Allister folds his hands on the table and peers at us for a reaction. None of us say a word for a few moments. We sit there as if made of stone. It's so…bizarre.

I mean, I've spent my life making sure I followed the rules while expecting Fae to do the same. Because Oberon always found out when we didn't. Because Trackers were everywhere.

Except they weren't.

They're four captive humans with an unfortunate talent Oberon used.

I lick my dry lips, swallowing once. Twice. And then give my stunned attention to Allister. "Did you know I killed Igor?" The thing that started it all. My one and only rule break.

Allister nods. "Soon after you did it, actually."

"And Oberon never knew?"

"He doesn't, no." Allister leans forward. "When Igor made your list with our future queen, I must admit I was relieved. Oberon couldn't punish you for breaking the rules, and I believed with everything in me you'd see our queen for who she is and protect her. You've proven me right, as your Order always has."

"Is that why you had her focused on my Order, because you trusted us?"

"That's precisely why, especially after your mother's death." Allister takes a deep breath. "Oberon had her killed when a Tracker revealed her and Finn's last meeting. He knew Miriam

252

was planning a rebellion, and he quashed it before she shared her plan with her Order and others, killing her and Casey, while capturing Lord Finn." Allister gives Finn a sorrow-filled frown. "Oberon wanted you to suffer after finally capturing you. He wanted you to pay for all you've done for the Fae, to die a slow death. He almost succeeded."

I press my hand on Finn's leg, needing contact with him. Anger bubbles inside him. Anger and memories of the time he spent in the prison, starving and burning from the iron, being poisoned by it.

"You never thought to tell us all this?" I say, my voice feeling like broken glass in my throat. Fresh pain ripples across my skin. "If you had, my father would still be alive."

Allister has the decency to look ashamed. "I wanted to. Truly. If I'd had known Oberon's plans, what he planned to do... I never in my wildest assumptions believed he'd take the army to your door. Before then, I believed I was protecting you. I was gravely wrong."

I don't even know what to say.

After a few uncomfortable moments of silence, Ben places both palms flat on the table. He stares at his fingers, clenches his jaw until his cheek tics. "You said Alexie is your future queen." This part of Allister's story would definitely have the strongest impact on Ben.

"She is."

"No, she isn't."

Allister opens his mouth. Closes it. Inspects his hands again as if they hold all this world's secrets. "The day a Tracker uttered Alexie's name, a Tracker I could not silence, is quite possibly the worst day of my life thus far." The misery in his voice fills the air between us. "She is the rightful queen, and it is high time she takes the throne. Our people need her."

"No," Ben repeats, voice lethally quiet.

"Please, let me explain." Allister gives Ben his attention. "I understand. She's young, not ready. She would need trusted allies around her to keep her safe." Allister then shifts his gaze to Finn. "She would need you."

My body goes numb as I focus on Finn's impassive expression. He doesn't say a word, barely acknowledges Allister's statement. I want him to deny the request. I want him to be enraged. But all that comes from the Bond is a resigned acceptance that replaces his prior fury, like he knew this would be the endgame.

He can't be here for Alexie because I need him. And fucking hell, I know how selfish that sounds.

"I'm not expecting an immediate coup," Allister goes on quickly, desperately. "This is why it's important to take care of the Trackers. We do that, and we'll have a window of time before Oberon retaliates. And he *will* retaliate, I assure you."

I tilt my head. "When do you think it's a good time to take on the fucking kingdom?"

He stares at me for the longest time. "When you say it's time. There can't be an end to this nightmare unless you're ready to back it. You know it as well as I do."

That's not fair. Not even remotely. Yet, I know he's right. And I know it will kill me to ask my Order and those who allied with us to risk their lives for the slim chance of success. "How do we take on the king, even if we wanted to?" Which I don't.

Allister smiles softly, as if my question has given him hope of my agreement. "He is not as powerful as you may think. Of his Mages, he has only Talia left. The rest are long gone from either old age or rotting in the dungeon for not performing well enough. All we need to do is take out his army, and with Finn and Alexie helping you and your allies, it is quite possible."

Ben lifts his hands in frustration. "Sounds pretty fucking easy. Too easy."

"Not easy, Assassin," Allister tells him. "But not impossible. For now, let's focus on getting the Trackers taken care of and rescuing Pia. The rest will become clearer after."

"About these Trackers," Ben starts. His hand moves to my thigh as if he needs the contact. "How are we to take care of them, exactly?"

Anger tightens Allister's face, another emotion that surprises me. "They are innocents. Victims. The honorable thing to do is

254

save them from that wretched prison and let them live the rest of their days in the world where they truly belong."

How the hell can you argue with that? We're done killing innocent people, even if those innocents are unwittingly threatening every person I love.

I nod. "I'm with you."

A grumble of agreement ripples from everyone else.

Allister sighs heavily, his face relaxing. "Excellent."

"Do all Messengers have the access you do to these Trackers?" I ask.

Allister hesitates and looks at Gavin, who gives him a subtle nod. "Ah, no. The king... He trusts me above most."

"Why?" I narrow my eyes. "How are you going to get Pia without no one growing suspicious?"

"Tell them," Gavin says. He stands then, only to take the spot beside Allister as if guarding him.

"Very well." Allister focuses on his folded, white-knuckled hands. "I know what I'm about to tell you might be shocking."

"Out with it, mate. We're all friends here, are we not?" Luca's polite words contrast with his deadly tone. Tension from all my men, from me, saturates the Bond.

"I'm... his brother."

Finn's hands light up with glowing balls of magic–right before he hurls them at Allister. The magic hits him square in the chest, the force of it knocking his chair backward. Gavin's strong grip under his arms saves the Messenger from hitting the floor.

Finn's hands light up again. "You lying, manipulating son of a–"

Gavin moves Allister behind him, his eye teeth lengthening to fangs as his eyes glow topaz. "Stop, Mage. If it weren't for this man, you would all be dead."

"And why has he kept us alive?" Finn's anger eclipses all of ours. We gather behind him, ready to do whatever it is he feels we need to. "To use us so he can lay claim to the throne when his brother is out of the way? Perhaps he wants Alexie seated so badly because she's a child, easily taken out with the proper

255

manipulations." Finn's rage is raw and black and terrifying. It's deep-seated in a long fear of history repeating itself.

Allister lifts his chin and moves from the safety of Gavin's protection. The ballsy sonofabitch walks up to Finn, looking him in the eye. "I understand your rage, my lord. I do. But I do not want the throne, nor have I ever. My brother is a madman who must be put out of his misery and ours." He lifts his hands. "Alexie Ulster is our rightful queen, and I will be the first to pledge my fealty to her once she is crowned."

Finn stares at him, seething with his magic glowing in his fists.

"Think about it! I've asked you to stay here, protect her until she's strong enough to protect herself. I could never overpower you, and I most definitely could not win a fight against a horde of Assassins."

"You obviously have allies of your own," Luca growls, his focus on Gavin.

Allister shakes his head. "I would never put them in harm's way for empty ambitions. I do not want the throne. I want peace."

Finn glares at Allister still, but a ripple of curiosity cuts through some of the rage brewing inside him. After a few more tense moments, he raises his glowing hand. "Prepare yourself, Messenger. This will hurt a bit." Finn then places his glowing hand over Allister's heart.

Allister gasps, the veins in his neck bulging. Gavin comes to his rescue, but Luca and Ben block his path. "Easy, wolf," Luca says. "He's not hurting him."

Finn isn't, and we all feel it. What he is doing is searching Allister's mind, his soul. All he finds flows through the Bond. We see snippets of Allister as a youth idolizing his brother, and then as a young man trying to understand his brother's penchant for abuse and torture and tyranny. We see him as the man he's been for decades, trying to end the tyranny, free the Fae, make up for his complicity. He doesn't want the throne.

On the contrary, he wants obscurity.

He wants to be left alone.

"Well, then," Finn says, his tone affable. He makes a show of smoothing out the wrinkles in Allister's tunic. "That's that. Would you be so kind as to show us to our rooms?"

Allister takes a shaky step backward, his face pale and confused. "Never do that again."

"I won't need to." Finn gestures to the stairs, his mood shifting swiftly back to his haughty self, as if the last few invasive moments into Allister's mind hadn't happened. "Shall we?"

Chapter 38

Once everyone calms down, and before we're led upstairs, I tell Allister about our red pill discovery, an act of diplomacy, a showing of reciprocal trust. Luca assures him he's brought some for tomorrow. We don't have an infinite stash or anything now, but Luca grabbed quite a few before scaring the hell out of that TikTok Pixie.

And after Allister and Gavin test the pills, with Ben sliding his iron dagger over their forearms, all hard feelings are forgiven. As Allister shows us to our rooms, he carries Ben's dagger, pressing it against his palm with as much wonder as Alexie had when she first took them.

"Make yourselves at home," he tells us, waving to all five doors. His smile is like a child's smile as he touches his skin with the blade. "I can't believe…"

"Aye," Luca says. "'Tis a miracle of science. A shame we killed the one person who could've produced more."

Except it's not. Adrina deserved to die as much as her brother had. The blood of Luca's Order and kin also coated her hands. Others helped her come up with that formula, and maybe someday we'd find them.

But I don't regret for a second that she's dead and gone.

"Miracles happen, don't they?" Allister shakes his head, blinks a few times, and then lifts his gaze to us. "Please, get some rest. We leave at dawn."

When he disappears downstairs again, Gavin gives us a nod. "Thank you, for the pills," he tells me softly.

I smile at his unsmiling face. "It's the least we can do for what you've done for us."

Finn snorts. "Oh, I don't know, love. I think sparing the lives of him and his pack was pretty considerate of us."

Gavin rolls his eyes at Finn before closing himself in a room. The wolf is already learning to ignore Finn's barbarous tongue. I'm impressed. It took me a lot longer.

Finn takes my hand without looking at either Ben or Luca. "I'll be across the hall from our canine friend." He pauses, studying my fingers as if it's the last time he'll see them. "Wherever you decide to sleep..." He doesn't finish his sentence, kisses my cheek, and slips into his chosen room.

Ben, Luca, and I stand in the hallway, all of us staring at Finn's closed door. I want to go in there, and that want travels to them without me having to say the words. No uncomfortable guilt or shame mars my happiness. All my men are here with me, and one day, I'm sure we'll all sleep in the same room, but Finn and I...

I need more time with only him.

And the real chance Finn will have to choose between our Bond and his people is imminent. I won't force a choice on him. I love him too much for that. It'll just tear my heart to let him go.

"No need to make this awkward." From his pack, Luca pulls out my pillowcase, filled with our weapons and a change of clothes for Finn and me. "We didn't come here to infringe on the man's time with you," he says, handing my things over. When I accept the sack, he bends to kiss me slow and long on the lips until my insides tingle with need.

When Luca pulls away, I palm his chest, where my father's name is forever enshrined. "I love you."

"And I you." Luca covers my hand on his chest. "I must tell you... We called the Orders, asked them to prepare. We're daft if

260

we believe we'll not be accelerating the war to come by our actions tomorrow. Allister's wish for a regime change may come sooner than we expected."

He's absolutely right, and I'm so thankful he and Ben did what needed to be done before coming here. We'll be prepared this time. No more surprise attacks in our backyard. "Thank you."

He nods before tipping his chin to Ben. "I'll be taking the room farthest down the hall. I don't want to be sharing a room with you while Nora and Finn…become more acquainted."

Right. Because they'll feel my pleasure, and I highly doubt either of them wants an audience when they have to take care of themselves.

I'll make it up to them.

But damn. I'm instantly wet knowing we're all going to be feeling what Finn can do to me. It's a gift, in my humble opinion.

"'Night, man," Ben says, pulling me to his side. He waits until Luca shuts himself in the room before backing me up against the wall. "Hey, you."

I smile up at him. "Hey."

His eyes glint with green fire as he takes the pillowcase from my hands and sets it next to us on the floor. "I'll let you go in there, be the bigger person like Luca." He leans in, touching his lips to mine. "But I want a taste of you first."

His kiss deepens then as he snaps off the button of my jeans. With the speed only he has, Ben's fingers slip into my panties and circle my clit until I'm panting against his mouth. "Ben…"

I wrap my arms around his shoulders, my mind free of everything but him and his fingers and the sharp pleasure blooming from my pussy.

He dips two fingers inside me, pressing them deep, his thumb now giving my clit luxurious attention.

And before I explode, he pulls his hand from me, steps back, and smiles as he sucks on the fingers he had inside me.

I sag against the wall, wet and aching and swollen. "God…"

He chuckles and gives me a chaste kiss on the forehead. "Most people call me Ben."

261

I laugh then, happy and horny and so fucking grateful my men are all here. "I'll have to remember that."

He shrugs and takes a few steps backward, toward the door next to Finn's. "I'll be on the other side of the wall... enjoying every noise you make, every sensation you feel." He opens the door, and before he closes himself inside the room, he winks at me. "Remember that every time Finn makes you come."

Holy fucking hell.

With shaky hands, I collect my things and enter Finn's room. It's quaint, with a decent-sized bed, hearth, and a dresser.

I plop the pillowcase atop the dresser, our weapons clanking against the fabric and wood, and go to Finn. He peers out the window, his hands behind his back. "So, Ben has given a little something to tide you over?"

I hate how my cheeks burn. "Finn..."

"I liked it, Assassin." He turns to me, his face dark with lust. "I liked it very much."

"Oh..." I tap my bottom lip, trying to find something to say. Relief makes it hard to find the right words. "Good."

"I'm trying to share you without..."

I wrap my arms around his neck, nipping at the sensitive spot behind his ear. "Without what?"

"I don't know, exactly. Bear with me." His breath quickens as I lick a path across his skin.

"I'll do anything you need me to do."

"Except swear to only fuck me?" Humor trickles in his voice as he captures my waist in his hands.

"Except that, yes."

He chuckles, and it's a rich sound that makes goosebumps prickle my skin. "Can't blame a man for trying, now, can you?"

I smile, and then ask, "Can you do what you did to Allister to anyone, see what's inside them?"

Finn presses gentle fingers into my hips. "I can, but never have before. It's invasive, and you can usually tell a person's intent without using it. But for this..."

Always the moral Fae underneath the sardonic shell. "And what Allister said about Alexie, about you being here for her...?"

His smile dwindles some, but he kisses my forehead, whispering against my skin, "It wouldn't be for forever, love. If it were to happen, I'd only be a Window away until I could be with you always."

He's right, but it doesn't make it easier, and it's not something I want to think about, not now. "Let's forget everything for one more night."

"I have no issue with that." His hands move to my breasts, his thumbs flicking over my already taut nipples. "You're so beautiful." His focus gravitates to his thumbs' ministrations. "I *will* hate to share you."

I don't know whether to be concerned or flattered by how much Finn is consumed by me. His possessiveness runs through him like lava.

Now, at this moment, I choose to bask in it. Let it consume me like it does him.

"You don't have to share me now." I dip my hands under his shirt, trace the muscles at the small of his back.

"No, I don't." He smiles then, and it takes my breath away. Then his lips come down on mine. The kiss is slow at first, exploring. With the Bond, it's more intimate, more everything. When he deepens the kiss, becoming more urgent, I moan and press closer to him. Our clothes are in the way. The very air is in the way.

Sensing my need, he strips off his shirt, and I do the same, only breaking our kiss long enough to yank the fabric completely away. Next goes my bra. His pants. Mine. Our underwear. We're grappling at every barrier, tearing them away.

The hearth isn't lit, but I'm on fire.

Finn lifts me, our mouths still melded, and whisks me to the bed. His weight is luscious on top of me. His hands are everywhere, matching the desperation of my touch as I explore and taste and worship every single muscle I can reach. Every single inch of tan skin.

His mouth leaves mine to follow the path of his hands. My neck, my collarbone. My nipples. He stops there and gives each lavish attention, licking, tasting.

"Please, Finn." As he rubs himself against my belly, I grip his hair and arch my back to get closer to his hardness. I don't want slow and cherishing. I want fast and brutally intense. I want our combined sensations to erase tomorrow and the "what-ifs" that come with it.

I want him to fuck me until all I can do is feel without thinking.

He moves lower on my body, nipping at my hip bones, splaying his fingers over my stomach. I squirm under him, trying to get closer. When his mouth finds my clit, I lace my fingers through his hair and pull him nearer. My climax builds and builds as he swirls his magic tongue against my throbbing core. When I come, it's explosive. I scream out his name, beg him to drive inside of me.

He doesn't make me wait long.

His strokes are urgent, without rhythm. He slams into me, going deeper and deeper. His building orgasm fills me with sensation, and it's so fucking intense. It triggers another orgasm of my own to blossom and build.

There it is. The perfect sensation.

"Finn! I... I'm coming. I..."

He whispers Fairy words in a ragged breath, and that ecstasy right before my body's release lasts and lasts and lasts until I swear I'm going to die from pleasure. I scream and buck under him. Claw at his back. It's too much... I can't...

And then my body combusts.

I cry out as waves and waves of undiluted release ripple through me, as it does him. His cock pulsates violently inside me, and that sensation with more broken, beautiful words from Finn sends another crashing orgasm through me.

Fuck...yeah.

As I float back into my body, I notice how I'm sweating and gasping. My bones are water. My muscles are vaporous.

Holy shit.

Holy. *Shit.*

I barely register Finn smoothing damp hair from my face with trembling fingers. When I open my eyes–and I had no idea they were closed until this very second–a mixture of concern and awe lights his gray orbs. "Are you okay?" he asks.

Okay? *Okay?*

What is racing through my veins isn't *okay*.

A thought flashes in my mind of Luca and Ben stroking themselves as they enjoy the pleasure. That makes me throb all over again.

"What was that?" I ask, my voice hoarse and throat scratchy from my screams.

Finn kisses my forehead, his breath not yet even, and whispers, "Magic."

Chapter 39

Drab morning light drowns this world in gray. It's fitting. It matches the dread sinking my stomach.

We stand not ten yards from the mouth of the prison, leaning against a shoe smith's store and hidden by a shielding spell Finn has cast. If we remain still, we're golden.

I'd be too stunned to move, even if we could. We didn't have to infiltrate the castle–where dungeons usually exist. No, Oberon's prison stands in the center of this village like a foreboding iron watchtower. I'm sure it's intentional. A blatant warning to Fae who dare betray their king.

Oberon is a monster in beautiful skin.

Allister converses with two Seelie Guards at the door, smooth-talking them. He's good at convincing people. Good at making them feel as if they need to listen to him. He is the king's brother, after all.

But he needs to hurry it up.

The strain it takes Finn to maintain the spell even saps some of my strength. Ben's and Luca's, too. How did he manage when his blood was iron-touched, before our Bond healed him? Before he had our strength to pull from?

His struggle heightens the desire to end Oberon. That fucker deserves to die for so many reasons. For what he's done to his people, how he's used Assassins.

For trying to murder Finn with a slow, torturous iron death.

For having my mother killed. My fathers.

For everything I've seen in this world, everything he's done to his people and mine...

Anger builds and builds and builds inside me, begging to throw all caution out the window and attack. Attack now. Attack without a plan. Find him. Kill him. Make him pay.

He deserves to die.

I can't let him live.

Fuck.

Calm. Down.

I close my eyes for a moment and concentrate on the shopkeepers' early morning bustle. I take in the scent of baking bread and brewing teas. Listen to the muffled conversations and some distant tinkling of laughter.

The Fae living here seem to have an easier life than others I've witnessed over the past few days. They're nothing like the downtrodden souls in Rutsk. I don't know whether to be relieved for them or angry about Etherias's blatant chasm between social classes. This society is made up solely of the haves and have-nots. No middle exists here.

Finally, Allister convinces the Guards to open the heavy iron door. When the Guards, protected by lirium gloves and armor, unlatch the thick bolt, Allister gives an imperceptible nod in our direction.

"We're on." As soon as the words leave Ben's mouth, Finn's camouflage spell dissipates.

Finn moves quickly into another spell, mumbling words and twitching his fingers in the Guards' direction. They freeze instantly. No one pays any mind to the lirium-plated statues. The Guards simply appear to stand watch.

We pull the hoods of borrowed cloaks farther down on our faces before stalking to the prison. As we pass the Guards, everyone rushes inside.

Except for me.

I take Allister's elbow when he hastens to leave. "Wait."

"We don't have much time, child. Go. Take the first flight of stairs to the left once you're in there. The Trackers are in a cell on the bottom floor at the very end of the hall. Hurry, before the Guard does their rounds."

I nod as he speaks, listening and not really. We've hashed out this plan more than once since last night. As he speaks, I pull two red pills from my front pocket. "Take these for you and Pia." Gavin and Finn have already downed theirs.

Allister accepts them from me, clenching them in his fist. "Thank you."

"Be careful."

"I always am. We will be at the Window waiting for you."

Excitement and anxiety run in tandem up my spine. I'm so fucking ecstatic to have Pia back, and I'm terrified of what she'll admit to me once I confront her. "Okay, ah…" I glance over his shoulder. Still, no one gives us their attention. "Tell your brother I said hello."

"Perhaps next time." He smiles a conspirator's smile. "See you soon." Allister turns on his heel in the castle's direction. He walks with that confident stroll I've known my whole life. It's part of his mask.

Once Allister makes it to the castle gates, I do one last recon of the bustling village. No one screams or points with alarm. No one looks in my direction.

We're ghosts in a crowd.

With a heavy exhalation, I rush into the prison.

The moment the heavy iron door closes us in, I yank my hood down. "How long will the Guards stay immobile?" I ask Finn while Ben and Luca do a quick scan of our immediate surroundings. Finn's magic is shit when surrounded by iron, like nonexistent.

"Difficult to say." Finn rips off his cloak and tosses it near the door. "But we don't have much time before they sound the alarm." He then gestures to Gavin. "Now, wolf, if you please."

"No problem." Gavin strips down without hesitation, leaving his clothes next to Finn's cloak. In seconds, he's shifted into his wolf. He fills the narrow hall in his animal form, and for the hundredth time, I'm thankful this Fae is on our side. If he catches scent of a Guard, he'll take them out. Fancy armor won't have a prayer against the steel trap of Gavin's jaw.

"Keep your eyes open," Luca says as he and Ben shed their cloaks. "We won't be alone for long."

"We'll be ready for them." Ben grins at me. "Lead the way, gorgeous."

"Down here." I point left toward an iron-walled stairwell. "Single file, fellas. No need to get stuck while saving the humans."

Gavin takes off ahead, his paws quiet on the iron-laced floor.

All this fucking iron, man. I'd love to strip every Guard of their lirium protection so they could feel what these captives feel. Feel what Finn felt for five years. Feel what almost killed him.

Thank the gods for those pills. Finn may not be able to use his magic in here, but at least the iron won't hurt him. It won't burn Gavin's paws, either.

Once we reach the landing on the bottom floor, with only torchlight illuminating the space, the cells aren't very distinct. But we don't need to see what's behind every thick door to inhale unclean bodies. It permeates the air, sticking to our clothes and skin. Soft moans come from a few of the cells. Wailing cries bleed through the small windows of others. Fae who wronged the king, many for minor infractions, are rotting away in their own filth while having their skin burned by the iron surrounding them.

Anger boils inside me. I want to save them all. It kills me that we can't.

Finn slips his hand in mine as the four of us follow Gavin. His anger matches my own. Same with Ben and Luca. Yet, more than anger runs through Finn. Misery coats him from an acute flash of memory. I can see it through our Bond, him lying on the iron floor, hungry, thirsty, feeling the burn of the metal kill him inch by slow inch. His desire for death saturates his memory.

I squeeze his hand, let my love for him flow through the Bond.

As we get to the end of the hall, the two scribes Allister warned us about are sitting at small, wooden desks outside the last cell. They're frail, old Seelie, who have a quill in hand and heads bent to parchment for any information the Trackers might scream from their cell. Gavin takes care of one and Luca the other before the men lift their heads to see what's happening.

The sounds of their death ricochet in the hall, triggering the prisoners' wails and pleas to double in sound and urgency. My stomach churns. I want to leave this place and never come back. And I hate myself for feeling it. None of these Fae will be coming with us, only four humans.

"This is wrong," Luca growls, cleaning his bloody dirk on the robes of the Fae he just killed. "Why would they leave this place so unguarded? Leave these old men down here alone?"

"What can these prisoners do but wallow in their own feces and despair?" Brittle anger coats Finn's voice. "This is where you go to die a slow, hungry, burning death. Not even the King's Guard want to see that."

"They starve the Trackers?" Ben's furtive gaze darts from cell to cell, his eyes dimming with sadness every time a Fae pleads for death.

"I suppose we'll find out soon enough." Finn's hand trembles over mine. "No being should be subjected to this."

"You're goddamn right." Ben knocks on the Trackers' door, softly at first. When no sound emits from behind, his knocks become more urgent. "Is there anyone in there?" he whispers through the barred window. He peers inside, squinting against the dark, reeling against the foul stench, the only thing greeting his voice.

"Let's get the fucker open and be done with this," Luca says.

"Right, yeah." I bend to the dead scribes, search their robes for the key. My shoulders slump when all I find is a sealed pot of ink and a crust of bread. "Nothing."

"Let's do it the hard way, then." Luca grasps the handle. He yanks until the corded muscles in his neck strain. The door barely creaks.

He's the strongest of us, and his strength barely made the rusted iron door groan.

But a locked door has never stopped us before. I glance at Ben and Finn. "One more on the handle and two pulling the bars on the window." I then tip my chin to Gavin and hope his wolf understands me. "Keep watch. You see anyone, rip out their throats."

The wolf huffs from his nostrils and moves to the middle of the hall, his back haunches tense and the hair along his spine standing at attention.

"Okay, on three, y'all." I take the spot by Luca as Finn and Ben grip the iron bars.

We pull and tug, and with every centimeter of movement, the door squeals in loud protest. It echoes through the hall, rousing the prisoners even more, making them scream and beg and demand to be let free.

Their pleas are razors scraping the inside of my skull. I keep pulling, keep trying to free these humans who have made us miserable while Fae after Fae beg for our help.

It's not fair.

It's never fucking fair.

A deep growl erupts from Gavin as the door gives. With a loud yell, Luca tosses the offending thing to the side as the rest of us rush in. I shoot Gavin a quick glance to find him fending off two Guards, both lirium-protected. Both wielding those poisonous swords.

"Ben!" I tug on his arm. "Help Gavin."

He peers behind me, and with a quick nod, leaves us to dodge the same kind of weapon that took out my father.

I can't think about that now, even if my brain demands it.

Forcing my gaze from the fray, I fumble in the dark with Luca and Finn until we stumble against metal bed frames. We don't wait for the beings who occupy them to give us permission.

Finn and I each lift a skeletal body. Luca takes two, one over each shoulder.

To the fighting and grunting in the hall, we tote our cargo into the dim light of the corridor. I gasp when I see who Finn carries. An older man, wizened and small and unmoving.

The woman I carry fares no better. She's all bones and loose skin. The fetid smell of their unwashed bodies is the strongest thing about them. My eyes water with every inhalation until I force myself to breathe through my mouth. That's worse. I can almost taste it, and it makes me gag a few times.

Luca holds the young girl and another man in no better shape than the one Finn carries.

Saving them, forcing them to live, seems worse than leaving them in their cell. But we can't stay in this hall and debate what would be best for these frail humans.

The Guard knows we're here, and they won't stop at the two fighting Ben and Gavin.

"This is not mercy, Nora," Luca says, reading my thoughts. He gently places his cargo on the ground. "'Tis cruel to all but the girl to let them live."

He doesn't wait for my answer and rushes in to help Ben. Before he makes it to them, Gavin has the throat ripped from one, and Ben has the other in a grip that snaps his neck, the sound a dull *thunk* in the narrow corridor.

It gets the Fae trapped in cells screaming their pleas with more fervor. Their hope and desperation and fear bleed from the barred windows, and I have to refrain from clapping my hands over my ears. Hearing them makes me falter. Hearing them makes me rethink the objective of our entire mission.

Fuck.

Ben rushes to us, takes one look at the four, and frowns at Finn. "We'll never make it to the Window with them." Pity coats his voice. Pity and the urgent desire to get the hell out of here.

Finn shakes his head. "Once we've left the prison, my magic will work. No unnecessary killing."

"They're already half dead, mate," Luca growls above the din of pleading Fae. "Killing them would be a mercy."

Finn opens his mouth to speak.

But then the girl struggles to her feet. She's waif-thin, hollow-cheeked, dressed only in a decaying gown, and the way she lifts her chin, she reminds me of our warrior Pixie. "I've known you my whole life, Nora Waters, and I've helped protect you, even at the risk of Oberon torturing me and what is left of my family. Please. Do not kill them. Let them die peacefully in your world, where we belong. They deserve it."

Finn looks at me, challenge in his gray eyes. He's daring me to deny this slip of a girl with dark, matted hair and filth smudged across her face and exposed skin.

Goddamn it all.

"We're taking them with us." I nod toward the stairwell. "We gotta go. Now."

Gavin takes off as soon as the words leave my mouth. Ben grabs the old man, and Luca lifts the frail girl once more, this time cradling her in his arms.

"We'll not be able to fight," Luca says as we rush to the stairs. "Not with our cargo."

We don't have to worry about it.

Gavin is savage as he pounces on four Guards coming down the stairs. They don't have time to lift their poisonous swords, or maybe fear prevents them. Gavin snarls and gnashes his teeth. He's viciously graceful, ripping into them with lightning speed and herculean strength. None of them have a chance.

They're dead quickly and gruesomely.

Gavin's coat is covered in their blood, his snout drenched in guts, as he rushes the stairs, making sure our path is clear. On the main floor, four more Guards await us.

Gavin doesn't make them wait long.

He makes quick work of three, while Luca flings his iron dirk into the exposed neck of the fourth. The skin around the blade sizzles and pops as the Guard gurgles his last breath.

Once we reach the exit, which is still shut against the world, Gavin shifts. He uses his cloak to wipe the blood from his body before donning his clothes with enviable speed.

I huff out a calming breath, and then another. "Time to go home." I then nod to Gavin. "Mind carrying Finn's load? He'll take it from here."

Gavin curls his lip at the old woman slung over Finn's shoulder. "I won't get her smell from my nose for weeks."

Says the guy who still has Guard-insides smeared on his face.

He takes her with surprising gentleness, anyway.

"Thank you," I tell him. "For everything."

He shrugs like it's no big deal that he saved all our asses. "I'm only doing my part, Changeling."

"Right." I hike my delicate load higher on my shoulder and give Finn a concerned frown. "You gonna be okay using so much magic?"

He grins and bends to kiss my lips, ignoring the fact I'm carrying a smelly human. "You healed me." He kisses me lightly once more. "Though I wouldn't refuse another round of healing once we're home."

I grin despite the situation. "Deal."

He winks before tipping his chin to the door while cracking his knuckles. "Prepare yourselves. This will be messy." Hesitating only a moment, Finn grasps the iron handle and heaves open the door.

A sea of lirium-protected Guards awaits us. When they see who has infiltrated their prison, their helmets can't hide how wide their eyes grow with shock.

And then fear when Finn smiles at them.

Foolish Guards. They gave him space to leave the confines of the iron structure, and their shock gives Finn the tiny window to step away from the offending metal to wreak havoc. He lifts his arms in a flourish, his mouth moving in whispered words.

The Guards scatter as if they were shot from a cannon.

We don't let the shock of his abilities paralyze us and run. Finn leads the way, knowing exactly where to go. We run through the cobblestone streets, dodging stunned townsfolk and tipping our chin to the Fae whose faces shine with hope and pride as they voluntarily move from our path.

We race by the towering stone wall surrounding the castle, reaching a gate in moments. Twenty Guards await us. They don't make the same mistakes as those who surrounded the prison. Shock doesn't stop them from attacking, and they don't attack with poisonous swords. They shoot poison-tipped arrows at us.

It's still not enough to stop Finn.

He swipes them from the air as if wiping dew off a windowpane. Arrows fall to the ground, useless. Finn then focuses on the archers, says his beautifully deadly words, and balls his fists. They fall to the ground, ripping their helmets off and clutching their heads in agony.

Finn doesn't kill a soul.

I wouldn't have his restraint.

Once we rush the gate, Finn leads us toward a cluster of stone buildings. He stumbles some and sweat saturates his hair. His face is the color of freshly fallen snow.

We don't have much more time.

People scatter out of our way as they had in the village. Some don't appear as relieved to see us, mainly Fae who wear rich clothes and aren't covered in a morning's worth of work and sweat.

"Here!" Finn points to a place near the buildings. The dead and yellowing grass surrounding the area is the only tell. But it's enough.

We've found the Window.

Guards, of course, surround us like sharks with blood in the water. I give Ben, Luca, and Gavin a knowing glance. We need to ditch our cargo and help Finn.

As Finn swats each attacking Guardsman away, the four of us set our humans against a smokehouse beside the Window.

"Avoid their weapons," I remind everyone. "Just shove them the fuck out of the way." Which is pretty much all we can do because of their armor.

Gavin rips his clothes off and shifts quickly–and then we surround Finn as a unit, shoving, throwing, avoiding poisonous weapons. Gavin is the only one who can kill, his snout narrow enough to find vulnerable, exposed necks. Finn may not kill, but

Gavin has no heightened moral code. Kill those who try to kill us. Period.

We protect Finn's back as he focuses on the Window. I try not to think about his weakened state, try to remember I healed him and all he'll need is some rest to recover from this. But his fatigue and pain rush through me, rushes through all of us. Our strength seeping into him is the only thing keeping him on his feet.

Finn's magic pours from his mouth, as he chants and chants, his voice getting louder with every second the Window stays closed. Alexie's magic is strong, and he's struggling to override it with his own.

"Hurry, Finn. Please fucking hurry." I push and fight and heave gasping breaths as they keep coming.

"Nora!" a small voice screams.

A familiar voice.

A voice I haven't heard in over two months.

Pia.

I turn my attention toward the castle, find Allister and Pia running for us. My fear for her safety gives me a surge of adrenaline. It's enough to clear a path between the Guards for my friend and Allister to fit through unscathed.

There's no time for a reunion. No time for hugs and questions and tears.

We fight. We fight as Allister and Pia rush toward the Trackers, helping to lift them, to prepare them to jump through the Window.

It's chaos. It's blood and dirt and screams. Poisonous weapons and tired opponents.

We're winning. We have the edge.

"Now!" Finn yells.

That's all he needs to say.

Ben, Luca, and I collect the Trackers. Gavin protects Allister and Pia.

All of us dive through the Window.

Chapter 40

Finn doesn't waste time once we've safely crossed and secures the Window. He chants and lifts his hands, the veins in his arms and neck straining. No Guards come through. None seemingly want to get trapped here.

Thankfully, fear works both ways.

As soon as the Window is locked, Finn slumps to the snow-covered boulder beside it, his chest heaving with each labored breath he takes.

I set my burden on a fallen trunk, make sure he's stable, and go to Finn. Sitting next to him, I press my palm tightly against his upper back, massage his tense muscles. He rests a hand on my thigh, needing the contact. Luca and Ben, still holding their cargo, come to my side. It's an unspoken desire we all understand. We need each other. Our Bond demands it.

No one speaks. Gavin is still in his wolf form, sniffing the foreign soil, pacing as if he's in a cage. The Trackers look around them in amazement and fear. This is the world they see in their thoughts. This is the world that has only been an idea until now. And their reality is met with the bitter cold of winter.

I glance at where Pia stands with Allister. She watches me, her face pale, her fingers twisting in knots in front of her. She's wearing rich clothing, a gown made of deep purple silk and gold thread. So many things I want to say, so many things I need to ask, but right now, I just want her in my arms.

I smile at her and hold out a hand.

She runs to me with a sob and wraps her tiny body around mine. I hug her like a child, like an eighty-six-year-old infant. Ben rubs her shoulder and whispers soothing words.

I take a moment to absorb the quiet. Winter blankets the forest. It muffles sound and folds us in. Snow falls in a lazy drizzle and the early evening light is already surrendering to the dark.

Home.

It's only been a week since I left it, and it feels like a thousand years.

"Holy shit! Nora!" Seamus is barely in eyesight, but not even snow can silence the way he tramples through the woods or cusses with his usual fervor. Jessie follows him, her face not as tense, not as panicked.

The sight of them releases something inside me. Our cherubic giant and hardcore Assassin. *They* are home.

And when Helene flies above them, Callum trailing behind them, I let go of a sob.

Ben takes Pia from my arms with a soft smile. "Go. The kid's been a fucking mess since he got back from New York."

"He was tied in knots there, as well," Luca says. "You'd think the lad lost an arm."

I nod, because words can't leap over the emotion in my throat, and then take off.

The snow is deep and cumbersome, angering me. It makes me slow when I need to be fast. When I finally reach my surly Haunt, he wraps me up in his arms and rests his head on my shoulder like a child.

I feel like he's mine.

Because he is.

He's family.

"Hey, kid," I whisper, running my fingers through his tangled blond curls. "Missed you, too."

"Next time, I'm fucking coming with you."

280

I smile, even as tears blur my vision. "You got it." I then focus on Jessie, Helene, and Callum. All of them give me relieved smiles. "It's good to be home."

Everyone surrounds us then. Gavin's wolf and the human Trackers in the arms of Ben, Luca, and Allister. Only the girl stands on her own. Pia is tucked under Finn's arm as he uses her as a crutch. His face is still so pale, but thankfully only exhaustion saps his strength now.

Shocked expressions are exchanged. Hesitant smiles.

Introductions and explanations will wait until we're safe and warm in the cabin. Strategy for our next moves will be on the agenda, too.

Because this isn't over.

All those Fae I saw, all their misery and hunger and pain. Regina's, Gavin's pack, the child begging for food, those desperate prisoners. I thought I could leave doing nothing to help them.

I can't.

I won't.

I promised to kill Oberon, Kellen, and Talia after my father died.

And I will.

Soon.

∞ ∞ ∞

Home is…home. It's familiar and comfort and safety. Being here, surrounded by warmth and quiet, makes it hard to feed the fire of retribution after what we've been through. We have the power to stop fighting now, to keep the Windows locked, especially with both Finn and Alexie at their strongest.

But even if we wanted to wipe our hands clean of Oberon, forget him and the world he exists in, there are Windows we don't control. Windows he'll always have access to.

We can't forget him.

He'll never allow us to.

281

And we'd never allow ourselves to forget the desperate Fae in need of saving.

Allister is right. Oberon will repay us for taking his Trackers, his eyes into this world. And he'll still torture Regina, Gavin and his pack, that hungry child, and those desolate Fae prisoners. He'll have them and so many more like them to torture and starve and kill.

Oberon's reign must end.

I've already contacted our allies, asked them to send everyone they could to our woods. We will fight. There's no question about it. We're already preparing.

Jessie has agreed to see Gavin to Ontario's Window tomorrow. Finn will open it as soon as Jessie calls. Gavin said his pack will be ready to fight with us. We've set a date, a week from tomorrow.

Now, we need some rest. Tomorrow is the true start of the end. Tomorrow is soon enough.

The Trackers are in my and Ben's room. We've brought in an extra bed and some cots. Callum has taken over their care with a little help from Malcolm, who has EMT training and a huge slice of empathy for the weak and dying humans.

Alexie and Helene stay in Ben's old room. Pia has asked to stay in Topher's room, and I agreed. It seems fitting. I haven't spoken to Pia yet, not privately. It's a conversation I'm not excited to have.

Everyone else has found their own spot. No need for me to play hostess. They can sleep wherever they can find a place to rest their heads. Except in the largest bedroom in the house.

My men and I have claimed it. I don't want to be without them, even while sleeping.

Luca and Ben shoved the double beds together, and it's large enough for the four of us. Finn already sleeps in the middle. It's been a few hours, and he hasn't made a sound.

The rest of us sit on a bunk bed mattress that Ben dragged to the floor and shoved against the wall. If we survive what's coming, it'd probably be prudent to buy a couch–because this is our new room. All of us.

"We have the resources to take out the king, relieve him of his throne. I'm confident of it. But…" Luca doesn't need to finish. We know what he's saying.

Alexie.

She's a child.

She isn't ready.

And yet, she is a powerful child.

And we would make her ready, help her until she is.

I sigh out my resignation. Allister is right about something else. Alexie is the only one worthy of the throne, the only one who will be strong enough to keep it once she's ready. And until she's ready, she'll need Finn at her side. "We all know the answer to this problem." My voice is calm, even as my heightening blood pressure pulses against my temples. "Alexie was made to rule. She could do it."

Ben stiffens, his hand going still on my thigh. I hold my breath until he says, "It's not our decision."

Luca's quiet. No matter. Ben is the one to convince, not him.

I lean against Ben then, covering his hand on my thigh with mine. "What would you say if she were willing?"

"She's eight, Nora Jean. She doesn't understand."

"Yes, she's only eight, but she understands. And she's not a child. She hasn't been since the day Oberon had her mother killed. She also understands this has been her path all along. It *is* her choice, but we wouldn't leave her to the wolves. We'd make sure she'd be protected."

"Protected by Finn." Ben's gaze drifts to the bed, his expression full of regret.

I close my eyes against the burn of tears. "Yes."

"And by us," Luca says. "The Window would be at our disposal. We'd not truly be separated, Nora."

No, we wouldn't be. But Finn wouldn't be at my side every night. There would be a space between us.

Ben remains quiet. So damn quiet the loudness of it scrapes at my skin. Finally, he rests his cheek on the top of my head. "If she agrees to it, and if Finn agrees…okay. I'm with you."

Weight remains on my shoulders, even with his approval. I can already feel Finn's absence. "Thank you, Ben."

He kisses my head again. "Don't thank me yet. She still has to agree."

"She will," I say with an exhausted sigh. She has to.

A soft knock echoes against the door, and for the life of me, I don't want to deal with whoever is on the other side.

But a Leader can't ignore duty. My father never did.

"I got it." I tear myself away from Ben and Luca to crack open the door.

And the weight sits heavier on my shoulders, getting good and comfortable.

"Hey, Nora." Pia's face is all pale anxiety. She wrings her hands in front of her, her chocolate eyes peering into mine. She no longer wears that ridiculous gown. One of Topher's sweatshirts drowns her small body, and the sight makes pieces of my heart splinter. "Can we talk?"

I don't want to talk. Don't want to ask her the questions and listen to her answers. I don't want to hear her tell me how she's been lying to me since the day we met. But I need to hear it. Hear it all and decide how much further this friendship is going to go. She's here because she loved my father. She's here because she tried to save him.

She's here because our friendship, real or not, gave her leverage.

I glance over my shoulder at Ben and Luca. Both give subtle nods, sending comforting murmurs of emotion through the Bond.

Fine.

I don't say a word to Pia as I pull on a coat, socks, and boots. I still don't say a word to her when I hand her Ben's coat. I leave my new room and expect her to follow.

When we reach the kitchen door, I push the iron shield away and step out onto the porch. Pia is right behind me. I stand at the steps, look over the snow-covered yard, and wait for her to begin.

"I want to explain," she says quietly. "I want to… tell you…"

I try to relax my jaw before finally turning to give her my attention. "You used me. You've used me the entire time we've known each other."

She steps forward, her eyes wide. "No! No." Her gaze darts to her feet. "Well, yes… in the beginning. But, Nora"–she gives me her liquid eyes, full of unshed tears and regret–"things changed. I never wanted to hurt you, though, even in the beginning. I only wanted your protection."

"From Oberon?" I ask like it isn't obvious.

She nods.

"And you've known who I was, who my people are?"

Again, she nods as tears slip to her cheeks. "Allister always said yours was one of the most honorable Orders."

I ignore her statement and push on. "What changed, Pia? Tell me."

A smile lifts the corners of her mouth even as tears flow from her eyes. "Well, I love you, silly. You grew on me with your surly temper and kindness." She lifts her hand as if to touch me, but then lowers it. "You're my favorite person in the world."

My heart lurches. Pia's so genuine, so *her*. She's my friend who has tucked me into bed during drunken rants, made me laugh, kept me sane when I forced a separation between myself and my family. She's been there for me without ever asking for anything in return.

No, that's not true. My protection was payment for her friendship.

Gods, that hurts.

I stuff my hands in my coat pockets, try not to tug on the distressed fabric there. "You love me? Like you loved Oberon? So, what was I? Witness protection from an ex-lover? From a fucking mad king?"

Confusion ripples over her expression. "Lover…? What?" She shakes her head until understanding widens her eyes. "Oh, wow, no. That's not… You have it all wrong."

"Enlighten me, then."

"Jesus…" Her shoulders sag in defeat. "Everything I told you about how I left Etherias as a child is true."

285

I don't respond to that.

And so she continues. "He's my father, Nora. The asshole's my father, and he killed my mother. She was one of many unwilling Fae he kept in a morbid harem, another Pixie he abused and raped and tossed away into the streets. She died because she refused to give me to him when he deemed me old enough to live in the palace. He summoned her, demanded she tell him of my whereabouts. I'm alive because she gave her life for mine. My gran… She whisked me away as soon as word got to us."

My mouth hangs open in shock. *I… What the hell?* "So… Allister is your uncle."

She gives a watery, sad smile. "He has always been kind to me, helped me hide here. Oberon has been looking for me since I was a girl. Who knows why he wanted me, but I can tell you it wasn't because he loved me." She pauses, her gaze drifting toward the snowy yard.

"What…um…what happened to you while you were there?"

A single tear travels down her left cheek. "He made me pay for hiding from him." She stares down at her feet. "I… I don't want to talk about it, not yet. I'm just happy I'm here"–she lifts her gaze to mine–"with you."

"I'm so sorry, Pia," I whisper.

She wipes tears from her cheeks with a shaky hand. "And I loved Topher. I can't believe…" Pia breaks then, her tiny shoulders hunched, her hands now cupping her face as she sobs. "I still feel him in his room. I still… He was…"

Her pain activates mine, and I can't take it anymore. I pull her quaking body into my arms, and for the first time since he died, we mourn Topher together.

Chapter 41

Six days. Only six short days until we storm the castle. It's some medieval shit. The kind of scenario I never envisioned for my Order.

But here we are, with so many others from Orders we're now allied with. The cabin is already getting crowded with Assassins after the calls I made yesterday. The outbuildings are filling up. Some of the more daring ones even pitch tents in the snowy yard. We have an army, a strong one. An army willing to end the tyranny of a deranged king. And to our massive advantage, Oberon no longer has his Trackers to see us coming.

After supper, my core group finds solace in my shared room. Alexie sits at the edge of the bed, Ben on one side of her, Helene on the other. Finn squats down in front of her, Allister at his back. The Messenger peers at Alexie as if she's a god. He has since yesterday. He idolizes her, an eight-year-old child. A child who is compassionate and strong and gently fierce. A child who could take out every single person in this room if she chose to.

Finn has been working with her all day, picking up lessons from where they left off before we went to Etherias. She's honing her spells, testing her strength. She's strong, as we all know, and when she's able to focus her strength, she's formidable.

And now we're going to ask her to take on the burden of a kingdom.

We've warned Helene. Let her know our intent. With the promise of Finn at Alexie's side, she relented. She insisted on being at Alexie's side, too.

Fair enough and wholly expected.

I stand by the door with Seamus and Luca, Pia wrapped in my arms, feeling my heart tear inside my chest. I know I'm not losing Finn, but...

I *am* losing him, at least for a little while.

"Well then, little queen," Finn says, taking her tiny hands in his. "We must ask you a favor."

Alexie tilts her head, her silver hair a bright curtain. "What kind of favor, my lord cousin?"

Finn smiles at her, his love shining so vividly on his face it brings tears to my eyes. He tells her of the wrongs Oberon has done, of what we saw. He asks her to remember her own experience in Etherias, to remember the desolation of the people there. He tells her she's worthy. He tells her he'll not leave her side. And he asks her, "Are you ready, my queen?"

Ben purses his lips, emotion flooding through him. He loves this little girl who almost killed him. He loves her as if she were his.

Alexie shifts her attention to him, her cherubic face scrunched in uncertainty. "Do you think I could do it, Ben?"

I press a hand to my heart, my own tears spilling as Ben's green eyes fill. "Oh, yeah, little witch," he says, his voice gravelly, "you got this. And I'll be here if you need me."

Alexie nods, her gaze then shifting to everyone in the room, stopping on Allister, the only one she doesn't know. "Who are you?"

Allister kneels at her feet as if she commanded it. He's no longer the apathetic Fae, and it's still jarring. He bows his head. "I am forever your servant, my queen." He then tells her who he is and how he'll help her navigate parliament and the mess she'll surely be stepping into. He pledges his fealty to her as he swore he would while in his cottage.

It's humbling to watch.

When Allister finishes, Alexie lifts her tiny chin and says to Finn, "I will serve my people, and I will help save them." She cups Finn's cheek in that childlike way that shows absolute trust. "Show me how."

Yes, she's only eight, but I was right. She's no child.

She's truly a queen, one who will mend her world and ours.

As she and Finn speak quietly, with Helene and Ben looking on like proud parents, I give Pia one last hug before letting her go. I then place a soft kiss on Luca's mouth.

When I pull back, he says, "Go on, lass. Take some time. We'll be here when you come back."

I cover the hand he has on my cheek for a moment. Thank the gods for our Bond, for his ability to know what I need. "I won't be long."

Luca then opens the door for me.

I'm out of there before anyone gets the chance to question me.

Downstairs, the house is loud and full and bloated with the tension of what's coming. I wave at some Assassins, nod to others. Try not to step on any sleeping bodies as I make my way to the kitchen door. The shields are down, as they have been since everyone has arrived, and I'm thankful that my escape is quick. I slip on boots and a coat and rush outside.

I start for Topher's woodshed and change my mind. Ontario's Order, as well as some of another Order are camped in there. Four or five people are crowded in the small space. I don't envy them.

With a sigh, I head into the woods. I don't need light to guide me. These woods are ingrained in my DNA. They're my haven and my oxygen.

The moon is effervescent, and the air is crisp and clean. With every deep breath, anxiety gets washed away. We can do this. We have the numbers and the magic.

We *will* do this.

I walk until I reach the Window. Snow covers the ground, and it's frozen over. It's made clearing the trees surrounding the area difficult. We've worked today, many of us cutting and hauling away timber. There's a bit more to clear, something we'll be tackling tomorrow. The naked spot in the middle of my beloved forest causes a twinge of sadness. So much beauty destroyed.

I shake my head.

Stop.

It will grow again. Sometimes it takes tragedy to make life beautiful.

We've all learned that the lesson.

"What's brought you out here, love?"

I latch on to Finn's voice. It's quiet and calm, as quiet and calm as the winter woods.

I turn to him, take the few steps until I'm in his arms. He hugs me close, planting tiny kisses on the crown of my head. Despite his question, he understands what has brought me here. He can feel it as sharply as I can. Our fight to Bond has been the hardest, the most intense. "I don't know how I'm supposed to be here without you."

Finn smooths my hair down the length of my back. "You'll never be without me."

I can only nod and cling to his coat, gripping the fabric in my hands as if that alone is enough to change the inevitable.

We let the cold and muffled quiet envelop us, hide us. His chest is warm, and the steady rhythm of his heart against my cheek helps me focus. Helps center my thoughts on the here and now, not on what happens in the future.

"I need to be with you, Finn," I finally whisper into the darkness. "Before we leave… I need you." One last time.

I already miss him.

"Then let us not waste this moment," he whispers. His hands explore my back, ride my spine through my shirt and coat. Finn then captures my lips with his. He's not gentle. He's persistent. Starving.

And so am I.

Teeth and tongues clash together, our hands desperate for skin and heat as we both roam and lift coats and shirts.

I need this. *Need* it.

Finn whispers in Fairy, and the button closing my jeans pops off. His fingers find the hem of my panties, sliding past it. He groans into my mouth when his touch finds my wet folds, his index finger circling my clit. Again, he whispers his words, and the air around us warms, even as we stand on the packed snow.

My breath hitches as pleasure erases anxiety, washing it away like a wave eating sand. He knows how to touch me, knows where I need him to touch me. I scream into his mouth as I come around his fingers, my hips moving, riding the ecstasy of his touch.

He doesn't give me a chance to come down from my climax. He lifts me, my legs wrapping around his waist as he carries me to the boulder by the Window. Without letting me touch the cold stone, Finn holds me up with a hand firmly on my ass, bracing us both with one hand planted on the boulder. His mouth again moves in whispers, making the stone's face warm and as soft as our bed. As he sets me down on the surface, I get busy yanking his pants down, freeing his cock. Even with Finn's spell, our breath puffs out in vapor any time we come up for air.

Finn drags off my pants, letting out a frustrated sound when they get caught around my boots. He strips each one off with hard tugs before finally ridding me of my jeans. It's awkward and ungraceful, and I don't care. We're ravenous, eager. Both wanting to feel. Wanting to embrace what we're fighting for.

We're fighting for us.

We're fighting for family.

We're fighting because we're so tired of fighting all the time.

In one swift motion, Finn slams into me. His hand is on my ass, bringing me closer, and I rock my hips in rhythm with his. My eyes flutter as I feel his orgasm building, the intensity of it hitting all my nerve-endings. I moan and pull at his coat, hating the barriers against his skin.

"Finn," I whisper into his mouth, my hands frantically searching for hems. "Our clothes…"

Finn leaves me to pull his clothes away, his tan skin glowing in the moonlight. I admire him, his erection throbbing and all mine. He comes back to me, stripping me of my own barriers.

The rock is warm, and so is Finn's body as he presses against me. As his lips find mine, he plunges into me again, pumping, searching, building his orgasm that triggers mine.

I grip his shoulders, my fingertips pressing into his warm skin. "Finn, I'm... *Please...*"

I don't know what I want to ask for. I don't know. I just want... more. More of Finn. More of this feeling.

As I plead with incoherent, broken words, Finn gains his rhythm. He's not gentle, and I don't want him to be. With each stroke, each whispered, "I love you," in my ear, I climb higher and higher. I cling to him, meet every thrust, my back arched and hips circling. When he comes, I explode with him, my scream echoing off the trees. He breathes out a moan against my lips.

My body feels like liquid, my eyes drooping with the afterglow.

But Finn isn't done.

He doesn't curl next to me or help me up. No, he slips out of me and kneels on the ground between my legs. His hot tongue and soft lips capture my sensitive clit. I jerk at the touch, my hands lacing through his hair. I don't think I can take any more sensation.

Until my clit throbs and swells again with need.

The heat from his tongue and the cold from a gust of wind are a heady combination. I arch closer to his mouth, pull on his hair. Repeat his name over and over as waves and waves of pure ecstasy wash over me. "Finn... Finn..."

And when my body explodes, my world comes back into balance.

Finn kisses a soft trail along my inner thighs, my stomach. He captures my nipple, suckling a moment before helping me up to dress and then dressing himself. After he slips on his coat, he takes my face between his hands and kisses me possessively. I taste us both on his mouth. When he breaks our kiss to take my hand, he leads us out of the woods with a soft smile on his lips and no words whispered.

We don't need them.

Not tonight.

Chapter 42

Time doesn't slow down for anyone. On the morning of *the* day, I'm acutely aware of that.

We left the warmth of the cabin not fifteen minutes ago, trusting Malcolm and the iron shields to keep Pia and the Trackers safe.

Now, the wind screams at us, and snow pelts our faces. Fifty of us wait in the woods in the early morning light by the Window. Fifty of us dressed in clothes for Etherias's spring. Fifty of us armed and ready and willing to accept what's waiting on the other side.

Ben, Luca, and I stand behind Finn, who has yet to open the Window. Alexie stands in front of us, wearing lirium armor. Callum wears the other suit. Allister stands close, his face serious, concerned.

We all shiver and brace ourselves against the cold. Soon, the cold won't be our problem. Our problem will be what waits for us on the other side of the Window.

Jessie moves up behind me, her face a mask of boredom, a mask she wears well. But she can't fool me now. Excitement runs through her. We've chosen to use her expertise. She's strapped to the teeth with explosives. Fancy, sophisticated ones that will give us the advantage when we need it.

Fuck the rules of war. Oberon doesn't deserve that respect.

"Look behind you, Nora," Jessie says softly. "Look at how our people have come together."

I do as she says. For the first time, I give myself a few moments to really absorb what I'm seeing. Seamus and Callum stand behind me as Helene flutters above them. The Ontario Order stands beside them, ready and prepared. The Pacific Northwest Order is behind them, Madera and her Bonded, all regal and fierce. So many others have joined us, including my father's old Order. Each Assassin is stronger than ten Fae. Each Assassin possesses a lifetime of training.

We can do this.

I give Jessie my attention again, the pride in my chest mingling with the responsibility of so many inevitable deaths. Yet, we're on the right side of history for once. We're fighting for the Fae. We're fighting for ourselves.

Luca slips his large hand over mine, and his warmth sends another jolt of confidence through me. We spent last night together, and I spent the night before with Ben. One more moment with each of them. One more memory to stow away if anything should happen to one of us.

"We've passion on our side," Luca says to Jessie and me. "I'm proud this day. Honored to fight at the side of my new clan."

My heart swells, and I don't miss how Jessie's eyes mist over at Luca's words. She gives him a genuine smile. "Glad to be part of it, gorgeous."

He winks at her and squeezes my hand once more before releasing it. I glance over at Ben, who has his hands on Alexie's shoulders. He gives the look he reserves only for me, and mouths, *I love you.*

I press a hand to my heart and send love gushing through our Bond. I send it to all my men and feel theirs warming me in return. We have so much to fight for.

Finn turns to address all of us. Before he speaks, he smiles at me, and then gives that heart-stopping smile to Alexie. "Stay by my side, little queen. I will secure the Window while you kill the magic on their weapons. Those are our first tasks."

We've been through the plan a thousand times, but I have no issue with Finn repeating it to her.

Alexie stands straighter, moving from Ben's protective touch. "I will not fail, cousin."

Pride for her gleams on his face. "I know you won't... Your Highness." Finn then lifts his gaze to everyone. He tugs on his fitted thermal and then pulls his hands behind his back. "They are waiting for us directly on the other side of this Window," he starts, yelling over the howling wind. "Talia has tried valiantly to break my magic, but the poor girl has failed. She will be exhausted, unable to protect the king. This will be an advantage we must take."

Seamus steps beside Jessie, and my heart swells to bursting. My grumpy, foul-mouthed, ridiculously brave Haunt. "You think the fucker's gonna be in the field?"

Finn's lips twitch at Seamus's colorful words. "Highly doubtful. Our Order will storm the castle, so to speak, like we planned."

Seamus nods, gripping his ax with both hands.

I love how he understands he's part of our Order. Part of our family.

Allister clears his throat, and even that sound is melodious. "Infiltrating the castle will be tricky." He lifts a finger as if someone interrupted with a question. Not one of us did. "But I can get us in with minimal risk. It will be a sight to behold, watching Oberon's reign end."

Finn arches a brow, his smile still pleasant. Deadly. "It will, indeed." He then faces the Window. "Now, then. Be ready, as they are well ready for us."

Chapter 43

They are, indeed, waiting for us. At least a hundred of them.

Yes, they're waiting, but they're not ready.

Pitched tents are scattered everywhere. Guards lounge around fires, pulling meat from spits. Hell, there's even a fiddle player strumming out tunes. Torches light up the darkened field as the two moons glare down at our intrusion. Guards who notice us filing into their world frown in disbelief, like they're surprised we have the nerve to bring the fight to them.

I shift my weight, acclimate to the warmer temperature. My daggers are up, waiting for the Guards' first move as the last of us slip from the Window.

Talia exits a tent and stares at us in shocked horror. Before she can lift her hand with a chant, I toss the dagger in my left hand, catching her in the throat. Her gushing blood and gurgling moans as she slumps to the ground give me sadistic joy.

And her death wakes the crowd from their stupor.

We don't give the Guards a chance to organize. Some of us go headfirst into the melee, killing before Guards grab their poisonous swords. Ben, Luca, and I surround Finn and Alexie while their magic recuperates from crossing over. They need less than a minute. In less than a minute, the Window will be relocked, and those swords won't be anything but pointy metal. In less than a minute, we will systematically overpower them.

Ben gives a sharp, loud whistle as he fights by my side. He gives it again. And again. And one more time.

Howls answer him after the last piercing sound. Distant at first but coming closer. Gavin's pack answered our call, and they'll be here to fight alongside us soon.

Our wolf cavalry.

The shock and fear in the Guards' eyes as they hear the answering howls gives me almost as much pleasure as watching Talia die. Fuck them. Let's see how they enjoy us in their backyard.

We get as many as we can, some coming at us without donning their helmets. They wield their poisonous swords, and it's all we can do to dodge their thrusts while aiming at any unprotected skin. A few of our brethren get the deadly end of those swords. Their deaths, even in the midst of battle, weigh me down, fighting with the adrenaline pumping through my veins.

Only a few more seconds. A few more, and then–

"Now!" Finn yells.

And I smile at my opponent.

He knicks me in the shoulder with his impotent sword, and I'm still alive to plunge my iron dagger into his throat. His skin sizzles and burns as blood spurts from his carotid.

Howling and snarls render the air as Gavin and his pack race to us from the lower village. They're magnificent and large and deadly. They gnash and rip at skin, the lirium a joke against their strong maws.

Villagers' screams echo to us, their fear traveling to my stomach. My big concern is collateral damage. None of us want any more innocent blood on our hands.

More and more Guards infiltrate the yard. Hundreds more. Their armor is a glinting wave in a moonlit ocean. They box us in close by the Window, even Gavin's pack. They mean to corral us, maybe pick us off like fish in a barrel.

They don't get the chance.

Jessie yells, "Take cover," seconds before she tosses flat disks into the Guards' ranks. They light up instantly, their armor melting into their skin. Burned flesh stings my nose and makes my eyes water. I do a search, find my people, make sure everyone's accounted for.

Because more soldiers come. And more.

It's overwhelming.

I retreat with Ben, Seamus, and Luca, again moving toward Finn and Alexie. Helene and Callum follow.

Finn protects our queen and Allister, using small amounts of magic, conserving his energy. Jessie tosses another bomb, and another.

More Guards continue replacing their fallen. They pour from the castle like cockroaches.

"Finn!" I yell over the fighting and dying and mayhem. Ben and Luca position themselves so their backs are to mine. Seamus fights at my side, Callum on the other, as Helene dives in and wreaks as much havoc as she can.

Finn glances at me before throwing thirty Guards fifty feet away with a wave of his hand. "Quickly, love," he says, ridding us of all the attacking Guards at our heels.

When we get to him and Alexie, I take a moment to squeeze his hand, mine covered in blood and dirt. "They keep coming. We can't risk losing anyone else."

He gives a slight nod, kisses my lips hard and fast, and then steps in front of me. "Have everyone fall back."

Luca, Ben, and Seamus rush to get the message to our allies. Helene screams it from the sky. Wolves and Assassins fight their way behind Finn, who holds the first line of Guards frozen, a barrier their comrades have trouble pushing past.

All are our allies are fierce. But we can't keep this up.

Finn needs to end this battle so we can infiltrate the castle and end the war.

And he does—with Alexie's help.

It takes moments.

It feels like a hundred years.

But then the lirium sea frosts over like a field in winter.

Finn and Alexie don't kill them. Don't slaughter them as they would have slaughtered us.

Finn smiles down at Alexie, his face pale as sweat beads his skin. His expression is full of awe and pride. "You've done well, Your Highness."

She gives him a tired smile. "I will not kill them, cousin. They only fight us because they're forced to." Alexie has more restraint than all of us put together, and the way she controlled her power...

She's come a long way since we first met her.

Finn smooths her hair. "Are you ready, my dear?"

"I am." Alexie slips her hand into his.

Finn looks at me, his tired eyes worried. "We must hurry. This spell will not last long."

I gesture to Allister. "You're up, Messenger."

Allister straightens his coat as he smiles at me. "My pleasure."

I stare at his back as he traverses the frozen-Guard maze. Brother against brother. It's almost fitting to end this way.

It's eerily quiet as we weave our way around frozen bodies. Distant cries from the villagers drift on the wind, and the heat from Jessie's explosives mingle with the cold emanating off the Guards. None of us disrupt the quiet. We twist and dodge around bodies. Gavin and his wolves aren't so careful, knocking some of them down, their bodies too large to slink through the gaps.

It's claustrophobic, wretched.

Ben takes my hand as we navigate the yard. His touch steadies me, keeps me present. Luca's towering presence behind me also helps to block out the chaos.

Once we reach the castle gates, Allister turns to Finn and Alexie. His face is tight, serious, as he stands among the frozen Guards. "Would you be so kind as to open the gates, my lord?"

"My pleasure." Finn flicks a hand toward the lirium gate, and it flings open as if made of paper. I feel Finn's energy waning, feel him losing steam. He can't keep this up for much longer.

Allister gives him a grateful smile. "Thank you, my friend." He then tips his chin at me. "It's almost over now."

I hope so.

Once we're all inside, Finn uses his magic to relock the gates. "Just in case," he tells me, his eyes worried.

Shit.

When the spell breaks on the Guards, he won't be able to cast another one so large.

I cup his cheek. "It will be okay."

Finn glances at Ben and Luca, before meeting my eyes again. "The freezing spell couldn't reach anyone lurking inside. We will have to fight."

"I've no problem with that, mate." Luca waves his hand to our core people, all close, all hanging on every word Finn says. "Are ye ready for a bit more?"

Seamus lifts his ax, his angelic face smeared with blood and dirt. "Fuck, yeah."

Callum winces at Seamus's words but refrains from admonishing him for once. He simply nods his agreement.

"Couldn't have said it better myself," Jessie says to Seamus. She pulls out a gun stashed in her belt, giving us all an exasperated frown. "But enough with this medieval bullshit. I'm tired."

Ben chuckles and shakes his head. "That's our girl."

I take them all in for one selfish second, smiling up at Helene, who flaps her battle-worn wings above us. My family. "Let's go kill us a king, then."

As we near the towering main entrance, I turn to Madera, who stands with her Bonded, and to Gavin, whose pack surrounds him. They're fierce and ready for more. "If the spell breaks, and they make it through the gate before we succeed..."

Madera grins at me, her iron sword glinting in the moonlight. "We will not be as generous with their lives as our young queen."

Gavin's low growl concurs.

I nod. "Kill only as many as you have to." I then follow the rest of my Order.

Helene flutters above us as we walk as a unit behind Allister. Before he has a chance to ask Finn to open the heavy doors, I go to them, Luca, Ben, and Jessie behind me. "We got this one," I tell the Messenger as he backs out of our way.

He nods before taking a place at Alexie's side. "Of course, Assassin."

The four of us take a spot at the doors, two on each one. With Luca's strength flowing through Ben and me, along with Jessie's power, we still struggle. Lirium doors. Of fucking course.

The metal is warm against my palms as I push and push. We give it everything we have, but just like our weapons can't penetrate it, our strength is no match, either.

Finn runs up next to me, his hands glowing as he presses them against to door. He gives me a tired wink. "I may have a bit more steam in me. On three, love."

I grin at him, and then concentrate on the door. We try again and again and again. The door creaks and complains.

It does not let us in.

I look up, around us, desperate to find the answer.

The only thing I find is archers gathering on the parapets above. Their weapons are still poisonous, protected from Alexie's spell behind the castle walls. They aim right at us.

"Take cover!" I yell behind me as a volley of arrows rains down into the courtyard. Wolves' cries and Assassins' screams ricochet off the walls. They're killing us. Cowards behind walls.

Alexie breaks free from Allister's grasp and lifts her hand, tears streaming down her cheeks. She whispers words until some archers fall to the ground in grotesque, unnatural piles of bone and blood.

But the arrows keep coming. One hits Seamus's arm.

"No!" I run to him, catch him as he falls. We go to the ground together. I push sweaty hair from his eyes, my own filling with tears. *Please, don't die. Please!*

Seamus's violet eyes still glow their ethereal light–and his mouth still spews his beloved curses. "Motherfucker! Shit, man. Shit!"

I hold him, rocking him even as arrows fall around us.

302

Alexie places her small hand on my shoulder, her young face pale. "Their magic is gone, Nora. No more poison."

As I register what she's saying, Ben snatches her out of the way of the volleying arrows, tucking her in the safety of his arms by the doors, out of the arrows' paths.

Relief washes over me as I drag Seamus to safety. The arrow only grazed his arm. A scratch. He'll live.

Jessie shoots upward, emptying her clip, and reloading as more fall to the ground. "Get inside!" she yells to us as she shoots. "Hurry!"

We all take our places at the doors again. This time, Callum joins us. Helene and Seamus contribute their strength, too. So does Allister.

We push and push. Nothing.

Until Alexie takes a place at Ben's side. She sets her glowing palm on the door, and as we all give it one last hard shove, the doors swing open.

Alexie is the first inside, her lips moving in a chant as Guards come at us, swords drawn. Ben again takes her out of harm's way, shoving her behind him. "No poison," she tells us, her voice trembling. Sweat glistens her forehead, her silver hair wet and plastered to her skull. Her magic is waning.

But she's done enough.

It's our turn now.

All of us fight, even Allister and wounded Seamus, as the Guards come at us. The hall is wide, but we still fill it. Weapons clang. Screams render the torch-lit hall.

And then Gavin's pack rushes through the open doors.

They snarl and pounce, the Guards' swords not fast enough for the wolves' attack. It's bloody, a massacre, and it clears a path to Oberon.

"This way!" Allister races down the long hallway.

Ben, Luca, Finn, and I, with Alexie tucked in the middle of us, follow him. Helene and Callum trail behind, with Seamus between them.

The castle is immense, filled with paintings, gold, jewels, and lavish furniture. It infuriates me. All this wealth while the Fae of this world are starving.

Allister takes us up a flight of stairs, and then another. A few Guards confront us along the way, and as soon as Alexie's chant leaves her mouth, we dispose of them.

When we reach doors as tall as the ceiling, ones that rival the main entry, Allister stops, sweating and heaving for breath. "This is it, Assassins. The last step." He gives me a compassionate frown. "Kellen became part of Oberon's personal Guard after the slaughter at your home. Now is the time to avenge your father."

No. Now is the time to avenge all of us.

Excitement chases away exhaustion from battle. I grip my dagger tighter. "Let's get these fucking doors open."

Alexie steps up before any of us can take a place at the lirium barriers. She presses her glowing palm to the door, chanting with her eyes closed. After a few moments, Finn joins her. As they chant, we wait behind them, ready.

When the doors fling open, we don't have a chance to rush inside. Kellen is there, ready and defending the king. He lets his poisonous dagger loose, aimed at Finn's chest.

"No!" I move to protect him, my hand whipping up as if that's enough to stop the blade.

It is.

White light flashes off my palm, the energy knocking the blade to the ground. Shock ripples through me as I give Finn a wide-eyed stare. Pride and relief light up his face. "You share your strengths, and apparently I get to share mine."

I nod once, take no more time to wonder about it, and run for Kellen.

He's ready for me, a sword up and waiting for my heart.

Ben races to flank him on one side, Luca on the other. Yes, we'll all take him out.

For Topher.

Kellen is huge, as massive as Luca, but against the three of us, he's nothing. Hate is on our side. Vengeance runs through our veins. He took from us. And now, finally, he'll pay for it.

Ben lunges first, dodging Kellen's attack with lightning-quick speed. As Ben advances, Luca takes the chance to grab him around the neck, getting a solid choke hold on his exposed throat. As Kellen grapples at Luca's arm, Ben knocks the poisonous sword from his hand. With Luca restraining him, Ben wrenches the lirium helmet from his head and tosses it away with a loud clang against the marble floor.

He looks at me. "He's all yours, Nora Jean."

I don't waste time with words or accusations or give voice to all the horrid thoughts that have run through my mind since the day Kellen drove his sword into my father's heart. I walk to him, look him in the eye–and drive my dagger into his temple. Warm blood covers my hand, and it doesn't give me the joy I've been dreaming of.

It gives me relief.

My father's memory can finally rest.

When Kellen slumps to the ground, all of us turn to the king. He's beautiful and frightened and cowering on a red velvet chair fit for the king he isn't. He's not the formidable Seelie king on horseback with a Mage's protection and an army at his back.

Oberon lets out a mewling cry as we advance on him, Finn taking the lead.

Allister moves to the king's side, bends until the two are eye-level. "Your reign is over, brother." Allister's voice is soft, full of resigned sadness.

"You betrayed me." Oberon spits in Allister's face. "You betrayed your people to side with these heathens."

Allister doesn't answer him. He simply straightens, wipes the spittle from his cheek, and takes a step backward. His resolute stare points to Finn. "Do what you must, my lord."

Finn gives Allister a slight bow. He then moves in front of Oberon, kneels at his feet, and peers intently into the mewling king's eyes.

Memories ripple through our Bond. Finn's memories. They're of him as a child, being remanded to the kitchens, of being cuffed on the side of the head by haughty royals and parliamentary members like Oberon. They shift to when he's older, maybe Seamus's age. He's running with Alexie's mother and other Mages, fleeing to Mystic when Oberon and his uncle had his father and half-siblings murdered. The memories transition to when he tried to keep his people alive while hiding.

He thinks of his lifelong mission of bringing innocent Fae through the Windows, of setting them up in my world, trying to keep them safe and off the Trackers' radar.

He thinks of his time in the prisons, burning, beaten, starving.

Dying.

He thinks of his people now, scared and nervous and not knowing what the hell is going to happen to them.

All because of the sniveling, gorgeous, evil man in front of him.

I place a hand on Finn's shoulder, try to give him as much comfort as I can through the touch. It will never be enough to erase what he's suffered.

Finn presses his hand to Oberon's chest, directly over his heart and rich clothes. Looking into the king's frightened eyes, Finn slowly freezes him from the inside out. Oberon screams and thrashes under Finn's touch.

Luca and Ben each clamp onto one of the king's shoulders, forcing him to die without struggle, forcing him to die while looking at my serene Fae, who continues to kill him. Slowly. Painfully.

After a few long minutes, Oberon no longer struggles. His face is frozen in terror. Or maybe regret.

I don't care about his regret.

When Oberon's body slumps to the floor, Finn stands, caresses my cheek with a trembling palm, and then goes to Alexie. On shaky legs, he bends a knee before her.

Chapter 44

The kingdom is in ruins.

Bodies lay everywhere. Children cry in the distance, and grown men and women sob. The smell of fire and blood and burning flesh pollutes the air. It's almost dawn here. The soft orange light of the sun casts a glow of false pleasantness. The light can't change the devastation we've caused.

It makes me sick to know we had to take more lives. Lives of Guards who fought us on order of their dead king.

I'm tired of killing. Tired of all of it. I want to go home, fire up the oven, and bake until flour seeps through my skin.

I want to sleep for about a hundred years.

And… I don't want to go home.

Because Finn isn't coming back with us.

Yes, the kingdom is in shambles, but Alexie and Finn are already working to repair it.

We've ferreted out the parliament members. Royals cowering in rooms. Alexie has already relieved them of their duty, even before she's spoken with her people. Most of those outside know Oberon is dead, though. That kind of information is tough to keep secret.

And there hasn't been one wail of mourning echoing from the courtyard and beyond. Yes, Fae are stunned. They are scared. They are crying from the devastation. But they are not sad the king is dead. Not even the Guards who survived are mourning their king. They meander around, shocked as if awakening from a trance. No one wails Oberon's name. No one pleads for his resurrection.

Alexie speaks to all she confronts in the castle with authority, her tiny voice unbroken and strong. Finn stands at her side. He's her advisor now. Her protector until she is old enough and wise enough to trust all those surrounding her.

Allister has found himself a seat in her new parliament, something he wasn't expecting, and frankly, claims he doesn't want. But he does as his queen commands.

Helene and Callum have also found a spot, as has Gavin. More will be added. More commoners, more of the people who have been living in poverty and understand what it will take to help the masses.

I think of Regina and that child crying from hunger. I know Alexie will surround herself with people who want to help them, and others like them. I know she will not allow children to starve.

Seamus is coming home with me. He has asked, and I would never tell him no. I'm glad he's chosen to make my home his. He fits there. Fits with me.

The beginnings of the new parliament have happened in the first hours after Oberon's death. Finn insisted. The sooner a governing body is in place, the easier it will be to convince the people this isn't another coup orchestrated by another monster bent on claiming power. They'd start proving themselves today. Alexie has already taken tours of the kitchens and supply rooms. Food will be distributed across the country. Medicines and other supplies, as well.

To watch her, dirty from battle and still wearing her lirium armor, she reminds me of Joan of Arc. She's a crusading heroine who evaded the pyre. Who won. And her prize is serving those lost souls who have only known hunger and fear.

She'll also be releasing those suffering Fae from the prison. I hope she demolishes it. Having a prison is a necessary evil in any society. Having one riddled with iron that burns and eventually kills every occupant is torture.

We surround Alexie and Finn, now in the foyer. The battle here has been cleaned away. Haunts who served Oberon volunteered to take care of the bodies. Seamus did, too. The souls of the dead he consumed healed his arm. He's soul-drunk now, what I've decided to call it. He stands by Helene and Callum, wavering but content.

Ben and Luca each clasp one of my hands. Their touch warms me, and it helps to fill the burgeoning hole Finn's future absence is already making. It won't be forever. And it won't be as if I'll never see him until he's able to come home permanently. He's only a Window away.

He's always belonged to his people. I understood that going into our Bond. I can share.

I don't have a choice.

"Are you ready, Your Highness?" Finn tucks a curl behind Alexie's ear. She insisted on bathing and dressing in clothes that weren't armor stained with battle before addressing her people. She's stunning. Innocent. And those she's placed around her will keep her safe.

Alexie looks up at Finn. Nerves dance in her eyes, no matter the smile she wears. "I'm… scared, cousin."

"Don't be." Finn gestures to the closed doors. "These people have been waiting for you their entire lives."

Not all of them, and it will be a mess to sort out. One we'll help clean up on the other side of the Windows.

Ben squeezes my hand once before going to Alexie. He takes her hand, giving her that gorgeous smile of his. "Come on, little witch. Let's go introduce ourselves."

Alexie's face instantly softens as she moves closer to Ben's side. "Okay."

When the doors open, we're greeted with our allies, including Gavin's pack, who are all in their Fae form. We're also greeted by townspeople and battered Guards. Pride dances on the faces of our allies, and trepidation mars the expressions of those who have no clue what happened outside of our invasion and the death of their tyrant king.

As Alexie walks out on the steps, Ben and Finn at her sides, she lifts her chin and studies the crowd. After a few moments, she says exactly what Finn has advised her to say. "I am Alexie Ulster, niece of Louis Ulster the Fifth." At the mention of her name, excited chatter ripples through the crowd. "And I am here to serve you."

Epilogue

One Year Later

Ben, Luca, and I stand in front of Topher's memorial stone. Snow drifts down onto the barren field, and the cold pushes against us. It demands access to our skin, protected underneath layers of clothes and thick coats. No one complains, all content to let winter surround us. We're grateful, even. We fought hard to have the right to stand in this field and feel the bite of frost.

I can't believe it's been an entire year since the start of our new life.

"Topher would've been proud of you, Nora Jean." Ben leans in to touch his lips to my cold cheek, warming it instantly. "He'd have been pissed a time or two, but I can picture him rocking back on his heels, smoothing that thick-ass beard, with the proud smile he always shot your way."

"Aye, the man could grow a beard." Luca chuckles. "And he'd have been mighty proud of you, for certain."

I grin at their words, even as tears threaten. My father would've definitely questioned a few of my decisions, but... yeah, he'd have been proud of what our Order has accomplished. He would have also been impressed by my magic skills. Nothing as powerful as when I blocked the dagger Kellen threw has happened since, but Finn's been trying to coax the power out of me. I've been an eager student.

"I wish he were here to see it. To enjoy it." I don't hide how my voice hitches. I don't need to hide anything from Ben and Luca. I couldn't if I wanted to.

Luca takes my hand in his. "If the humans are correct, he's watching from somewhere, lass. He knows."

I squeeze Luca's palm. It's a nice idea. A comforting one. "I like that. Him, Mama, and Casey somewhere causing all kinds of mischief."

My gaze shifts to the stones beside Topher's, one with Casey's name and one with my mother's. No matter what, they're together in this field in a way. I've come here often in the last few months. During the quiet of the morning, after a long run through my beloved forest, I stop at this spot and talk to my parents, keep them filled in on how our lives have changed.

Ben, Luca, and I live in the cabin full-time now. As much as I love my bakery in the Poconos, I love my home more. I ran away from it once, and I'll never do it again.

Pia runs the bakery now, and she's damn good at it. She's taken over my tiny apartment and won over Carl and the rest of the townies with her bubbly attitude and excellent baking skills. Luca and I go back once a month or so to check on things, his bar now managed by a loyal employee—Malcolm. He and Pia have become fast friends, and they look out for one another.

Seamus lives with us, going back to Etherias to visit his family when I go see Finn. I met them a few times. They're as colorful and amazing as Seamus, and they love that he's getting an education that isn't yet available in Etherias. Alexie's parliament is already working on the educational system, though. Callum has taken the helm on that project. It won't be long until the schooling system is at a quality the children there deserve.

Layla, the teen Tracker, lives with us, too. Allister, come to find out, gave her the name. I guess no one else cared to. The poor girl is the only one left of the four Trackers. Her grandfather, great-uncle, and great-grandmother all passed on shortly after arriving. They're buried here, across the field from my parents. We gave them a proper burial, and it's not uncommon to find Layla sitting in front of their stones during my morning visits.

I believe Seamus is a little in love with her, and I don't blame him. She's strong. With all her trauma, she's fighting to truly live for the first time in her seventeen years of life. He's her protector in school and everywhere else. Her gentle presence and unquenchable curiosity drives our Haunt to be her teacher, her tour guide, and her shoulder to cry on when the past sneaks up on her.

I love them both, and so do Ben and Luca.

So does Finn.

My heart pinches at the thought of him. I see Finn often, spending time on both sides of the Window, but I'm looking forward to the day he gets to come home for good.

I shake the gray threatening to cloud my mood. I won't let it. Today is all about celebrating. Pia and Malcolm are here, and so is Jessie. In a little while, we're all going through the Window to spend the day with our queen. I'm excited to see her. Helene and Callum, too. Allister and Gavin, as well, if I'm honest. They're all family now. We're celebrating the one-year anniversary of our freedom from a tyrannical king. We're celebrating the absolutely amazing job Alexie is doing, with help from Finn and the rest of their hand-picked parliament. Fae are happier on both sides of the Windows. So are Assassins.

It's not all unicorns and rainbows, though. Most Orders are still working for the Queen. We track down known Dust dealers and Fae who threaten our existence with being too open with humans. We don't kill anymore, the biggest change. Everyone deserves a fair trial, even the Dust dealers. We make sure they get one by taking them back to our queen. She's reasonable, and when punishment is needed, no Fae suffers from the wrath of an iron prison. It's been torn down and rebuilt.

It's hard not exacting immediate punishment on Pixie murderers, but honestly, only a few dealers are around anymore. Believe it or not, Queen Alexie is loved and respected. So many of her subjects want to please her as they witness what she's doing for the Fae. Hell, not many cross over here anymore since the living conditions in Etherias have improved exponentially.

But today, my Order is off duty, and so are others across the country who helped us fight a year ago. Today, we reinforce the notion that Assassins are Fae allies. We are no longer the killers they once feared.

I sigh and squat down to brush snow off the tops of my parents' stones. "You all should be here to see the results of what you started," I whisper. I swallow as emotion fills my throat. "Thank you... for everything."

I stand, and Ben takes me into his arms, Luca folding himself around my back. My men cocoon me, and my heart swells to bursting as the Bond sings between us. I still can't believe I ran from this for so long.

"I suppose we should be getting back," Luca says, his chest rumbling with his deep voice against my back. "They're expecting the lot of us soon."

I nod into Ben's chest as Luca stands back. With one last glance at my parents' memorials, I turn toward the path leading to the cabin, holding Ben's and Luca's hands. As we head home, our Bond vibrates in my chest. It begs me to stop in my tracks. A smile spreads across my mouth and hurts my cheeks, as it does every time when the Bond is at its strongest.

When all three of my Bonded are in the same place.

I glance up at Ben and then Luca, both grinning as they focus on the direction of the Window.

"He's here," I breathe out, happiness on the verge of exploding from my chest. They obviously know as well as I do, but the words needed to burst from my lips like a trumpet call.

Ben and Luca are almost as ecstatic as I am.

Both release their grips on my hands. "Go on, then," Luca says. "We'll be right behind you."

I give Luca a soft kiss on the lips, do the same with Ben, and take off toward the Window. My feet are clumsy with anticipation. I saw Finn a week ago, but a week is too long.

A day is too long.

When I finally see him sauntering toward me with that haughty smile painted on his lips, and his love for me storming through the Bond, I let out a whimper and pick up my pace.

Finn captures me in his arms when I collide with him and doesn't waste time finding my lips with his. He kisses me deep and with the hunger of a man starved. I press against him, wanting to feel the heat of his skin.

When he lifts his mouth from mine, he takes the time to smooth tangled hair from my face as he looks down on me with the same adoration that still baffles me. "I've missed you, Assassin."

I cup his warm cheek, drink him in with a thirst that will never be satiated. "I hope so."

He quirks a brow with a slight grin. "Do you doubt me?"

"Never again."

His grin widens. "Good."

"What are you doing here?" I lean in, resting my cheek against his white tunic. "Not that I mind."

His chest rumbles against my cheek. "I couldn't wait any longer. Call me impatient."

I shift to stare into his gray eyes, eyes like liquid moons. "I'm glad you're impatient."

He kisses me until I'm breathless and then moves to take my hand. With a glance over my shoulder, he waves at Luca and Ben. "Gentlemen."

"Good to see you, brother." Ben clasps Finn's hand for a moment. "It'll be nice when it's permanent."

"Aye, when do you wager that'll be, mate?"

Finn's pride shoots through the Bond, his admiration for our new queen matching what we all feel. "Oh, a few more years, at least, but the queen can out-magic me already. I've no doubt she'll be holding her own sooner rather than later."

"That's my little witch." Ben gestures toward the path home with a tip of his chin. "Let's get the troops. I'm ready to leave this cold-ass world for a little while."

"It's as good a plan as any." Luca chuckles and starts walking, Ben at his side.

Finn peers down at me as Ben and Luca take the lead. He lifts my hand to kiss my knuckles. "Come on, love. It's time to prepare ourselves for one hell of a party."

Author's Note

Reviews are important for new authors! Thank you to everyone who takes a moment to leave one, even a line or two! Flip the page for information on how to contact me, I love to hear from readers!

About the Author

Rachelle is a librarian by day and a writer of spicy romance at night. She lives in the Pennsylvania woods with her husband and their gaggle of children, who happen to be pretty amazing. She writes about kickass heroines and the men who love them. If you're into strong women, guys who make you swoon, and a lot of magic, she's got you covered. Rachelle drinks way too much caffeine and is completely addicted to audiobooks.

Connect with Rachelle:

Other Works

Assassin's Pull Series

To Hunt a Fae
To Tempt a Fae
To Avenge a Fae